A LON

Slocum drew a deep breath and shifted his gaze to the low-slung, stunted bush. A round shape peered from beside a lower limb. Sunlight winked off metal.

Slocum thumbed back the hammer of the Ballard. The heavy thunk of the big hammer seemed loud in his ears. The round object snapped into focus as the Indian started to raise his rifle. Slocum let his breath out slowly, swung the Ballard to his shoulder, dropped the sight in line in one smooth motion, and stroked the trigger.

The brass crescent buttplate of the Ballard slammed against Slocum's shoulder; the heavy recoil carried the rifle barrel upward in a jarring muzzle blast. A split second later, Slocum heard the solid *whop* of lead against bone and flesh. . . .

JAKE LOGAN

RENEGADE TRAIL

JOVE BOOKS, NEW YORK

RENEGADE TRAIL

A Jove Book / published by arrangement with
the author

PRINTING HISTORY
Jove edition / November 1995

ISBN: 0-515-11739-0

A JOVE BOOK®
Jove Books are published by The Berkley Publishing Group,
200 Madison Avenue, New York, New York 10016.
JOVE and the "J" design are trademarks
belonging to Jove Publications, Inc.

PRINTED IN THE UNITED STATES OF AMERICA

10 9 8 7 6 5 4 3 2 1

RENEGADE TRAIL

1

Slocum battled his way back to consciousness, fighting through the thick, heavy blanket of darkness toward the light that seemed just beyond reach.

The dull throb in his skull gave way to the first bright slash of pain, a saber cut that sliced cold and brassy through his brain. The sting quickly built into a fiery lance through his temples as he tried to force shattered images into focus before watery eyes as the faint light gave way to the aching glare of a high, hard sun.

The position of the sun confused Slocum for a moment. It had been a lot lower in the sky, warm against his back, the last he remembered.

Slocum lay still, his muscles unwilling to move, as he tried to regain his bearings. His sense of smell was the first to return. It brought the scent of death, the coppery smell of blood. Blurred shapes wheeled against the summer sky, shimmered into vague forms, then fuzzed again before Slocum could finally focus his eyes.

The sky was full of buzzards.

One of the carrion eaters lumbered to earth and made an awkward, stumbling landing, wings flapping for balance, on the parched brown grass at the crest of a low hill a few yards away.

"Not this time, damn you," Slocum muttered to the bird. His voice was weak and raspy to his ears, barely audible through swollen lips and tongue. The buzzard cocked its ugly, featherless head at Slocum, hissed, and settled down to wait. The obscene patience of the big bird sent a wash of anger through the relentless pounding in Slocum's head. A ripple of returning strength flowed into his muscles.

He ground his teeth against the effort and forced his right hand across his body, reaching for the Colt revolver he carried cross-draw style. He would blast the bird into a pulpy mass of feathers. The hand touched only cloth. His gun belt was gone. He muttered a curse and tried to sit up, but managed only a weak shuffle. The simple act of trying to grip a handgun that wasn't there had sapped the bit of strength his anger at the buzzard had given him.

Slocum turned his full concentration to staying awake. He struggled against the urge to slide into the comfort of darkness that would still the raging agony in his head. The buzzard might have its meal yet, Slocum silently vowed, but it wasn't going to answer this chuck call without a fight. He lost track of time as he fought to stay awake and waited for strength to flow back into his weakened muscles.

The barely audible crunch of a boot on parched grass jarred Slocum. His heart quickened. He doubled a fist, knowing the effort would be futile at best; he didn't have the strength to put up a decent scrap. But he vowed to go down fighting as best he could. It was the only way he knew. After a couple of heartbeats, the cautious footstep sounded again, nearer this time. The metallic click of a hammer drawn to full cock chilled his blood. He braced himself for the slam of lead.

"I'll be damned," a deep voice rumbled from just beyond Slocum's view, somewhere behind his right shoulder. "Never expected to find a live one."

Slocum didn't try to speak. He willed what strength he had into the muscles of his arm, ready to try a desperate punch.

"Easy, mister," the voice said. "I'm not one of the bunch that jumped you. How bad you hurt?"

"Don't—know," Slocum said. His words were little more than a croak.

"You look like hell."

"Feel—like hell."

A muted chunking sound told Slocum the man behind the voice had lowered the hammer of his weapon. Seconds later, a stocky man squatted beside Slocum. The man's face was broad and dark, with eyes set wide apart below a shapeless felt hat. Flat black eyes stared at Slocum without expression.

"Can you sit up?"

Slocum dug his elbows into the dirt and tried to lift his shoulders. He managed only a few inches before his arms started to tremble. A thick arm slipped around Slocum's back and lifted, powerful but gentle. The pain in Slocum's head grew into a screech as he sat up. He heard a steady roaring in his ears; the change in position left him dizzy and blurred his vision again.

"Take it slow," the stocky man said. "Don't try to move too much too quick."

Slocum heard the whisper of leather against cloth, the gentle slosh of water, and an audible pop as the man plucked a wooden stopper from a water bag. The container appeared beneath Slocum's nose. He managed to raise a hand, grip the soft, leathery material, and downed two quick swallows. The water was sweet and cool against Slocum's tongue. He lowered the bag reluctantly. Too much water taken too soon would just hit bottom and come back up.

Slocum licked his swollen, cracked lips, and tasted the slippery salt bite of blood on his tongue. His wavering vision cleared. He turned his head slowly, ignoring the fresh blast of pain from the movement, and studied the man at his side. The man was thick of shoulder and thigh, the cloth of a sweat-stained homespun shirt straining across bulging chest muscles. Twin bandoliers of large-caliber rifle cartridges crossed his chest. The barrel of a Winchester rifle rested against a heavy upper arm. A thin, jagged scar snaked from beneath his hatband across his left cheek and down to the point of his square jaw. Thick black hair cropped square at the shoulders framed the deep copper of the sun-weathered face. Indian, Slocum thought.

Slocum tried to shrug away the supporting arm, disgusted at the thought of depending on anyone but himself. It was a weak effort. The Indian ignored the gesture.

"Easy, now," the deep voice said. "Don't rush it. You might pass out again."

"The—the others?"

"Dead. Know what happened?"

Slocum started to shake his head and immediately gave up the idea. Any movement sent a blacksmith pounding on the anvil in his temples.

"No. Don't remember—anything since sunup." Slocum sipped at the neck of the water pouch and realized the bag was made from the stomach of an animal. This time, the water had a slightly bitter aftertaste. Slocum wasn't sure if the flavor was the lingering taste of animal gut from the container or the bile in his own throat. At the moment, he didn't care. He became aware of a thick stickiness above his right ear. He raised a hand to the side of his head. The effort sent his vision swimming again. His fingers came away dark with drying blood. Slocum stared at the hand for a moment as if it were on the end of someone else's arm.

"Might as well see if your brains are showing," the Indian said.

Slocum winced as rough, powerful fingers probed the thick, matted hair above his ear. After a moment, the Indian grunted. "Doesn't look good," he said. "You've got a deep cut over the ear. Bled like a stuck pig. Big bruise over the cheekbone and lower jaw. You took a nasty wallop there."

"I had that much figured out," Slocum said.

"That's the easy part. Big question is if your skull's cracked. Or if your brain got bounced around in your skull enough to bruise it. That's the case, I can't help you much." The Indian pulled a sack of Bull Durham from a pocket. "Saw a man die from a brain bruise once. Head swelled up so bad his eyes near popped out before he died, tongue all lolled out his mouth and turning black. Nasty way to go."

"Thanks for the encouraging words," Slocum said. He watched as the Indian opened the drawstring of the tobacco sack with his teeth and deftly rolled a cigarette with one hand. He fired it with a sulphur match, took a drag, and offered it to Slocum, who took it with trembling fingers. He sucked in a lungful of the rich, heavy smoke, and exhaled slowly. The tobacco seemed to ease his raging headache a bit.

"Reckon you can sit up by yourself?"

"Think so." The supporting arm fell away.

"I'll take a look around. Got a good idea what happened, but I'd like to make sure." The Indian stood and strode away, his footsteps silent in the dry grass and blowing sand.

Slocum finished the smoke, twisted the stub until the final grains of tobacco trickled from the shredded brown paper, and scooped a handful of dirt over the remains of the quirly. It was an unconscious gesture driven by long habit; in dry grass country, a single spark from a discarded cigarette could touch off a wildfire that might burn thousands of acres.

It seemed to Slocum the Indian was gone a long time, but the position of his shadow told him only a few minutes had passed before the blocky man again squatted at his side. Slocum startled at the Indian's sudden appearance. He hadn't heard a thing. For a heavy man, he was light on his feet.

"It was them, all right," the man said.

"Who's them?"

"Bunch of bronco Indians. Been tracking them better than two weeks." A wrecked coach gun thumped onto the dirt at Slocum's side. "Reckon that's what kept you from getting killed."

Slocum studied the shotgun for a moment. The twelve-gauge double-barrel was wrecked. A dull splash of lead marked the point of impact of a heavy slug against the top part of the receiver. Both hammers were twisted, the crossbolt latch bent, and the barrels had separated along the sight rib. Slocum remembered now; he had been riding on the wagon seat, the butt of the shotgun resting on his thigh, before the lights went out.

"Looks like it took a hit from a big-bore rifle, likely a buffalo gun," the Indian said. "I'd guess the impact of the slug whapped the barrels up against your head. Otherwise you'd have been dead now."

Slocum said, "Shotgun's saved my life a time or two before, but not this way." The simple effort of forming words fuzzed his vision again. He dropped the useless shotgun at his side.

The Indian jabbed a thumb toward the ridge where the buzzard waited. The bird hissed and spread its wings. "Tracks say a jasper on the crest of that little hill over there cut down on you. Probably figured you were dead before you hit the ground. My guess is you bled so much those renegades thought somebody'd already taken your scalp. They peeled all the others."

Slocum looked around. Blow flies buzzed over the gory remains of the teamster and a downed mule nearby. A few yards away, dark clumps marked the huddled bodies of two outriders.

The wagon he had been riding on was gone. Slocum muttered a curse. The wagon had held twelve cases of new repeating rifles and more than a thousand rounds of ammunition.

"Feeling better?"

Slocum nodded gingerly. Pain still hammered through his head, but it didn't feel bright white now. It was more of a throbbing gray.

"Good." A broad, callused hand with scarred knuckles reached out. "Name's Jim Stonekiller."

Slocum took the hand. "Slocum."

"Well, Slocum, if you're up to riding, we best move on a ways. There's a spring twelve miles southwest of here, on the edge of the Cimarron breaks. It's more of a seep, but the water's good. I'll need more water than I've got with me to patch you up." Stonekiller slipped a powerful arm beneath Slocum's shoulder blades and helped him to his feet. The skyline of the rolling southern Kansas prairie listed to one side, then the other. The thump in Slocum's head grew worse. "Wait here," Stonekiller said. "I'll fetch my horses."

Slocum blinked until the horizon settled down into a straight line again, then looked around. Both his horses were gone, along with his saddle and weapons. He felt naked without the comfortable weight of the pistol belt, knife sheath, and Winchester rifle that had been a part of him for so long. And the missing saddlebags had held the hundred and ten dollars he'd managed to save over the last eight months. At least he still had his hat. It lay crumpled and dusty in the ruts left by passing wagon wheels. Slocum knelt cautiously, knocked most of the dirt from the hat, pushed it back into a semblance of its original shape, and eased it onto his head. He winced at the sting of the hatband against the torn flesh above his ear.

His gaze settled on a jumble of canvas rolls and burlap sacks lying beside the dead teamster. The raiders had tossed personal belongings aside before making off with the wagon. They had left his bedroll. He went to the pile, still unsteady on wobbly knees, and tugged his bedroll from beneath the dead man's legs. The teamster had been shot half a dozen times. His shirt was soaked with blood. A spot of pink-stained bone shone where his scalp had been. Slocum ignored the dead man's sightless stare and patted the bedroll. He sighed in relief as his fingers tapped the solid metal lump. At least he wasn't completely defenseless now. His spare handgun, a .44-40 Colt Peacemaker, was safely tucked deep inside the canvas groundsheet and blankets. He loosened the straps, retrieved the weapon, and spun the cylinder. The Colt held five rounds; Slocum carried the hammer down on an empty chamber until the need arose to plunk a sixth cartridge home. Five rounds wasn't much, but it was a hell of a lot better than nothing. He tucked the weapon into his waistband and looked up at the sound of horses' hooves.

Stonekiller led a saddled, deep-chested bay and a twitchy sorrel carrying a heavy pack. The sorrel snorted and shied nervously at the smell of blood and death.

"I'll give you a leg up on the bay," Stonekiller said.

Slocum lifted an eyebrow. "How about you?"

Stonekiller shrugged. "I'll walk. My people used to cover forty, fifty miles a day on foot, easy. Lift your boot."

Stonekiller boosted Slocum into the saddle. The stirrup leathers were a good six inches too short for him, but Slocum wasn't about to complain. He knew he was too weak to walk more than a few steps.

"What tribe were your people?" Slocum asked.

"Kiowa. Half of them, anyway. Mother was full-blood Kiowa. Pappy was pure Irish. I've got more of her than him in me. At least on the outside."

Slocum couldn't argue the point. Except for the white man's clothes he wore, Stonekiller looked like he might have just stepped out of a buffalo-skin lodge. All he needed was a shield and war paint to finish the picture. His weapons were as much from the white man's culture as his clothes. He carried a Bisley Colt with gutta-percha grips in a slick-worn holster that rode high on his right hip. A Bowie knife almost as big as a short sword nestled in a rawhide scabbard against his left hip. A second rifle that looked to be a big-bore single-shot rested in Stonekiller's saddle boot.

The bay fidgeted a bit at the feel of the stranger in the saddle, but quieted down as Slocum gathered the reins and patted the animal's neck in reassurance. The bay fell into step alongside the skittish sorrel as Stonekiller shouldered his Winchester and moved out at a steady walk. The half-breed's heavy legs produced a surprisingly long, ground-eating stride. Slocum was relieved that the bay had an easy way of moving. The way his head felt, this was no time to be aboard a rough horse. They had covered less than fifty yards before the sound of ponderous wings and quarrelsome hisses told Slocum the buzzards were already at the bodies. Slocum thought they should take the time to bury the dead men he had ridden with, but finally conceded it didn't matter much to them now.

"Not that I'm complaining, Stonekiller," Slocum said after a time, "but stopping to help me is costing you tracking time. That bunch has gained several miles on you already."

Stonekiller shrugged. "They'll keep."

"I'm obliged," Slocum said. "I owe you."

"Nobody owes me, Slocum, except that gaggle of bastards out there. And they'll pay, sooner or later." The set of the Indian's square jaw and tone of voice told Slocum the man was deadly serious. And plenty deadly.

Slocum rode in silence. When Stonekiller decided to talk, he would talk. It wasn't in Slocum's nature to pry into a man's affairs—or to have men pry into his. Besides, Slocum had other worries at the moment. Waves of dizziness washed over him and dimmed the sunlight from time to time. He concentrated on staying awake and in the saddle.

He wasn't too woozy to notice Stonekiller's wariness. The Kiowa paused frequently to stare at the ground, study the horizon, and then turn to gaze along their back trail. Slocum's dizzy spells came less frequently as they rode. His vision had cleared; the low, rolling hills and sun-browned prairie were now sharp and clear except for the heat waves that shimmered in the distance.

The sun had dropped well toward the western horizon before Stonekiller finally grunted in satisfaction as they topped a low ridge. He nodded toward a green swatch in a shallow valley ahead. The green strip snaked south as the valley narrowed and deepened, twisting its way toward the Cimarron breaks a few miles away.

"Antelope Springs," Stonekiller said. "My people used to camp here on hunts when I was just a kid. It has water, wood, and some graze for the horses. We'll lay over here a day or so, get you patched up and the horses rested."

Antelope Springs still bore the signs of previous visitors, man and animal, Slocum noted. Sun-bleached bones from the size of rabbits to buffalo flashed white as the breeze rippled scattered clumps of knee-high prairie grass. Some of the bones looked reasonably fresh. Slocum figured it was a favored hunting spot of predatory animals, including man, in a land noted for its scarcity of water holes. A horseshoe-shaped line of stunted oak and cottonwood trees rustled in the breeze at the south end of the marshy seep. Trees and firewood were almost as valuable as water in this part of the world, Slocum knew. This likely had been a campground for many generations of wanderers.

Slocum swung down from the big bay a couple of yards from the edge of the spring. A faint odor of mud and animal droppings wafted to him. The hum and buzz of insects was clearly audible over the whisper of the breeze. A dragonfly hovered curiously before Slocum's face, then darted away. Slocum leaned against the bay's shoulder and waited for the pulsing throb in his temples to ease.

Stonekiller waved off Slocum's offer to help set up camp. The Kiowa wasted no motions. He had the camp set, the horses tended and staked, and a fire started within minutes, tindered with tall dry grass and a few small limbs from a deadfall at the edge of the trees. A coffeepot warmed on a bracket of stones above the smokeless blaze, along with a washbasin filled with water from the spring. Even as he worked, Stonekiller paused every few minutes to cock his head, listening, and to sniff the breeze.

The basin began to steam. Stonekiller spread a blanket, motioned for Slocum to sit, and fetched one of the canvas packs. Slocum noted that Stonekiller kept the Winchester rifle close at hand as he worked. He had also slipped the hold-down thong from the hammer of the Bisley Colt.

Stonekiller pulled a rag from a pack, dipped it into the steaming water bowl, and turned to Slocum. "Take your hat off and we'll check out the ouch on your skullbone," he said.

Slocum tried not to wince as the half-breed's powerful fingers swiped away the blood and probed the cut. It started bleeding again.

After a moment, Stonekiller grunted. "Not as bad as it looked at first," he said. "If your skull bone isn't cracked or your brain bruised, you'll mend." He rummaged in the pack again and produced a small leather pouch, a cloth bundle folded and tied with rawhide strips, and a full quart of Old Overholt. Slocum licked his parched lips at the sight of the whiskey. It had been days since his last drink.

Stonekiller lifted an eyebrow at Slocum as he finished threading a needle. "You want a shot of that whiskey before I start? Could be this might sting a bit."

Slocum reluctantly shook his head. "I'd rather wait until you're finished," he said. "Might need it more then."

"Suit yourself." Stonekiller opened the small leather pouch, pried Slocum's cut open with his fingers, and dribbled a powder onto the raw skin.

Slocum's breath whistled through his nostrils. It felt like Stonekiller had just poured a handful of red ants into the cut.

It got worse.

Slocum's face was pale as Stonekiller tied off the last of a half dozen stitches and leaned back to survey his work. "Never was much of a seamstress," he said, "but I think it'll hold. We'll rig a bandage later. Fresh air's best for it now, as long as you keep it clean. Ready for that drink?"

Slocum nodded and took the bottle from Stonekiller's bloodied fingers. The whiskey went down smooth and lit a fire in Slocum's gut. The ants seemed to ease up their attack on his scalp.

Stonekiller lifted the bottle, swirled the contents, downed a quick swallow, and sighed in satisfaction. "Too bad us Injuns can't handle whiskey. Makes us red men plumb crazy, you know. Maybeso this Injun scalp you now."

A wry grin touched Slocum's lips. "I thought you just did," he said.

Stonekiller almost smiled. "White man firewater better'n rotgut Injun trade whiskey. Want another?"

Slocum shook his head. "It's a hanging offense to drink up all a man's whiskey. What was that stuff you put in my head, anyway?"

Stonekiller stowed the whiskey back in the pack. "Old Kiowa cure. Dried moss and a wad of spider web to stop the bleeding. Ground nettles, bloodwort, a touch of antelope droppings, and some crushed herbs to pull out the bad spirits so it doesn't get infected. Learned it from a toothless old medicine woman up on the Arikira."

"It work?"

"Judging from that old woman's looks it works on everything but a toothache. I haven't lost a patient yet. I'd appreciate it if you didn't spoil that record." Stonekiller rose in an easy, fluid motion. "Set easy, Slocum. I'm going to take a little scout around."

Slocum waited patiently, straining his own senses to pick up any unfamiliar sound or smell. None came. Slocum decided that either his senses had been dulled by the lick on the head or Stonekiller just had a case of the yips. He doubted it was the latter.

The Kiowa was back in a quarter hour. His sudden appearance caught Slocum off guard. He had been watching the tree line; one minute Stonekiller wasn't there, the next he was. Stonekiller strode casually to the fire, lifted the lid, and peered into the coffee-pot.

"Coffee's ready," he said.

"Sounds good to me."

"Hope you don't mind drinking after an Injun. I only brought one cup."

"If you can stand the idea, it doesn't bother me a bit." Slocum probed in his shirt pocket and mouthed an oath. His last two cigarillos were squashed and broken, shredded in his fall from the wagon. He turned his shirt pocket inside out and dumped the crumbled tobacco. Stonekiller offhandedly tossed his Bull Durham sack to Slocum and poured a cup of coffee as Slocum rolled a quirly.

Stonekiller blew across the tin cup to cool the liquid, sipped, and traded the coffee to Slocum for the tobacco sack. The two smoked and drank in silence for a time.

Stonekiller refilled the cup and lifted an eyebrow at Slocum. "Hope you got enough of your wits back to shoot, Slocum," he said. "We got company coming. Injuns."

Slocum's gut tightened. "I suppose you wouldn't have mentioned shooting if they were friends of yours."

"I know them."

"Part of the bunch that jumped me?"

Stonekiller shook his head. "No. Three Kickapoos. They've been wanting to get me in their sights for over a year now. Been on our trail several hours. Hate to drag you into a personal spat, Slocum, but it looks like we don't have a choice. Unless you want to lose your hair."

"I'd as soon not."

"Sort of figured that." Stonekiller shucked the long-barreled single-shot rifle from its saddle boot. "You know how to use a Ballard?"

"Never fired one."

"Handles like a Remington Creedmore. Target rifle for long-range work. Given to me a year back by a grateful rancher. This one's a .40-60 caliber. Hit something and it stays hit. There's a cartridge in the chamber." Stonekiller flipped up the folding tang sight with its sliding notch and scored brass slides. "Each mark is a hundred yards to target, out to a thousand. It's sighted in for a six o'clock hold at a hundred yards. Light trigger. Breathe on it and she goes blooey. Rolling block action." He handed the weapon to Slocum. Stonekiller cocked an ear, listening, then nodded. "They'll split up. Two will come at us from the trees. Don't worry about them. The third one will sneak up on the west crest across from us, to that stunted juniper standing off by itself. See it?"

Slocum nodded.

"When he shows himself, take him down," Stonekiller said. "They'll make their move in about fifteen minutes, just before sundown. I make it just over a hundred and twenty yards to that juniper. You'll be looking almost into the sun. It'll be a tough shot."

"I've had tougher."

Stonekiller stood, brushed dirt from his rump, stretched, and shouldered his Winchester. "Stay loose, Slocum. Just like you were settled in for the night. We don't want them to know we're on to them until it's too late. But be ready. That Kickapoo up on the hill's their best rifle shot."

"I'll be ready," Slocum said, his tone tight. "What about you?"

A slight, cold smile touched Stonekiller's lips.

"Thought I might wander off into those trees, take a leak, and wait for a couple Injuns."

"Watch your hair," Slocum said.

"Don't worry about me. Just nail the shooter on the hill." Stonekiller turned, then glanced back. "By the way, Slocum. Do the job with one shot if you can. Ballard ammunition's expensive as hell."

Slocum watched as Stonekiller strode casually toward the trees, whistling as if he had not a care in the world. That, Slocum thought, is one tough hombre.

Slocum settled down to wait.

2

Slocum ignored the persistent buzz of flies and shrill hum of mosquitoes about his ears, all his attention focused on the ridge across the valley.

He didn't stare directly at the juniper bush; a man's eyes tended to play tricks on him if he stared too long at the spot where he expected to see something. Instead, he fixed his gaze on a grass clump a few feet right of the juniper. He knew from long experience that he could trust his eyesight to more quickly pick up a movement slightly off center from his focus point.

He sat outwardly relaxed, the Ballard rifle resting across his thighs, right hand relaxed over the cool metal of the receiver, thumb resting on the hammer. The balance of the Ballard was considerably different from that of the more familiar and lighter Winchester lever action, but the rifle was comfortable in his hands. He didn't doubt Stonekiller's word that the Ballard shot where it pointed.

Despite his outward calm, Slocum felt the tension in his chest muscles. He knew he would get only one clear shot. If he missed, he would be the target, sitting in the open with no cover to dive behind. Stinging sweat trickled into the cut above his ear. His head throbbed with each pulse of his heart. Slocum willed his muscles to stay relaxed, his senses to remain alert. A lack of patience had cost many a hunter his game. It had cost a lot of them their lives. Patience was one thing Slocum had learned in the Confederate army. A sniper without patience soon found other work—or a shovel full of dirt in his face.

He had not heard a sound from the trees where the man had disappeared. Stonekiller might be half Irish, but on the hunt he was all Kiowa. Slocum blinked against the lowering sun. It was a bit to the south and a hand span above the juniper now, not directly in his face but bothersome enough to make for a touchy shot. Lining the sights on a strange rifle while squinting against the glare of a low sun wasn't Slocum's idea of a simple turkey shoot. Especially when the turkey could shoot back.

He drew a quick breath at the distant snap of a twig from the direction of the trees. He did not look toward them. A few seconds later, the sound of a muted scuffle and muffled grunt drifted to his ears—and something moved beside the juniper. Slocum shifted his gaze to the low-slung, stunted bush. A round shape peered from beside a lower limb. Sunlight winked off metal.

Slocum thumbed back the hammer of the Ballard. The heavy thunk of the big hammer seemed loud against his ears. The round object snapped into focus as the Indian started to raise his rifle. Slocum let his breath out slowly, swung the Ballard to his shoulder, dropped the sight into line in one smooth motion, and stroked the trigger.

The brass crescent buttplate of the Ballard slammed against Slocum's shoulder; the heavy recoil carried the rifle barrel upward in a jarring muzzle blast. A split second later, Slocum heard the solid whop of lead against bone and flesh. Slocum didn't fight the recoil. He let the weapon fall of its own weight, racked back the rolling block action, and chambered another big cartridge. Through a hole in the billow of powder smoke, Slocum saw a rifle skid downslope from beneath the juniper.

The echoes of the Ballard muzzle blast were still rolling when Slocum heard the flatter thump of a handgun shot from the trees. He swung the Ballard's muzzle toward the tree line, no longer concerned with the rifleman across the valley. A sudden silence fell over the camp, broken only by the outraged squawks of a startled jay.

Slocum waited for what seemed to be a long time, ignoring the beads of sweat on his forehead and the steady thump of his heartbeat. Finally, a call came from beyond the lip of the west ridge: "Slocum! I'm coming in! Don't get twitchy on me!"

Slocum lowered the Ballard's hammer. Moments later, Stonekiller's stocky bulk appeared beside the juniper. The half-breed knelt briefly beside the stunted tree, then rose and disappeared behind the ridge.

As he waited, Slocum picked up the spent Ballard cartridge case, puffed the dust from it, and dropped it into his pocket. He never wasted good brass when it could be recovered, even if they didn't have the equipment for reloading at the moment. Old habits died hard.

Stonekiller reappeared just before sunset, riding a gaudy paint horse and leading two others, a nondescript roan and a rangy dun. Stonekiller was packing a fair load, Slocum noticed. He carried three rifles across the pommel of the paint's saddle, had a pistol belt draped over one shoulder, and what looked to be a couple of leather pouches slung around his neck. Something—Slocum couldn't make out what—dangled from a saddle string at Stonekiller's right knee.

The something else turned out to be three scalps.

The blocky man casually tossed aside the gory trophies and captured weapons before dismounting to squat beside Slocum. The left sleeve and upper chest of his shirt was soaked in blood.

"You handle a long gun pretty good for a white man, Slocum," Stonekiller said casually. "Nailed that Injun between the nose and upper lip. Slug took the back of his neck off when it came out. Made a hell of a mess. You want the scalp? You earned it."

Slocum shook his head. "Never had much use for scalps."

Stonekiller shrugged. "Grew out of that stage myself a spell back, but lifted these anyway. Could have some use for them later on. You okay?"

"Sure." Slocum inclined his head toward Stonekiller's shirt. "That blood yours or theirs?"

"Theirs. Never got a scratch, myself. Damn Kickapoos never were all that good in an eyeball-to-eyeball scrap."

"Mind if I ask what happened in there?" Slocum said with a glance toward the trees.

"Nothing much I didn't expect," Stonekiller said. "They weren't paying attention. Didn't even know I was around until I'd already cut the first one's throat. Had to shoot the other one." Stonekiller sounded apologetic about having to waste a pistol cartridge.

Slocum handed over the Ballard. "Nice weapon. Kicks like a mad mule, though."

"You ought to see what it does to the man on the other end," Stonekiller said. "I brought the Kickapoo guns and ponies back. The guns look to be mostly junk, but you might find something you could use. The saddle on the paint's in passing fair shape. I think the stirrup leathers will let out enough for those long legs of yours. Long as I'm feeling generous, take your pick of the mounts and weapons. The Kickapoos won't be needing them now."

Slocum studied the horses for a moment, then nodded. "The dun will do."

Stonekiller grunted. "Good eye for horseflesh. Ugly as sin, but the best of the sorry lot."

"I never had a dun that wasn't a passing fair horse," Slocum said. "All of them seem to have a lot of bottom, plenty of speed, and a smattering of smarts."

A coyote yelped in the near distance. An answering wail came from farther away. Stonekiller listened to the scavengers' cries, then nodded. "Chuck time on the prairie. I dragged the bodies off a half mile or so." His nose wrinkled in contempt. "Never could abide the smell of a stinking Kickapoo. Even a dead one. Coffee still hot?"

"Should be," Slocum said. "Probably thick enough to whittle on by now." He rummaged through the Indian weapons as Stonekiller knelt by the fire, cup in hand. Slocum immediately discarded one rifle, an old Henry rimfire so worn out that the barrel was almost a smoothbore. The second rifle wasn't much better. The barrel throat of the battered single-shot Remington falling block was scarred by deep rust pits and badly fouled with black powder residue. It looked like it hadn't been cleaned since day one, Slocum thought. He tossed that one aside, too.

The third was more promising, a reasonably new Winchester carbine, .38-40 caliber. Slocum worked the action to clear the magazine and dry fired the weapon. The lever was stiff and the trigger pull about twice what he liked, but it could be tuned up if he had the proper tools. The best thing the .38-40 had going for it was a full box of ammunition in one of the leather pouches. Fifty-seven rounds, counting the ones ejected from the magazine. It would do for now.

With the long gun problem solved, Slocum picked up the handgun, an old Remington Army cap-and-ball job. Its accuracy would be questionable at best—the barrel wasn't in the greatest shape—but the leather pouch held powder, caps, and ball to fit the weapon. He stuffed the revolver and its equipment into a pack. It could be sold for a few dollars somewhere down the road. He kept the pistol belt. A few swipes of his pocket knife recontoured the belt and holster to a reasonable fit for his Colt. It was nowhere near the custom fit of his own design, and it rode a bit awkwardly, but he could live with it until some better leather came along. He was strapping on the gun belt when he became aware of Stonekiller's steady gaze.

"Figured you knew your way around guns," the half-breed said. He nodded toward the improvised crossdraw rig. "You cavalry? Horse soldiers wore their handguns like that."

"I was for a time." Slocum didn't elaborate.

Stonekiller didn't press the point. He tossed aside the dregs of his coffee and stood. "Getting on toward chuck call," he said. "If you'll feed the fire, I'll stake the ponies and rustle up some grub. There's a haunch of antelope tied behind the saddle on the roan."

"I'll handle it," Slocum said. "I need to carry some of my weight around here." He started to turn away, then paused. "Kind of curious about something, Stonekiller. How did you know those Kickapoos' plan of attack?"

The faint smile touched Stonekiller's lips again. "Snuck up on them and listened in. I speak the language. There never was a Kickapoo could hold a Kiowa's breechclout when it comes to sneaky. Skillet and other truck's in that pack beside you." Stonekiller scraped a fingertip across the crimson stain on his shirt. "I'd best wash this out before it develops maggots, the way it's drawing flies."

Slocum stripped the saddle from the paint, set a picket line with one of the Indian riatas, and secured the horses where they could reach grass and water.

Stonekiller had waded into the spring and was washing the bloodied shirt when Slocum returned after tending the horses. The light was all but gone now, yet Slocum could see that the stocky man's back and chest bore several scars. Whatever he was, he was a warrior, Slocum thought. A timid man didn't accumulate that many battle marks.

Stonekiller spread the wet shirt over a small bush to dry and squatted by the fire as Slocum laid out cooking utensils and sliced thick slabs from the antelope haunch. "Well, that's the last of them," Stonekiller said casually after a few minutes.

"Last of who?"

"It's a long story."

"I'm not going anywhere."

Stonekiller sighed. "I suppose you earned the right to know, since you helped out. Those three were the last of old Yellow Shirt's brood. I buried another four of his litter over the last three years." He traced a finger over the scar on his face. "One of them gave me this to remember him by. He was a better knife fighter than I thought he was. Turned out that he thought he was a better knife fighter than he really was. You know, those Kickapoos carry a grudge something fierce. They've been after me ever since I brought their old man in to hang for murder, back when I was wearing a star."

"A star?"

"Kiowa Tribal Police. I quit the force a spell back. Had a nice little place up on Saschaqua Creek until that damned Bloody Hand went crazy." Stonekiller's voice trailed away. He had a far-off look in his eyes, Slocum noted.

The strips of meat began to sizzle. Slocum turned his attention to refilling the coffeepot, adding a palmful of fresh grounds to the old ones. He had ridden enough long trails to learn how to make supplies stretch.

"Grub will be ready in a few minutes," Slocum said. His brow furrowed. "Stonekiller, I don't like prying into a man's business, but I have a feeling you might be wanting to talk about something."

Stonekiller sighed. "You're right, Slocum. I keep it bottled up inside any longer, it'll eat my guts out. Bloody Hand's bunch raided my place while I was two days' ride off, tracking a horse

thief. They burned the buildings, made off with my livestock—
and my woman.''

Slocum glanced up. "Damn. For what it's worth, I'm sorry.
For you and your woman."

"I'll get her back, Slocum." Stonekiller's tone was as cold as
a Montana blizzard. "That's why I'm out here."

Slocum speared a slab of antelope meat with his pocket knife,
dropped it onto a tin plate, and handed it to the half-breed. He
waited silently until Stonekiller had eaten his fill, then took the
plate and snared a slice of meat for himself.

"If you were tracking Bloody Hand, it must have been his
bunch that jumped the wagon," Slocum said.

Stonekiller nodded. "It was. Finish your chuck and we'll talk
about it. I've got some studying to do." The blocky half-breed
ate quickly, then strode to the edge of the clearing and stared at
the thin, red-gold strip of sky that lingered from sundown. The
stars had appeared overhead before Stonekiller returned.

"How's the head?"

"Still aches a bit," Slocum said. "Nothing serious."

"Vision blurred? Ears ringing?"

Slocum shook his head. "A little buzz from that Ballard muzzle
blast is all."

"Good," Stonekiller said. "Seeing how you handled the rifle,
I believe we can quit worrying about a brain bruise. Still might
have a crack in your skullbone, but that's not something that
could kill you." The half-breed produced his tobacco pouch,
rolled a quirly, and tossed the sack to Slocum. "What'll you do
now?"

Slocum pondered the question while he rolled and lit a smoke.
"Up until an hour ago, I wasn't sure," he said. "Now, I've got
a horse, saddle, and weapons of a sort." He dragged at the cigarette. "And I've got a mad on. I'm going to track down those
bastards who bushwhacked me, stole my horses and money, and
took the wagon I was paid to guard. Things like that piss me
off."

"Didn't figure you were one to just roll over and whimper
about bad luck," Stonekiller said. "Know what you're getting
into? That's a mess of Injuns you're talking about taking on."

Slocum shrugged. "I've been outgunned and outmanned before. I've got to give it a try. It's the only way I know."

"You could get yourself killed."

"I could also get bit by a rattlesnake or have a horse fall on me. Nothing's guaranteed about life except that it will end someday."

Stonekiller dragged at his cigarette, let the smoke trickle from his nostrils, and leaned back against his saddle to gaze at the night sky.

"Bloody Hand's a crazy son of a bitch," Stonekiller said after a moment. "He's also got twenty young bucks with him, all of them full of scorpion piss. Those are mighty long odds for one man, Slocum." He paused to stub out his smoke. "What was in that wagon?"

"Twelve cases of new Winchester rifles. More than a thousand rounds of ammunition. And nearly nine hundred dollars in cash," Slocum said.

Stonekiller pursed his lips in a silent whistle. "Damn. That's not the best news I've heard in a spell. Give Bloody Hand that many guns and he'll have renegades from all over the Southwest riding to join up with him. Fits right in with his medicine vision."

"Which is?"

"Probably more of a whiskey dream than anything else. But the crazy bastard believes it. Thinks he's the red man's messiah. Believes he's the savior who can drive the white man back past the Mississippi and make the buffalo come back." Stonekiller shrugged. "The same sort of nonsense that medicine man Isatai told Quanah Parker before the buffalo hunters shot the shit out them at Adobe Walls."

Slocum finished his cigarette and started cleaning up the supper mess. "You believe in medicine visions?"

"Maybe. Maybe not. Lots of things in this world I don't know," Stonekiller said. "What I do know is that Bloody Hand's got my wife. And I'm going to get her back." The Kiowa leaned forward, forearms across his knees, and stared at Slocum for a moment. "We've got some things in common, you and me," he said. "For starters, we both want what Bloody Hand took from us. Alone, neither one of us would stand much of a chance. Together, we might be able to pull it off."

Slocum lifted an eyebrow. "You mean join forces?"

Stonekiller half smiled. "Hell, yes. The two of us could surround the whole bunch." The smile faded. "What do you think,

Slocum? You have any problem with the idea of working with a half-breed who's more Injun than Irish?''

"I usually work alone." Slocum paused to refill the community coffee cup. "But I usually don't take on a whole tribe on the warpath, either. What makes you think you want to work with me?''

Stonekiller sipped at the cup, then handed it back. "I think I've got a handle on you now, Slocum, and I like what I see. I know you can handle a gun. I know you're tough. And I've got a better than fair idea that you don't back down from anybody.''

Slocum scowled. "Just when did you get to know me so well, Stonekiller?'' He didn't try to hide the irritation in his words. Having someone tell him who he was rubbed Slocum the wrong way.

"Didn't take long," Stonekiller said calmly. "I have an instinct for sizing up people, Slocum. I look at you and I see a man who asks no quarter and gives none, takes no survivors in a fight, and is savvy enough not to get stupid at the wrong time.'' Stonekiller finished his smoke and ground the butt under a heel. "Teaming up might work to your advantage, too. I know Bloody Hand. I know how the bastard thinks. I know his strengths and his weaknesses. And now, I know where he's going. Arizona.'' Stonekiller paused for a moment, staring into the distance, his brow wrinkled. "He's one dangerous son of a bitch, Slocum. I'm not too proud to admit I could use some help.''

Slocum fell silent, studying on the idea. Ten to one odds were long, but a damn sight better than twenty to one. He had seen Stonekiller in action; there was no questioning the man's intelligence, guts, tracking skill, and ability with weapons. And, Slocum had to admit, he owed the half-breed. If not for Stonekiller, he would have been dead already. Still, the prospect of taking on a partner, even a good one, went against Slocum's grain. He had ridden many a long and dangerous trail alone and lived. So far.

"Well," Stonekiller finally said, "how about it?''

"What you're saying makes sense," Slocum admitted. "But it's a hell of a long trail from here to Arizona. It will take twice as many supplies for two men as for one, and it looks like you're already traveling light, yourself.''

"Money's a problem," Stonekiller said. "I've got thirty dollars left. You?''

"Bandits took everything I had except one gold eagle I keep hidden in the top of my boot," Slocum said. "My twenty and your thirty makes fifty. That won't finance a long hunt."

Stonekiller stared at the ground, frowning in silence for a moment, then looked up. "If it comes down to it, I'll live on rattlesnake meat and jackrabbit. I've done it before. But then, I'm half Injun."

"I've lived off the land, too," Slocum said, "but that doesn't mean I enjoy it. Also, we're going to need plenty of ammunition. The horses need to be reshod before we hit the badlands and mountains, or we'll be afoot within a week. We'll need grain for the mounts. Some of the country between here and Arizona doesn't have enough grass to keep a sheep alive."

Stonekiller lifted an eyebrow. "You know the country?"

Slocum nodded. "I've been through it."

"Another reason we ought to team up," Stonekiller said. "I've never been south of Santa Fe, myself." He rolled a smoke and tossed the tobacco sack to Slocum. "There's always a good poker game going on down in Raton. You play?"

Slocum nodded as he rolled his cigarette. "Some."

"Good at it?"

"Better than most, I guess," Slocum said with a shrug. He lit the smoke. "I'm not a professional poker player. I could lose what little money we have. That's why they call it gambling. It's risky."

"Life's risky." Stonekiller dragged at his cigarette. "It could be worth your while, Slocum. There's a thousand dollar reward on Bloody Hand. Dead or alive. You can have the money. All I want is my wife back."

Slocum fell silent for a moment, thinking. It was possible. He had lived off poker winnings for many a cold winter or hot summer. A thousand dollars wasn't a sum to be swatted away like a blowfly. All that stood in the way was a couple of dozen dangerous renegades with big guns and nasty tempers, and a few hundred miles of bad country.

"There's one more thing," Slocum finally said. "I wouldn't ask if it wasn't the most important of all."

Stonekiller nodded. "Ask away."

"I know how Comanches treat women captives. I've seen the results. So have you, Stonekiller. I don't know what that might do to your mind when we catch up to them. She'll be damaged goods.''

A wince creased Stonekiller's face. "I know that. I've come to terms with it. I won't go loco on you. Regardless of what's happened, I want her back.'' He sighed. ''She's my whole life, Slocum. You ever love a woman?''

Slocum stared off into the distance, faces from the past flitting across his memory. Two or three of them were more than hazy remembrances from the back rooms of saloons and red light districts from New York City to Matamoros. After a moment, he shrugged. "I guess I came close a few times. Close enough that it stung some when I lost them.''

"Close counts in artillery fire," Stonekiller said solemnly, "but when the right woman comes along, you take a direct hit. I did.''

"You realize they'll probably kill her if they're attacked," Slocum said after a moment. "Killing captives is the first thing Comanches do if they have a chance.''

A brief flicker of pain dulled the bright black eyes. "I know. Maria knows. I also know her well enough to say that she'd rather die like that than stay alive as Bloody Hand's woman. It's a chance we have to take.''

Slocum wasn't sure if by "we," Stonekiller meant Slocum and Stonekiller or Maria and Stonekiller. The woman might already be dead, but Slocum didn't think so. A white woman might kill herself to escape the horror of Comanche captivity, but suicide was the strongest of all Plains Indian taboos. To take one's own life meant to walk in the darkness of the night between worlds for eternity.

"Tell me about her," Slocum said.

Stonekiller's scarred face softened. "She's Cheyenne. The daughter of a war chief killed in a fight with buffalo hunters up on the Republican River not long after she was born. Her tribal name translates as Dove Wings Soft on Morning Wind. Maria is less of a mouthful, so she's been Maria most of her life." Stonekiller sighed, his gaze fixed on the stars that blanketed the western sky. "We met at a sun dance three years ago. She's a beautiful woman, Slocum, and a gentle soul. No child or old person went hungry or cold when Maria was around. She could have had anybody. She picked me. I still don't know why.''

Stonekiller fell silent for several minutes, obviously lost in his thoughts and memories. Slocum left him alone. At length, Stonekiller shook himself back to the present. "It's hard to describe Maria, Slocum. There's something about her that a man can't put into words."

Slocum could see that talking about Maria was causing Stonekiller pain. But there was one more knife he had to twist in the half-breed's gut.

"I wouldn't say this if I didn't think I need to know, but I've seen women who have gone stark, raving mad at the hands of Comanches. I've known of women who would rather force some buck to kill them than to endure what they have to put up with. Is Maria strong enough to handle it? And what will she be like when we get her back?"

The pain in Stonekiller's eyes faded beneath a glimmer of pride. "She's the daughter of a war chief, Slocum. She may be gentle, but she's also tough as rawhide. She's a survivor."

Slocum nodded solemnly. "Then she's worth going after, Stonekiller. You've got a partner." He extended a hand.

3

Maria Stonekiller sat beside the wheel of the captured wagon, her back straight, shoulders squared, and head held high despite the nagging pain of the bruises on her buttocks and thighs and the scabbing puncture wounds across her back and shoulders.

She tried to block out the muted whimperings that came from a few yards behind her. The pitiful mewings cut at her heart. But there was nothing she could do for the white woman. It was already twilight. The poor woman probably would be dead by morning. Maria hoped so. Death was the only escape for the woman now.

Exhaustion rode heavily on Maria's shoulders. They had been at this camp for two days and two nights, but there had been no rest for her. A coarse horsehair riata was looped around her neck and tied to a corner brace inside the wagon. A separate length of riata bound her wrists. The grinding abrasions of the horsehair left her skin raw and burned. The tether around her neck was not long enough to let her lie down at night. She had to sleep sitting up. If she drifted into a sound sleep and toppled over, the loop around her neck drew tight, choking her awake. Yet she refused to show her weakness before the renegades. Especially before Bloody Hand.

Bloody Hand's camp was noisy and boisterous with the cele-
bration of a series of successful raids. The sticks and bones gambling game had been going for two days and two nights now. A
dozen men knelt or squatted beside a blanket, whooping and yelling at each toss. Others stood alongside, craned necks to see the
results, and placed bets among themselves. Something of value
changed hands each time the sticks and bones fell—horses, blankets, knives, captives—anything a man might have that would
interest another in a wager. Several of the raiders had already lost
their fortunes of war and now stood watching the game.

The men were a mix of Comanche, Kiowa, Kiowa-Apache, a
couple of full-blood Chiricahua Apache, and a smattering of
Kickapoos. They were not warriors, Maria thought with a silent
snort of disgust. They were animals. Scavengers, thieves, mur-
derers who killed for sport and sport alone. They were the worst
the frontier had to offer. When despair and pain threatened to
overpower Maria, she had only to call forth her contempt and
hate for such men to renew her strength and resolve.

There were few women in the camp, fewer children, and less
than a half dozen lodges. The women showed little interest in the
gambling, even though it was possible one of their men might bet
them on a throw of the bones and lose. The women preferred to
entertain themselves tormenting the captives, anyway.

Almost a week had passed since the attack on the wagon on
the rolling plains, almost a month since the raid in which she had
been captured. Long, exhausting days of hard traveling, of feet
and legs leaden from carrying a heavy pack. And after the wagon
ambush, heaving against the tailboard when the sand dragged at
the wheels. Bloody Hand's band had eaten one of the mules the
night of the ambush. The raiders' taste for mule meat left them
short of animal power. The remaining mules were failing, their
strength sapped by constant straining against the traces to move
the heavy wagon.

Bloody Hand said he had called the halt to rest the mules.
Maria knew the real reason for the stop. It was the white woman
staked out behind her. She tried not to think about the woman.
Or the bodies of the woman's husband and grown son, scalped
and mutilated beside the wagon tracks known as the Santa Fe
Trail. They should not have been so careless or so stupid as to
travel alone in such dangerous country. The realization didn't ease

Maria's mind or silence the whimpers.

Maria's jaw clenched as a stocky Comanche strode past, grinning, repositioning his breechclout, heading for the fire and another round of the gambling game. Another Indian, a dirty, stocky Kiowa-Apache with a cruel face, called Natchee, walked toward the spread-eagled white woman. He was already fumbling with the buttons on the bloodstained breeches stripped from the body of the woman's husband. Maria didn't look directly at the two Indians, even though both cast leering glances in her direction. She had a measure of protection from the white woman's fate. Bloody Hand had put out the word that Maria was "his woman" until he said otherwise.

A toothless old Comanche hag jabbed a sharpened stick into Maria's back and cackled wildly as Maria flinched at the unexpected stab of pain. The old woman was as bad as the worst of the men in this clan. The puncture wounds on Maria's body had been her doing, as had the painful burn on her breast. Maria steeled herself against the pain with a promise that, should she be able to steal a knife, the old hag would never again torment a captive—even if it meant Maria's own life in exchange. It would be, Maria thought, a fair trade.

Despite her exhausted and painful state, Maria knew she had been lucky. Other captives had been less fortunate.

Two young Ute warriors, traditional enemies of the Comanches, had been wounded and captured while hunting only a few hours after the raid on the wagon. At dawn yesterday, the Comanches roasted the Utes alive over a slow fire. It was a long, agonizing death. The Comanches howled in glee at the screams of the tortured men. They sliced away strips of muscle with knives or poked sharp sticks into the slowly broiling flesh that gradually blackened, cracked, and fell away as the flames charred exposed skin and flesh before the two young Utes finally and mercifully died.

A pretty young Arapaho woman, run down while trying to escape a week ago, now huddled in a small, pathetic bundle near the lodge of her captor, one of the pure-blooded Apaches in Bloody Hand's band. Her left foot flopped uselessly when she moved. The Apache had severed the large tendon above her heel with his knife. She would never run again.

A fourth captive, a young half-Mexican, half-Ute girl barely thirteen years old, also had died within the last week, lanced through the belly and left to a lingering death because she had somehow offended her Comanche owner.

Only one of the captives had remained virtually unmolested. She was staked well apart from the others, securely bound, and closely watched by the sadistic old hag. She was Shoshoni, young, strikingly attractive, tall for her age and tribal heritage. She had been captured only two days ago, and she was menstruating. Even among animals such as the men in this camp, touching—or even being near—a woman who was in her blood moon was the worst possible medicine. It had saved the young woman for now.

The only male captive in Bloody Hand's band was a Mexican boy barely six years old. He was not tethered or bound at night like the others, and he ate with the men. Maria was reasonably sure the child would be spared and eventually adopted into the Comanche band.

She was less sure of the fate of a young Cheyenne girl now huddled asleep at Maria's feet. Maria knew the girl. She had been taken from the ranch adjoining the Stonekillers' place. The girl had not yet reached puberty. What happened to her when she grew to womanhood remained to be seen. In the meantime, it was enough that she lived and suffered little.

Maria inwardly winced at the grunting sound behind her. The Kiowa-Apache appeared moments later, fumbling with the buttons on his trousers. He stopped a few feet in front of Maria and glanced toward the fire. Bloody Hand had the sticks and bones, his face downcast, intent on his throw. He was not watching. Natchee leered and opened his trousers. His genitals were smeared with blood and globs of white fluid.

Maria's stomach churned, but she showed no emotion. Natchee laughed, buttoned his stained pants, and strode toward the fire. Another man, wiry and scarred, with a scraggly patch of chin whiskers, walked past the wagon. The parade of men had been constant since they pitched camp. Maria had no way of knowing how many times the white woman had been raped. It had been a constant thing. She had been given no rest, no food, no water during the entire time.

The young Cheyenne girl at Maria's feet whimpered in her sleep. Maria stroked the girl's black hair with her bound hands.

"Be still, young one," Maria said, her voice soothing. "Do not let the bad dreams rob you of your youth or your soul. Everything will be all right." Maria could only wish that her heart was as sure as her words sounded.

Darkness began to descend on the camp. Maria dreaded the appearance of the stars overhead. But tonight, she thought, perhaps she would be spared the indignity of Bloody Hand's touch if the gambling lasted until dawn. Unless Bloody Hand gambled her away. The thought chilled Maria's blood. As bad as the renegade Comanche leader was, many of his followers were worse. She knew her life lay in the coarse hands and unpredictable brain of the war party chief. She wouldn't live a day as a plaything of the others. Bloody Hand liked his women whole. The others didn't care. And each day she survived was a day more that Jim Stonekiller might reach her. Maria knew her husband would come. It was only a matter of when. And if Jim died in the attempt, so would she. Life without him would be a more cruel form of existence than death itself.

Maria peered toward the fire. The blaze was much too large. Flames leapt as high as a man's head. Embers spiraled skyward above the blaze, yellow dots against the darkening sky. Bloody Hand appeared to be winning; he still had the toss in the game. So far, her luck was holding.

The girl at Maria's feet whimpered again. Maria lowered her head to speak soothingly to the child. Tears trickled down the pale coppery skin of the girl's cheeks. For a fleeting moment, Maria wished her own pride would allow her to shed her own tears. But that would solve nothing. After a moment, she glanced up.

Her heart sank.

Bloody Hand strode toward her, outlined against the tall tongues of fire. He was a big man, even for a Kwahadi Comanche, a hand span over six feet tall, with long, powerful arms and a thickly muscled chest. His legs seemed out of proportion to the rest of his body. They were thin, almost without muscle bulk. He carried a bundle under one arm. His gambling winnings, Maria assumed. She dropped her gaze, hoping Bloody Hand would pass her by on the way to his buffalo-skin lodge.

The footsteps stopped before her.

Maria forced herself to raise her head. Bloody Hand's face was indistinct in the faint light, but Maria knew it well. A broad face, with thick scar tissue where one eyebrow should have been. Thin, cruel lips turned down at the corners below a humped nose that appeared to have been broken at least once. The most frightening thing about Bloody Hand was his eyes. They were cold, as cold as any wind in the Starving Time, and reflected a smoldering fire of hate.

Bloody Hand casually tossed his gambling winnings into the wagon. Maria heard the scratching as he untied the horsehair riata from the corner brace of the wagon. The big Comanche squatted, untied the bindings from one of her wrists, then rose and tugged at the riata still around her neck. He did not speak.

Maria drew a resigned breath, rose, carefully stepped over the sleeping girl at her feet, and followed Bloody Hand into his lodge. A heavy darkness fell inside the thick skins of the tepee as Bloody Hand dropped the entry flap into place and removed the tether from Maria's neck. The air inside the lodge struck her nostrils an almost physical blow. The lodge was fetid. It smelled of sweat, unwashed bodies, bear grease, and the acrid musk of scalps drying on thongs tied to lodgepoles. Maria's stomach churned at the scent; her Cheyenne heritage rebelled at the scent of filth. Her people had always been clean, bathing daily even in the worst of weather. She welcomed the darkness of the lodge as she silently stripped her doeskin dress over her head. At least she would be spared the further indignity of looking into the Comanche's face.

Maria's skin crawled at Bloody Hand's rough shove against her shoulder. She lowered herself onto the soiled blankets and vermin-infested buffalo skin that served as a bed. She heard the rustle of cloth as the renegade dropped his trousers. Callused hands closed on her full breasts. Maria ground her teeth as Bloody Hand brutally pinched and twisted her nipples. She would not give him the satisfaction of knowing he had hurt her. She knew better than to struggle against Bloody Hand. It was a lesson learned the hard way. Fighting him only fueled Bloody Hand's excitement and cruelty. She bore a deep bruise along her cheek and jawline from the first time. The skin beneath her dense mat of crotch hair was still tender where Bloody Hand had twisted his fingers and yanked hard enough to lift her hips from the robe, as if trying to rip away a trophy of his conquest.

She opened her thighs and raised her knees at the scrape of Bloody Hand's rough fingers against her upper legs. He groped at her for a moment in the pitch blackness. Maria flinched at the quick stab of pain as he rammed himself into her. It wasn't his size that hurt; he wasn't as big as Jim, but her canal was as dry as her mouth. She lay tense and unmoving for a moment, conscious only of the stinging friction inside her and the steady thump of Bloody Hand's hips against her already bruised crotch. Then she forced herself to move, knowing that the Comanche would beat her again if she showed no response. She began to lift her hips in time to his thrusts as she tried to focus her thoughts elsewhere, away from the foul breath in her face. She fought back the picture of her husband's face in her mind; she did not want him to see her humiliation, even in her thoughts. She focused instead on the image of a knife in her hand, its blade at Bloody Hand's throat, the quick gush of blood and gurgled cry as she swiped the keen edge across his dirty skin. Her body lurched beneath the renegade's furious humping, the scabs of the wounds on her back tearing open as the force of his thrusts scooted her across the grimy buffalo hide. The pounding against her crotch seemed to go on forever before she felt him swell, then the final, deep thrust as the first burst of fluid gushed into her. Bloody Hand grunted, his breath catching in his throat after each throb of his penis. Maria felt the hot stickiness fill her, then overflow and ooze onto the skin between her buttocks and smear against her thighs. Bloody Hand collapsed atop her, his heavy weight threatening to squeeze the breath from her chest. He lay still for a long time. His breathing gradually slowed; Maria felt him wither, and then his limp shaft slid from her.

After a moment, the renegade grunted and rolled off her. Maria sat up, reached for her dress, and slipped it over her head. The horsehair noose again settled around her neck. She rose and followed as Bloody Hand led her back toward the wagon. Maria felt the stickiness trickle down her thighs as she walked. A sliver of moon had appeared overhead. Maria glanced toward the spread-eagled white form a few feet away. The white woman no longer whimpered. Her eyes stared at the heavens without seeing. Raw flesh showed dark and bloody on her torso and between her legs. The renegades had skinned her breasts for tanning and carved away her crotch hair as a trophy. The breast skins and matted "scalp" would change hands many times at the gaming blanket before the sun came, Maria knew.

She sat beside the wagon wheel. Bloody Hand tied her neck rope to the wagon and again bound her wrists. Neither of them had said a word.

Maria's lips were a thin line, her eyes narrowed in hate, as the Comanche strode back toward the gambling game. Her hands unconsciously dropped to stroke the hair of the young girl, who was still huddled asleep, unaware of what had happened. Maria's hatred for Bloody Hand had grown even stronger this night. It was not his taking her to the blanket that darkened her heart; that was the way of the Comanche and of some other tribes, a part of the culture. It was that Bloody Hand had so cheapened and degraded the act of coupling itself that heightened Maria's desire to see him dead.

Maria slowly lifted her gaze to the stars overhead and tried to ignore the thick, sticky fluid against her thighs. She prayed to her Cheyenne spirits and the white man's god that the damned Comanche had not left her with child. She could bear the memory of the pain, the humiliation, even the rage. She could not bear the thought of bringing the devil's offspring into the world. Not when she and her Jim had yet to be blessed with a child. She had one additional prayer beyond that—to see Bloody Hand's head on a stake.

The thought of Jim Stonekiller brought a measure of uneasy peace to Maria. He was out there, somewhere. She knew he would come for her. It was her duty as a Cheyenne woman, and as his wife, to remain alive until then. The young girl at her feet stirred and whimpered beneath Maria's touch, lost in a bad dream.

"Be still, young one," Maria whispered soothingly. "My Jim will come for us soon." She lifted her gaze toward the gambling game. Bloody Hand once more had the toss of the sticks and bones. "And then," she said, "these animals who would be men shall know a real warrior."

Slocum checked the Kickapoo dun alongside Stonekiller's nervous sorrel on a ridge overlooking the bustling town of Raton.

The breeze from the Sangre de Cristos was dry and cool here. It carried the scent of pine from the mountain range along with a hint of woodsmoke from the town below. The dun snorted and fidgeted, restive despite the steady downhill ride through Raton Pass, but soon calmed under the steady pressure of Slocum's knees against its ribs.

Slocum eased the hat from his head and ran a kerchief across his brow and blotted sweat from the tender scar tissue beginning to form over the gash in his temple. He had always healed rapidly. It was a good trait to have, in his trade. The lingering headache had faded. Slocum's senses were as sharp as ever. He studied the town below. The streets of Raton were crowded. A pall of dust raised by the passage of horses, buggies, and wagons down the major streets drifted on the breeze. Slocum saw nothing out of the ordinary. It wasn't reassuring. Ordinary had a way of turning ugly on a man if he let his guard down.

"Must be a Saturday with this many people in town," Stonekiller said after a few minutes, "ready to go visit civilization for a spell?"

"No. I'd as soon ride around, if we had a choice."

"Me, too. Never had much good happen to me in a town before. But it wouldn't hurt my feelings any to have a cold beer right now, either." Stonekiller sighed. "Well, let's go sell some stuff and find us a poker game."

Slocum stepped inside the Silver Bit Saloon and paused for a moment to let his vision adjust from the white, bright sunlight of the street to the dimmer cantina interior. Oil lamps were lit although it was early afternoon. Weak sunlight filtered through two dirty, smoke-smudged windows overlooking the street outside. A haze of tobacco smoke hung against the ceiling of the lower floor of the two-story cantina. The smell of sweat, smoke, and stale beer lay heavy against his nostrils.

As his eyes adapted to the dim light, Slocum's gaze drifted around the crowded room. Cowboys, teamsters, and a handful of men who looked to be miners stood at the polished mahogany bar. The expensive bar with its shiny brass footrail seemed out of place in a saloon that seemed to cater more to Raton's working class. But the blacksmith down the street had pointed to the Silver Bit as the hottest gambling spot in town.

The cantina didn't look like a place where big money changed hands on the turn of a card. Three games—one monte, one blackjack, and one poker—were going on at tables in the far end of the establishment. All looked to be small-stakes affairs. The players were vaqueros, cowboys, railroaders, men whose occupations showed in weathered, sunbrowned faces and rough clothing. Men who worked for low wages and couldn't afford heavy betting. The smithy had said the real action was in a back room. The trick was to get there; a man with less than fifty dollars couldn't even get through the heavy door that stood at the near end of the cantina.

Slocum had just enough money to sit in on the big game, thanks to Stonekiller's sharp trading ability. The Kickapoo scalps were the big moneymakers. A drummer from back East who dealt in women's "intimate garments" had forked over ten dollars each for the scalps. Sale of the captured Indian horses and equipment brought another forty. After buying supplies and having the horses shod, the two hunters had just over sixty dollars left. That gave them enough extra cash for a couple of drinks each.

Slocum and Stonekiller eased their way through the crowd, found a space at the end of the bar, and waited as a young man with a pasty complexion scurried about refilling shot glasses and drawing mugs of beer from the wooden keg at the end of the backbar. Two hostesses drifted from table to table, taking orders, delivering drinks, pausing to laugh and joke with customers from time to time. One of the women was a thin, freckled red-haired girl who didn't quite fill out the bodice on her blue gown. The other woman was older, Spanish, with long, black hair and full hips. She more than filled her blouse. Her eyes twinkled when she laughed.

Slocum became aware that the redhead had stepped away from the table she had been hustling and stood staring at him. Slocum was used to being stared at, even if he'd never learned to like it. A man who stood nearly six foot two, with jet black hair, green eyes, and the lean build of a mountain cat tended to draw attention. The girl's thin cheeks colored under Slocum's direct, steady gaze.

"What'll it be, mister?" The bartender's reedy voice brought Slocum's head around.

"Two beers," Slocum said, "and a bottle of Old Overholt."

The young barkeep swallowed nervously, his gaze flicking from Slocum to Stonekiller. He cleared his throat.

"I can't—well, Mr. Martlee says—" His voice faltered for a heartbeat. "We don't serve Indians."

Slocum's eyes narrowed. He pinned a hard gaze on the nervous youngster and let him squirm for several seconds. Then he said, his tone cold, "What Indians? I don't see any Indians in here, son."

Sweat beaded on the young man's forehead. "Your—your friend," he said lamely.

Slocum turned to Stonekiller. "Jim, do you see any Indians around?"

Stonekiller flashed a disarming grin. "By the faith no, my friend, but I do spy a few of me countrymen from the auld sod. Ah, but the Emerald Isle has sent her sons to many an outpost here in the wilds."

The young bartender looked confused. Slocum understood why. The Irish lilt rolled effortlessly from Stonekiller's tongue. " 'Tis yet a wonder to find fellow Irishmen in such a town."

"You—you're Irish?"

"As Irish as a shamrock and the Blarney Stone, me friend," Stonekiller said cheerfully. "As Irish as the pope be Catholic, though I follow the Protestant road, meself. Now, how about it, laddie? 'Tis a thirsty world, this New Mexico."

"I—I don't know," the youth said haltingly. "You don't look Irish."

The flare of irritation in Slocum's gut gave way to a growing amusement. It didn't look like Stonekiller needed any help on this project.

"Aye, laddie, 'tis true," Stonekiller said. "The sun and wind of the West does darken a man's skin to the color of bark. No, I dinna look Irish—and ye dinna look like a tyke who'd hint a man was a liar, lest he get his skinny butt kicked as can be kicked not harder than by a mule or an Irishman." The cheerful tone was still in Stonekiller's words, but the expression in the black eyes was anything but jovial. "Now, laddie, kindly fetch those drinks, lest I swoon away from thirst."

The bartender's face went even paler. His Adam's apple bobbed. "Yes, sir. Right away."

Moments later, two mugs of beer, a couple of shot glasses, and a bottle appeared before the two men. "That'll be two fifty," the young man said. His gaze darted about nervously, as if he feared being caught in the act of defying the rules of the house.

Slocum tossed a five dollar gold piece on the bar. A man looking to get into a poker game had to look like he was well heeled. The bartender brought Slocum his change and hurried away. Slocum sipped at the beer. It was cool, a bit too malty, but not bad after a long, dry ride. He poured a splash of whiskey into each shot glass and slid one to Stonekiller. "Nice brogue," he said.

Stonekiller shrugged. "I do a passing fair coyote, too."

Slocum felt a hand on his shoulder. The thin, red-haired girl flashed a smile. Slocum noted the slight gap between her two front teeth.

"Hello, cowboy," the girl said. "I'm Angie. Looking for something special in Raton?"

"Yes, as a matter of fact," Slocum said with a smile. "I'd hoped to play some poker." He saw the quick flicker of disappointment in her hazel eyes. "Afterwards, maybe something else," he added to soothe her feelings. His comments were partly true. Any another time he would have tried her, if the price had been right. Up close she wasn't half bad. She wasn't the best looker he'd ever seen, but he had the feeling she was damn good at her work.

The hurt expression faded from Angie's eyes. "There'll be a seat open at the back table in a few minutes. I can get you in, Mr.—?"

"Slocum." He slid a silver dollar to Angie. "Thanks. I appreciate the help. But I was hoping for a game with higher stakes than these fellows are playing. What are a man's chances of getting into the back room?"

Angie slipped the dollar into her bodice. "Give me a few minutes. I'll see what I can do."

Slocum and Stonekiller stayed at the bar, nursing the bottle, as Angie disappeared behind the heavy door. Slocum went easy on the jug when it was time for serious poker playing. Too much whiskey fuzzed the brain and senses. Many a man had lost his bundle because of drunken bad judgment, not because of the run of the cards.

He had finished his beer and poured Stonekiller another whiskey before Angie sidled up and pressed her left breast with its erect nipple against Slocum's arm. The invitation was obvious. And effective. Slocum had to remind himself there was more important business at hand, but he made no effort to move his arm.

"You're in, Slocum," Angie said. "I'll introduce you around." She lowered her voice to a whisper and leaned closer. "Watch it. There's a professional gambler in that game. I think he cheats."

Slocum slipped an arm around her waist and gave her a brief hug. "Thanks, Angie. I'll stay alert. Maybe I'll see you later."

A hopeful glint, almost a leer, flickered in her hazel eyes. "I'll be here when you're ready." A bellow from a nearby table brought a sigh to her lips. "Let me take care of that braying jackass before he decides to wreck the place. Then I'll show you in."

Slocum stroked her hip as she turned away, then glanced at Stonekiller. "Are you sure you want to risk it? Going up against a card sharp could leave us flat broke. We've got enough now to carry us for a while."

Stonekiller shook his head. "We'll need a couple hundred, best I can figure. I'll keep an eye on the sharp. Know most of the tricks myself."

"Didn't have you figured for a gambling man."

"I'm not. But my sainted old Irish pappy could handle the pasteboards with the best of them. The old coot cheated me out of two dollars and three good ponies before he taught me the tricks of the trade." Stonekiller half smiled. "Speaking of Irish, it might be best if we used my Christian handle—James O'Hara—instead of my Kiowa name. Could be some of those men in the back room don't take kindly to an Injun standing around looking like he was about to lift a scalp."

Slocum handed the money to Stonekiller. "You handle the cash. That will give us an excuse to talk, if need be."

Stonekiller casually dropped the bills in a shirt pocket as Angie returned. "Ready to go play some poker, Slocum?" she said.

4

The back room, Slocum noted, had a lot more class than the rest of the Silver Bit. An expensive chandelier hung above the polished mahogany card table covered in green felt. A matching mahogany bar gleamed in the lamplight on one side of the room, its shelves stocked with costly name brand liquors. Slocum recognized one of the labels, a French brandy that cost as much per bottle as a good saddle horse. A heavy tapestry with ornate stitching hung along one wall. The scene on the tapestry looked to be something from fourteenth-century Europe.

Angie made the introductions. All but one of the men at the table were dressed in expensive, tailored suits and vests, and wore gold and diamond rings on their fingers. The fifth man was dressed like an ordinary cowhand, worn Levi's, scuffed boots, and a blue shirt faded from many washings. Wavy gray hair framed a face weathered almost the color of tobacco and intense hazel eyes that seemed to look inside a man instead of at him. Slocum pegged him as a rancher. He had the look of a tough old codger who had built his brand with sweat, blood, and guts.

Of the men wearing suits, one was a banker, one the owner of a merchandise firm known over three states, and another—a short, pudgy man with florid cheeks—was the owner of Raton's biggest growth industry. He was an undertaker. The names meant nothing to Slocum.

The fourth man was the gambler. It showed on him like a fresh brand. His name was Westphal. He was tall, slender, with long fingers and a face that had seldom seen the sun. He wore a string tie above a black silk vest adorned with a heavy gold watch chain. Slocum noted with interest that Westphal's stack of chips wasn't especially impressive.

As Slocum suspected, the roughly dressed player was a rancher. His name was Milt Hashburn, a name Slocum had heard before. Hashburn had been one of the first cattlemen in the open range country of West Texas and northeastern New Mexico. Even if he had never heard the name, Slocum would have known at a glance that Hashburn was not a man to cross.

Besides Stonekiller, there was one other nonplayer in the room. He stood behind the bar, his bulk seeming to dominate the entire room. His name was Turk. The moniker fit, Slocum thought. Turk seemed to have no neck. It was as if the massive head simply sat on shoulders that looked as heavy as a buffalo bull's. Cold brown eyes peered from beneath scarred brows. He made no move to acknowledge the presence of the newcomers, ignoring Slocum's casual nod of greeting. He wore a white shirt darkened by sweat at the collar and a suit coat with a telltale bulge beneath one armpit. Shoulder holsters were common these days. Westphal introduced Turk as an "associate." Bodyguard or shoulder hitter would be more like it, Slocum thought. He idly wondered if part of Turk's job was to retrieve any losses Westphal might accidentally incur at the card table. He didn't appear to be the kind of man who would have extreme convulsions of conscience after knocking somebody in the head in a dark alley.

Turk glowered at Stonekiller, then at Slocum. "What'll it be, gents?" His voice was thin and high-pitched for a man of his bulk. "On the house."

Slocum nodded. "Whiskey."

Stonekiller ordered the same. Slocum noted that of the men in the room, only Hashburn accepted the half-breed's presence without a frown or grimace. The rancher was the only one to shake Stonekiller's hand.

The banker waved toward an empty chair across from the gambler. "Game's five card stud or draw poker, dealer's choice, no jokers, no wild cards.'' His voice had an upturn at the end of each phrase, as if he were enjoying himself immensely. He probably was having a good time, Slocum thought; it was easy to have fun when you were gambling with other people's money. Slocum wondered how often the bank's books had been doctored and how many small ranchers and farmers foreclosed on because the man with all the money needed more. "Fifty dollar minimum," the banker said. "White chips are five, reds ten, blues twenty. Dollar ante, table stakes.''

Slocum sipped at his drink and waited as the banker counted out chips for the fifty dollars Stonekiller handed Slocum. The whiskey was the best he'd had since Saint Louis.

The banker had the deal. "Five card stud," he said.

Slocum caught a heart five in the hole and a spade jack up. The undertaker got an ace up, Hashburn a spade six, and the gambler a club five. Slocum folded when the bet came to him, then sat back and watched. Stonekiller leaned casually against the bar, his gaze drifting lazily around the room, outwardly relaxed.

Slocum folded twice more before he caught a promising hand. It was just promising enough to cost him ten dollars. Four hands later, he raked in a moderate pot, enough to put him a few dollars ahead and keep him in the game until he got a read on the players.

It didn't take long.

Slocum picked up the gambler's pattern within two hours. He lost more often than he won. That might have seemed odd for a professional, if it hadn't been for the banker. The pudgy man, who went by the name of Ely, had better than $500 in chips in front of him, by Slocum's guess. And he wasn't that good. But when the pot topped $100, the banker came up with the top cards on Westphal's deal almost every time. The big pots always seemed to come when one of the other players looked to be on a hot streak. Slocum knew the tactic. Let someone pull a few smaller pots until he thought the cards were running hot his way, then yank the blanket out from under him when the big money was on the table.

The ploy worked on Hashburn and the merchant. The two men were each down a hefty poke after three hours of play. The rancher seldom spoke, but Slocum saw the cold suspicion in the narrowing set of Hashburn's eyes. The undertaker, who seemed

a bit timid to be in a high-stakes game, was running a few dollars
ahead of even.

Slocum knew he was the target after he dragged four of six
pots and his winnings quickly topped the two hundred dollar
mark. The merchant had the upcoming deal, then the cards would
pass to the gambler. Slocum downed his drink and pushed back
from the table. He left his cash on the green felt.

"Deal around me this hand, gentlemen," he said with a nod
toward the back door. "Nature calls."

"Me, too," Stonekiller said casually. He fell into step with
Slocum toward the privvy behind the saloon.

"They're working the old in-law game, Jim," Slocum said.
"Westphal's fattening the banker's cards on all the big pots. It
wouldn't surprise me a bit to find out they were splitting the
winnings."

Stonekiller spat. "Sweetheart deal, sure enough. Keeps the professional's butt wiped clean if he doesn't win big. Westphal's
dealing seconds to the banker. He's not as good at it as he thinks
he is."

"We've got our two hundred," Slocum said. "We could
pocket the cash and move on. What's your pleasure?"

"Rather call than cash in," Stonekiller said grimly. "I never
did like a crooked game. Maybe it's time to teach somebody the
error of their ways."

Slocum half smiled. "I was hoping you'd say that."

"They're setting you up now, Slocum. If Westphal keeps up
his pattern, you'll catch three face cards to show a possible full
house on his deal, this time or next."

"And the banker will get lucky on the last card and nail a low
spot to a straight flush."

Stonekiller nodded. "That's my guess. Noticed that Westphal
likes clubs and diamonds when there's big money on the green."

"This time," Slocum said, his tone cold, "our banker friend
just might have a bit of trouble filling that straight flush. Let's go
do some gambling."

"Watch it, Slocum," Stonekiller said. "Never knew a gambler
who didn't pack a hideout gun. Banker could be holding iron, but
I doubt it. The no-neck mule behind the bar's got a pistol under
his armpit. Don't worry about Turk. I'll take care of him if it
comes to that."

The two went back inside. Slocum paused to pick up a fresh drink at the bar and returned to his chair, carefully adjusting the holster at his left hip.

The deal went around the table, Slocum winning two better-than-fair pots, before the gambler sprang the trap.

The game was five card stud. Slocum caught a queen down and a second lady on the first up card. The banker had a club eight showing.

"Queen bets," Westphal said.

"Ten." Slocum tossed a chip onto the table. The undertaker folded. Everyone else stayed. By the time the betting turned serious, Slocum had two queens and an ace up after the fourth card. The banker had the eight, ten, and seven of clubs showing. Westphal and the businessman folded.

"Queens have the power," the gambler said casually.

"Ladies bet twenty," Slocum said.

The banker chuckled. "Price of poker just went up, gents. Your twenty and another fifty."

Hashburn silently folded his cards. Slocum thought he read a look of curiosity, maybe anticipation, in the rancher's eyes.

"And fifty more," Slocum said. The banker called. It was head-to-head on the last card. The gambler had the trap baited.

At the corner of his vision, Slocum saw Stonekiller leaning against the bar within arm's length of the no-necked man.

"Last card," Westphal said. An ace dropped for Slocum. "Possible full house." The gambler's slender fingers ruffed the edge of the deck.

"Hold it a minute, Westphal," Slocum said casually.

The gambler quit fingering the cards, his gaze riveted on Slocum. "What's the problem?"

Slocum kept his eyes on Westphal. "Mr. Hashburn," he said, "I'd like you to take that deck and burn the second card."

"What?" Alarm flashed in Westphal's eyes.

"Nothing to worry about, Westphal," Slocum said coldly, "unless that second card happens to be a club six or nine."

The rancher took the deck from Westphal and flipped the second card faceup on the table. It was the club six.

"Looks like you've got a problem now, Westphal," Slocum said.

The gambler's face paled, then flushed. "What are you getting at, Slocum?"

"Our banker friend's been filling a lot of winning hands on the big pots on your deal," Slocum said. "Turn up his hole card, Mr. Hashburn. I'm betting it's the nine of clubs."

A silence fell over the room. Slocum could hear the tick of the undertaker's pocket watch. Slocum's gaze never left Westphal's eyes. He heard the banker's shallow breathing quicken, then the disgusted grunt from Hashburn.

"Club nine," the rancher said. "Damn curious."

"Not so curious, Mr. Hashburn." Slocum's eyes narrowed. "It isn't the first time Westphal has dealt seconds."

"Are you insinuating I cheat, Slocum?" A vein bulged on Westphal's temple. His hand crept closer to the lapel of his suit.

"No insinuation, Westphal. An outright statement." Slocum's tone was icy. "And I might add, you're not very damn good at it, either."

Westphal's hand darted inside his lapel. Slocum's right hand slapped on the grips of the .44-40, his thumb stroking the hammer as he whipped the weapon free. Light glinted from steel in the gambler's hand; Slocum swept the Peacemaker up, across, held back the trigger and let his thumb fall from the hammer as the muzzle fell into line. The blast of the Colt rattled the chandelier above the table. The .44 slug hammered into Westphal's chest. The shock of heavy lead slammed the gambler backward, toppling his chair. The spiteful pop of a small-caliber weapon sounded, the thwack of the little bullet against the ceiling barely audible above the thud as the back of Westphal's head cracked against the floor. Chairs clattered as the merchant and undertaker dove to the floor.

Slocum took his time, recocked the Peacemaker at the height of its recoil, and leveled the muzzle at the banker. The man's face was the color of ash gravy.

"Don't shoot, for God's sake!" the banker yelped. "I'm not armed."

Slocum wasn't the only man who had pulled a weapon. Milt Hashburn held a big, ugly Smith & Wesson .44 Russian, its bore centered on the banker's forehead.

"Naughty, naughty," Slocum heard Stonekiller say. He glanced through the powder smoke toward the bar. The keen point

of Stonekiller's oversized knife dug into the soft spot under the
shoulder hitter's left ear. A drop of blood trickled from beneath
the knife tip. "Little boys shouldn't play with guns." Stonekiller
reached inside the big man's coat with his left hand, brought out
a short-barreled .45 Colt, and tucked it beneath his waistband.

"What do you think, Slocum?" Hashburn said. "You want to
blow this bastard's head off, or should I do it?"

Slocum shrugged. "Suit yourself. Either way, he earned it."

The banker's pasty flesh seemed to turn whiter. His lips and
chin quivered. "For God's sake," he begged, his voice cracking,
"don't—please don't—it wasn't my idea."

"You lay down with dogs, you get fleas," the rancher said.
"What's your share, Ely? Half the winnings?"

The banker swallowed rapidly. His jowls trembled as he tried
to speak. Nothing came out but a strangled croak. After a moment, Hashburn lowered the big handgun. "Aw, hell. You never
have been worth killin', you sorry bastard. I reckon you're done
in Raton, soon's word gets around you were in cahoots with a
crooked gambler"—Hashburn glanced at the body on the floor
behind the table— "a dead crooked gambler. Wouldn't be surprised if there's a hell of run on that bank of yours come daylight." He glanced at Slocum. "Nice shot. Dead square in the
breastbone and a hand span under the neck. Likely he never knew
what hit 'im."

Slocum's ears still rang from the concussion of the Colt's muzzle blast. He glanced at Stonekiller again. The half-breed's knife
point drew a steady trickle of blood from Turk.

"Don't worry about this one, Slocum," Stonekiller said casually. "He won't be a bother. I haven't cut a white man's throat
in nearly a month now. I'm way overdue, and he knows it."

A babble of excited voices and footsteps sounded from beyond
the locked door.

"The rest of you gentlemen can come out from under the table
now," Slocum said. "It's over." He ejected the spent cartridge,
reloaded the chamber, and holstered the Colt. He rose, strode to
the dead man's side, and plucked the little .32 rimfire derringer
from the floor. He cracked the action, ejected the cartridges, and
dropped the pipsqueak handgun onto the dead man's chest. The
other men scrambled to their feet, faces ashen.

A tentative knock sounded at the door, then became more insistent. Slocum ignored the racket. "How much did you gents lose in this set-up game?"

"About five hundred," Hashburn said.

"I'm sure Brother Ely here would be more than happy to reimburse your losses, Mr. Hashburn," Slocum said, "and the losses of these other gentlemen, too. By my calculations, I'm owed five hundred, counting the last hand. I'll just help myself to Ely's winnings and fold for the night."

The rancher nodded. "Seems fair by me." He glanced at the door. The pounding and yelling was more urgent now. "Sounds like the natives are curious. The sheriff will likely be here soon. There'll have to be an inquest."

Slocum finished counting the money due him and tucked the cash into his pocket. "I'm afraid my associate and I don't have the time for formalities, Mr. Hashburn," he said. "Our horses are out back, we have a long trail ahead, and we now have what we came for in Raton."

"Then you better make tracks. I'll square things with the law. Shouldn't be too much trouble. The sheriff's brother-in-law is my ranch foreman." Hashburn holstered his revolver and offered a hand. "Wherever you're going, Slocum, good luck to you."

Slocum took the rancher's hand. "Thanks." He snugged down his hat and turned to Stonekiller. "Ready, Jim?"

"Have been for several hours," Stonekiller said. "If you're waiting on me, you're wasting time. Let's go."

Slocum and Stonekiller were fifteen miles out of Raton by sunrise. Slocum pulled his horse to a stop in a smooth, sandy clearing at the edge of a stand of piñon and lodgepole pines in a narrow valley of the Sangre de Cristos. A small but swift-running stream gurgled through the clearing, fed by snowmelt and showers from the northern mountain ranges. Lush, knee-high green grass flourished along the creek's banks.

"We'll rest the horses here a while," Slocum said as Stonekiller reined in alongside. The pack animals immediately lined up along the creek to drink. "See anything on the back trail?"

"Two mule deer and one eagle," Stonekiller said. He dismounted, loosened the cinches of his double-rigged saddle, and led his horse to the water. "Not a thing moving that looks to be men on horseback. I'd say we have the country all to ourselves. I could use some coffee.''

Slocum built a small fire and boiled coffee as Stonekiller tended and picketed the horses. Stonekiller squatted beside Slocum and nodded toward the blaze. "You make a fire like an Injun. Move like one, too. Never met many white men who didn't make more racket than a rutting elk all the time." He grinned at Slocum. "You sure you haven't maybe got a little redskin somewhere in your family tree?"

"Wouldn't be ashamed of it if I did," Slocum said softly. "I've spent a few winters in Indian camps. Coffee's ready."

"What tribes?" Stonekiller held out his cup.

"Northern Cheyenne, Crow, Blackfoot. Traded with the Nez Percé some. I always did fancy those spotted horses the Nez Percé breed. Nice animals." Slocum filled his own cup and leaned back against his saddle, watching the sunlight creep down the mountainsides toward the valley floor.

"Had to go into Crow country once, myself," Stonekiller said, reaching for his tobacco. "Only time I've been a little spooked, riding into a Crow camp to bring back a Flathead who'd developed a bad habit of stealing reservation horses and had a good hanging coming. The Crows still don't care much for Kiowas. Or a lot of other tribes, for that matter. Independent sorts." He rolled his smoke and lit it with a twig from the fire.

Slocum waved off Stonekiller's offer of the tobacco sack. He had replenished his cigarillo supply in Raton. He pulled one of the slim Mexican cigars from his pocket, nipped off the end, and lit the smoke. "Get your man?"

"I got him." Stonekiller sat quietly for a moment, smoking, then smiled wistfully. "You know, Slocum, I truly thought those Blackfoot women were the prettiest I've ever seen. Until I met Maria . . ." The half-breed's voice trailed away. He sat for a long time, gazing off toward the southwest. Slocum left him alone. There were times a man needed to climb inside his own memories.

Finally, Stonekiller sighed. "Sioux killed my father back in sixty-eight. He was with Forsythe's command at Beecher's Island, the scrap the Sioux still call The Fight Where Roman Nose Died. Some say James Dooley O'Hara was the one who fired the shot that killed Roman Nose. Maybe he did, maybe he didn't. I never disputed the claim. It made good medicine for a Kiowa police officer to be the son of the man who killed one of the Sioux nation's legendary war chiefs. I suppose Pappy saved me a lot of grief, even in death.'' Stonekiller finished his quirly, ground the butt under a boot heel, and reached for the coffeepot.

''Slocum, I had you pegged right off as a good hand with a gun. But I never expected to see anybody as fast with a six-gun as you showed back there in Raton.''

Slocum shrugged. ''I wouldn't call that fast. This borrowed holster has a tendency to drag. I plan to get some good leather when we stop over in Santa Fe to stock up on supplies. There's a harness maker there who can fit me with what I want. A man who doesn't have the best tools can wind up dead in a hurry. I'd also like to get a decent rifle.''

''I'd say you've earned whatever you want,'' Stonekiller said. After a moment's silence, he pushed his hat back and gazed at Slocum. ''I know it's none of my business, and if you don't want to talk about it, just say so.'' He leveled a steady gaze at Slocum. ''I wouldn't even ask if we weren't hunting some pretty dangerous game together. The lawman in me showing, I reckon. I'd be obliged to know why you're out here, and if you're on the run. Not that it makes any difference.''

Slocum fought back the slight irritation in his gut. He didn't like people prying into his background, especially a man who carried a badge—or who had carried one until just recently. But he supposed Stonekiller had a right to know who was riding alongside him when the shooting started. ''It's a long story.''

''I've got time.''

Slocum glanced at the sun. It was well above the eastern mountains now, its warmth bathing the whole of the valley floor. ''I'll give you the short version. I was the only one of my family who survived the war. We had a farm in Georgia. It wasn't much, but it was all I had left.''

He paused to sip at his coffee, then sighed. ''A little while after I came back home, a carpetbagger federal judge showed up with a so-called sheriff, who was really a hired gun. The judge said the taxes on the land hadn't been paid, which was a damned lie. He said he'd come to take the farm. I told him he wouldn't. His hired gun wasn't as fast as he thought he was. I killed them both, burned the house and barn, saddled up, and headed west. Been drifting ever since.''

"Any wanted flyers out on you?''

"On the far side of the Mississippi, maybe. But not this far west. You won't find many people out here who give a tinker's damn what happened to a carpetbagger land thief that far away. I quit worrying about it a lot of miles ago.''

Stonekiller reached for his tobacco again. "Count me among those who don't give a rip, Slocum. Sounds like the bastards had it coming.'' He rolled his cigarette in silence, his thick black brows bunched.

"Something else bothering you, Jim?''

Stonekiller said, "Now that you mention it, yes. Why would anybody send out a shipment of rifles with only three guards?''

Slocum drained his cup and tossed the dregs aside. "A plan that didn't work. The freight company sent a decoy wagon ahead, loaded with grain, flour, and beans with a dozen men riding shotgun to make it look like a valuable shipment. Bloody Hand somehow knew it wasn't. He let the decoy go by and hit the gun wagon a day later.''

"Curious,'' Stonekiller said. "Maybe in a few days we'll ask Bloody Hand how he knew which wagon had the guns.''

Slocum stood and brushed the dirt and fallen pine needles from his backside. "Speaking of which, we aren't getting any closer to the renegade sitting here. The ponies have had time to water and graze. We can be in Santa Fe by sundown tomorrow. It's time to move on. I'll fetch the horses.''

Stonekiller glanced over his saddle at Slocum as he tightened the front cinch. "Do me a favor, Slocum?''

"Sure.''

"Keep me on a short rein. We've got a long trail to ride, and I've got enough of Pappy's Irish temper in me that I might get impatient. It wouldn't do to get in too big a rush just yet.''

Slocum nodded.

Stonekiller swung into the saddle. "One more favor, since I'm in an asking mood. Leave that son of a bitch of a Kwahadi to me when we catch up with him. I plan to rip out his liver and hand it to him while he's still alive.''

"He's all yours.'' Slocum crushed the butt of his cigarillo beneath a boot heel and mounted, the creak of saddle leather and

soft snuffle of horses comfortable to his ears. He glanced at Stonekiller's face and saw the ache reflected in the half-breed's eyes
as he stared toward the southwest.

"We'll get Maria back, Jim," Slocum said.

5

Maria Stonekiller tried to ignore the constant, nagging aches in her back and leaden legs as she trudged behind the wagon.

The carry straps of the fifty-pound pack she carried burned into the raw skin across her shoulders. Blood seeped from beneath the narrow leather thongs of the carry straps and oozed down her back. She knew the scars of the pack would be with her for life.

Several times in the fading light she had stumbled and almost fallen, but she gathered her feet back beneath her as the coarse riata around her neck tightened, threatening to choke off her wind for a terrifying heartbeat. She knew that if she fell, no one would dare defy Bloody Hand to help her. She would be dragged until the life was gone from her body. Maria would not give the Comanche that cruel satisfaction.

The caravan had been on the move for almost a week since the extended encampment where the white woman died. The first three days had been brutal as they fought their way through the treacherous steep slopes and slippery shale slides of the Sangre de Cristo Mountains. Here the land was still rough and broken on the western foothills of the mountain range, but the going was less difficult. They were in a wide valley beneath blue-tinged mountain ranges to the east and west. Maria had no real sense of where they were. The land was strange to her, with no familiar landmarks. Only the sun told her they were still moving steadily toward the southwest.

Maria startled at the quick, sharp stab of pain in her right buttock. The high-pitched cackle of the old crone called Crow Woman sounded above the creak of wheels and murmur of voices. The old hag wandered away, the sharp stick in hand, tittering in delight over having slipped up behind Maria and jabbing her flesh in ambush. Maria steeled herself and waited for the sting of the puncture to subside. One day, she vowed again, the old hag would pay for her tortures.

Maria cast a concerned glance at the pretty young Shoshoni woman laboring alongside at the other end of the wagon tailgate. Fear and dread showed in the girl's dark, expressive eyes. Her blood moon had ended yesterday, and the Kiowa-Apache Natchee, he of the cruel mouth and dirty skin, had won her at the sticks and bones game. Soon he would take her. The girl tried hard not to outwardly demonstrate her growing apprehension, but it showed in her eyes, in the barely noticeable twitch at the corner of her full lips.

"Be strong, Willow," Maria whispered to the girl in the Shoshoni tongue. "There is hope."

The girl nodded, but it was obvious that the words of reassurance were hollow to her. Maria's resolve grew stronger. Natchee would not have Willow, even if it cost Maria her own life. Willow was too sensitive, too gentle for such a fate. Maria would somehow help her escape. She had been waiting for the opportunity since the two had first spoken days ago and quickly formed a bond of friendship and fear. In the meantime, Maria could only hope to delay the time when Willow fell into the cruel one's grasp. The Kiowa-Apache would not touch Willow until after the purification rites. The taboo was too strong even for a heartless animal like Natchee to break. Yet the time was not far off. Perhaps even tonight the old hag would lift Willow's skirt, cackle, and pronounce the girl's blood moon at an end. Maria's heart sank at the thought, yet she clung to the thread of hope that somehow she could help Willow.

The sun was near the western horizon before Bloody Hand called a stop for the night. The Kwahadi renegade trotted his horse to the top of a ridge to the west, shaded his eyes, and peered into the distance for a moment. Then he waved his rifle overhead, apparently a greeting to someone out of sight beyond the ridge, and reined his horse back toward camp.

Maria and Willow gratefully slipped the bonds of their packs and eased the heavy loads to the ground.

It was a brief rest. The sun had barely moved before a hunting party rode into camp, spoke with Bloody Hand, then kneed their mounts toward the captives.

The hunters dumped the still-warm carcass of a mule deer at Maria's feet. One of the warriors dismounted, gestured toward the deer, then to Maria and Willow. He casually tossed a crude flint cutting tool with no handle or protective wrap to each of the two captives. Maria and Willow set about dressing the deer, the sharp flint leaving cuts on their palms and fingers. At least, Maria thought, the old hag would leave them alone as long as Maria held a weapon. Maria knew she would have no chance to keep the crude knife; the warrior would retrieve it as soon as the work was done. And yet—

A glimmer of hope took shape in the back of Maria's mind as she sliced open the deer's belly and reached inside to cut away the entrails. Her hand closed around a thick, warm blood clot. She glanced around. The Comanche hunter had been watching them closely, but at the moment he was distracted, speaking with another warrior. Maria slipped the gory clot into Willow's hand.

"Put this high up between your thighs, Willow," she whispered, "as far as it will go. Squeeze hard with your legs. The old hag will think it is yet more of your blood moon time." The Shoshoni girl nodded and slipped her hand beneath her skirt.

Maria turned back to dressing the deer, practiced hands moving of their own will. Her thoughts turned to her own blood moon time. It should be coming soon. She had been unable to bring it on early by sheer force of will. She could only wait and pray that it did come. To carry Bloody Hand's child— She forced the painful thought from her mind.

The two women had the deer gutted and skinned before Bloody Hand rode back into hearing distance. Three men, all of skin nearly as dark as that of the black buffalo soldiers, rode beside him, talking and gesturing. Maria could make out only a few of the words, but enough to tell her the visitors were Apache.

Bloody Hand and the Apaches dismounted by the wagon tongue. The Comanche flipped aside the canvas cover and waved toward the cargo.

"Guns," he said. "Good rifles. New weapons, enough to arm your people and more, as my scouts told you. Others of my band are, as we speak, spreading the word across the mountains and deserts, even to our brothers in Mexico." Bloody Hand reached into the wagon, brought out two Winchester lever action carbines and two cartridge boxes. He handed the weapons and ammunition to the Apaches, who stood for a moment fondling the shiny new metal receivers and smooth stocks of the repeating rifles.

"Tomorrow, you return to your people and show them these," Bloody Hand said. "Spread the word that any warrior who would join us, no matter his band or tribe, will receive a new rifle and plenty of ammunition. And together we will kill the white man. Those who escape will be swept from Indian lands and chased back beyond the big river known as the Mississippi. Then the buffalo will return. Life will once more be for the people of all tribes, as the spirits so intended."

The Apaches nodded with growing enthusiasm, their eyes glittering as they examined the Winchesters.

"When the moon grows thin, we will meet again at The Place of the Bones," Bloody Hand said. He ignored the startled glance of one of the Apache warriors. "There we will feast and drink. There will be much tiswin, much white man's whiskey, enough for all Bloody Hand's brothers. All shall have their fill, and then we ride as the greatest war party ever seen by the white man. Tonight we will speak more of this great war. Then you shall go with the dawn to spread the word among your people."

The three men turned and strode off toward the center of camp, where a cooking fire was already blazing. Maria watched them go as she carved meat from the deer's carcass.

She glanced at the young Shoshoni girl. "When the time is right, Willow," she said softly, "I will help you to escape. You must remember the place of which Bloody Hand spoke—The Place of the Bones. Then you must find the American soldiers and tell them of the plan. Many lives, red and white, will be in your hands."

Willow nodded, her brown eyes wide. "I will remember. But what of you, Maria? Will you escape with me?"

"No, child. I am too closely watched. Perhaps Bloody Hand would not waste much time and effort attempting to catch you. It would not be so with me. Your chances will be better alone."

"How will we know when the time is right?"

"We will watch, and wait, and remain alert," Maria said confidently. "The time will come. It will be brief, and perhaps it will come but once. We must be ready."

"And until then?"

Maria lifted her head and stared toward the northeast. Jim Stonekiller was out there, somewhere. She felt it in her heart. "Until then, child," she said, "we do what we must to stay alive."

Slocum pulled the dun Kickapoo warhorse to an abrupt stop and stood in the stirrups, senses tuned to the gentle breeze that drifted along the winding valley of the Rio Grande in the shadow of the Ladron Mountains.

He heard nothing, saw nothing out of the ordinary. But the tickle in his gut meant more than his other senses. Many times that feather in his belly had saved his life.

Stonekiller reined in behind Slocum. He sat silently on his heavily muscled bay, the packhorses trailing behind on slack rein. They were four days south of Santa Fe, six days past the booming thunderstorm that had obliterated the tracks of Bloody Hand's band in the Sangre de Cristos. Losing the trail worried Slocum, even though he had a good idea where the renegade was headed before the storm hit. Still, in country as big as that to the southwest, two full Army regiments could pass within a mile and neither be aware of the other's existence.

Slocum and Stonekiller had gambled. They would follow the Rio Grande south to the village of San Acacia, cross the Galinas Mountains at Magadlena Pass, then strike straight west toward the Mangas Mountains. Unless Bloody Hand changed his course, they should cross the trail somewhere near Horse Springs or the Apache Creek Pass between the Mangas and Tula Rosa ranges.

It was a good plan.

If they lived long enough to follow it.

Stonekiller finally broke the silence. "Problem, Slocum?"

"Maybe." Slocum's eyes narrowed. "I can't shake the feeling we're being watched."

"Had the same twitch myself for the last hour or two." Stone-killer hiked his right leg, hooked the knee over the saddle horn, and reached for his tobacco pouch. "Thought I saw something a mile or so back. Glint of light, like somebody had a spyglass on us."

Slocum shook off Stonekiller's offer of the tobacco pouch. "A half mile ahead, the river makes a sharp bend to the west. This trail we're on hits a narrow stretch there. Rockfalls and dead timber along the side. If I was planning an ambush, I couldn't think of a better spot."

Stonekiller fired his quirly. "Outlaws?"

"Most likely. Some of the toughest men in New Mexico call this valley home."

"So what's your pleasure? Turn back and ride around?"

Slocum shook his head. "We'd lose a full day going back. That narrow cut we passed early this morning is the only trail out of the valley for miles behind us. Next pass is a mile or so up ahead."

"Then we'll go through them," Stonekiller said, an edge to his words. "We've lost too much ground on Bloody Hand's bunch already." He sat for a moment, smoking, his gaze flicking along the steep canyon walls. "How many?"

Slocum shrugged. "Could be as few as one or two. Or as many as twenty. If I was guessing, I'd say closer to a half dozen. Pat Garrett and his men have scattered the bigger gangs."

"Think it's the Seven Rivers bunch?"

"Not likely. They work the Pecos Valley. Don't often get this far west."

"That's good. I'd as soon not tangle with the Seven Rivers boys. Tough outfit." Stonekiller dismounted, ground his cigarette beneath a heel, and shucked the Ballard from its scabbard. He looped the reins of his mount through the ring of a rig on a packhorse. "Give me a half hour, then move on, slow and casual. I'll sneak up on top and cover your flank. My turn to do the long gun work." The half-breed didn't speak again. He strode toward the rocky, juniper-studded canyon wall and disappeared from sight seconds later.

Slocum checked his weapons as he waited. The new holster he'd had made in Santa Fe was still a bit stiff, despite the hours he had spent conditioning the leather with tallow and soapstone, but it would have to do. He waited until the shadows told him a half hour had passed, then shifted the crossdraw rig until he was satisfied with the angle of the .44-40's grips. He kneed the dun into motion.

He rounded the sharp bend of the trail and reined in. Three horsemen sat their saddles, fanned out a few feet apart, blocking the trail. Slocum recognized the man on the right, a tall, angular rider with a thin mustache. Slocum had noticed him watching them a couple of times back in Santa Fe. At the time, he had been with a short, stocky man with long, dirty blond hair. The long-haired one was nowhere in sight. Slocum figured the missing rider to be somewhere in the rockfall a few yards above and behind him, partway up the canyon wall. The man in the middle drew Slocum's immediate attention. He was a small man, narrow in the shoulders, with sharp features that gave him the look of a fox. He had the eyes of a gunman. His left hand rested on the grips of a revolver bolstered at his side. The other two men carried rifles across the pommels of their saddles.

"Howdy," the fox-faced one said.

Slocum inclined his head slightly, never taking his gaze from the small man's eyes. "Howdy."

"Mighty fine pony string you got there, mister," the little man said.

"I've had better. Had worse."

Fox-face's eyes narrowed. "I reckon you ain't heard this here's a toll road. Cost you a hundred dollars and them pack animals to use it."

"I think not," Slocum said. He casually rested his right forearm on the broad horn of the saddle. The motion put the fingers of his gun hand within inches of the holstered Colt. "I'm a bit short of cash right now."

"You got money." The little man inclined his head toward the rangy rider. "Nick here says he seen you back in Santa Fe, spendin' money left and right. You just hand it over—all of it— and maybe you'll ride out of here alive."

The tall rider called Nick glanced around nervously. "Spade, there was two of 'em in Santa Fe. I don't see the Injun."

Spade snorted in contempt. "Probably runnin' for his red hide. Never knowed a Injun to face a fight when he could cut and run." The little man's knuckles whitened on the grips of his handgun.

"Your play, mister. Step down or get yourself dead."

Slocum held Spade's stare. He knew he had to take the fox-faced one down first. Spade was the type who could handle a sidearm, a shooter who worked at close range when he didn't kill from ambush. The other two held rifles. It was a damn sight harder to fire a rifle from the back of a horse than it was to handle a revolver. Slocum also knew that if he made one mistake—or if Stonekiller wasn't in position or happened to miss a shot—he was a dead man. At three-to-one odds, he was still likely to catch some lead. He could only hope it didn't hit a vital spot. Slocum's muscles went loose in the relaxed calm that came over him before a face-to-face showdown.

"I think I'll stay where I am," Slocum said. "I like it horse-back."

Spade barked a sharp curse and yanked at his revolver.

Slocum abruptly kneed his horse sideways, his Colt clearing the holster as the dun moved; the .44-40's muzzle fell into line, and Slocum stroked the trigger.

The heavy lead slug took Spade in the chest and slammed him backward over his horse's rump. Spade's pistol, barely clear of the leather, blasted harmlessly into the air. Slocum's dun spooked at the gunfire and danced sideways. A rifle slug cracked past where Slocum's head had been as a Winchester cracked. A split second later, Slocum heard the heavy whop of lead against flesh, a grunt from the rockfall above and behind, and the jarring blast of Stonekiller's Ballard. Slocum didn't fight the Colt. He cocked the handgun at the peak of the recoil, waited half a heartbeat, even though he was looking into the bore of the thin man's rifle, dropped his Colt into line, and fired. The rider screamed, dropped his rifle, and sagged in the saddle.

The third man slapped a hurried shot that sailed wide, then yanked his horse around and rammed the spurs home, his heart gone from the fight. Slocum thumbed the hammer, sent a slug after the fleeing horseman, and mouthed a curse as the shot went high. Stonekiller's big rifle blasted again. The fleeing rider went out of the saddle as if hammered by a huge fist, his hat suspended in midair. He hit the ground, rolled, and lay still.

Echoes of the gunshots rumbled up and down the river valley as Slocum brought the nervous dun back under control and glanced at the tall man called Nick, who knelt in the dust, an arm pressed against his gut, his face slack and pale in shock and disbelief. In a few seconds Nick would start to hurt; in minutes he would be in agony, Slocum knew. The gun battle had lasted only a few seconds, but Nick could be a long time dying.

"Slocum! You all right?" The call came from near the rim of the canyon above.

"All right!" Slocum yelled back. He aimed with care and sent a slug through the gutshot man's head. Nick's boots cribbed at the soil in the convulsions of death. Shooting a defenseless man wasn't something Slocum particularly relished. The head shot had been an act of mercy. Slocum had seen gutshot men die before. It wasn't a pretty way to go.

Slocum reloaded the Colt and began sorting out the tangled leads of the pack mounts that had been spooked by the gunfire. He looked up as Stonekiller skidded down the last few yards of the canyon wall, his boots dislodging stones and shale. Stonekiller held the Ballard in one hand, a Winchester in the other, and had a pistol belt draped over his shoulder.

"Good shooting, Slocum," Stonekiller said. "Guess that's the end of that bunch."

Slocum nodded. "This bunch, yes. But these mountains are full of bandits. Could be some more attracted by the shooting." He glanced toward the mountainside. "The one up there dead?"

"Dead enough." The half-breed's tone was flat, almost without expression. "No reason to waste time burying these bastards. They sure as hell don't deserve it." Stonekiller glanced at the sky. Buzzards already wheeled overhead. "Coyotes and turkey vultures have to eat, too. We'll gather up the rest of their guns and ammunition and take a couple of their horses and saddles. Man can't be overequipped where we're going. And Maria will be more comfortable coming back if she doesn't have to ride bareback."

The buzzards began to drop from the sky before the two men finished gathering the outlaws' horses and equipment. Stonekiller grunted in satisfaction as he pulled a brass spyglass in a leather case from a recovered saddlebag.

"This thing might come in handy as hell," Stonekiller said. He tucked the tube into the middle of his bedroll. "Ready when you are, partner."

Slocum led the way, his rifle at the ready. The mile down trail to the pass seemed a mighty long ride, but there were no more shots or challenges. He spurred the dun to the top of the pass and paused to study the rolling country ahead. It seemed empty. Slocum wasn't reassured. Places that seemed empty could get a man killed in a hurry.

"Well, Slocum," Stonekiller said as he reined in alongside, "what do you think? How far behind Bloody Hand are we now?"

Slocum scratched his chin in thought for a moment. "Five or six days, give or take. A lot depends on how fast Bloody Hand moves. We'll have a better idea when we cut sign on them again."

"If we do."

Slocum kneed the dun into an easy, ground covering trot. "We'll find them, Jim. With a heavy wagon, there's only one trail they can take where there's water, grass, and a reasonably sound path for wagon wheels. They'll have to take the one easy pass between two mountain ranges. If we don't cut the track at Horse Springs, we'll find it at Apache Creek Pass."

Stonekiller frowned. "Even if we do, we've still got a hell of a lot of ground to make up."

"We'll make it up. We'll catch them." Slocum didn't add that he wasn't sure exactly what they would do after they caught up.

Bloody Hand squatted beside the cooking fire at the edge of Horse Springs and stared at the young Comanche scout digging bits of meat from the fire-blackened pot.

"How many soldiers, White Shield?"

The Comanche shrugged, chewing. "Thirty. Maybe more, maybe less. They will be no problem. We can kill them all and take many horses, many scalps."

Bloody Hand's frown deepened. "I must think on this, White Shield." He rolled a cigarette and stared into the distance. In normal times, an Army patrol less than two days' ride away would be a tempting target, an easy one. But these were not normal times. More was at stake than lifting a few soldiers' scalps. This was no simple raiding party to be measured in paltry trophies and a handful of horses. Bloody Hand must set aside his instincts as a warrior and plan as a white man's soldier general. The general of a great army. An army that was yet to reach the numbers to sweep the white man from the land of The People. The soldier patrol was bothersome. Where there was a thirty-man patrol, more troops could not be far away. He could not risk an all-out battle with the horse soldiers. Not yet. His forces were not yet strong enough.

Bloody Hand sighed. "The time is not right, White Shield. We will let them pass."

White Shield's gaze went cold. "Is Bloody Hand afraid of a few soldiers?" The question was a challenge tinged with contempt.

For a moment, Bloody Hand struggled to control the surge of rage that boiled in his belly. Such an insult was not to be ignored in normal times. He reminded himself sternly that these were not normal times. And despite his lack of respect for his leader, White Shield had a sizable band of followers. To kill him now might cost Bloody Hand's band a potentially powerful force in the big war to come. For now, Bloody Hand decided, he would ignore the young Comanche's sharp tongue. Later, when the war was over and the white man vanquished, the insolent White Shield would die. This was not the first time the man had challenged Bloody Hand's authority and questioned his courage. In the end, he would pay. Bloody Hand squelched his rage and shook his head.

"If we kill the soldiers now, their chiefs will send many more. Maybe they would send the big guns on wheels. We let them pass and send out scouts to watch the soldiers until they are far away."

White Shield snorted in disgust, but made no comment.

"We camp here for three suns," Bloody Hand said with finality. "By then our messengers will have returned from the northern mountains, bringing more warriors to join us."

White Shield rose and stalked away, puffs of dust rising from beneath his moccasins at each angry stride. Bloody Hand waited until the Comanche was out of earshot, then motioned to an older, wizened Kiowa warrior who had been standing a few feet away, rifle in hand.

"Watch that one closely, Antelope," Bloody Hand said.

The old Kiowa nodded and patted the receiver of his rifle in understanding. Bloody Hand put the young upstart from his mind. White Shield would be no problem with Antelope watching his every move, and Bloody Hand wouldn't have to worry about watching his own back. He smiled grimly to himself. He wondered how many insults White Shield would mouth when he found himself staring into the barrel of a rifle one day. The Comanche leader put the enjoyable vision from his mind. There was much work to be done.

Bloody Hand rose, passed the word that the band would camp here for a time, and paused for a moment to stare at the women tethered to the back of the wagon. The Shoshoni girl sagged, exhausted, against a wheel, her chin on her chest. The Cheyenne woman stood, back straight, head held high, her gaze sweeping the horizon to the northeast as it had so often in the past few days. The sight sent a ripple of concern through Bloody Hand. It was as if the Cheyenne knew someone was out there and she was biding her time. It was not a good sign.

Bloody Hand abruptly turned away. He found the Kiowa-Apache Natchee standing watch at a stone outcrop overlooking the camp. Bloody Hand squatted beside Natchee, offered his tobacco sack, and waited silently as Natchee rolled and smoked a cigarette.

"Natchee," Bloody Hand said after a time, "I sense trouble from behind. You are my best scout and strongest warrior. Take men of your choosing, as many as you think you need. Scout far behind us. If we are being followed, you know what to do."

Natchee nodded, his thin lips drawn tighter. Bloody Hand saw the Kiowa-Apache staring toward the young Shoshoni woman at the wagon and understood. Natchee owned the woman.

"There is no need to leave until tomorrow," Bloody Hand said. "Crow Woman says the Shoshoni girl's blood moon will end tonight. Tomorrow morning the toothless one will perform the purification rites. When that is done, take the Shoshoni with you. Put her on a slow horse. If she can't keep up, kill her."

Natchee grunted in satisfaction, hitched up his soiled white man's trousers, and strode toward the camp.

6

Slocum squatted on his heels beside the small fire at a bend of the trickle of water that passed for a creek in the dry, rolling hills a half day's ride south of the Galinas Mountains. He flexed his shoulders, trying to relieve the stiffness in his back, as he waited for the coffee to boil.

The last twenty hours and sixty miles, broken only by three brief stops, had been a drain on even Slocum's trail-tough muscles. The ride had been more brutal on the horses. Most of the mounts, even the shod ones, were footsore, the tender frogs of hooves bruised from the rocky mountain trails and shale slopes of the Sangre de Cristo range, and the volcanic rock fields and hardpan below the western foothills. Then came the rolling, wind-whipped sandhills west of the mountains, which had left them lean of flank from lack of water, decent graze, and sleep. Horses needed sleep as much as men did.

A horse could travel on grain rations, but it took grass to re-build stamina and strength. And now they were running low on grain. Slocum never worried all that much when a man suffered, but it got under his skin to see horses so drawn down. He was particularly worried about the leggy brown taken from the outlaw string after the shootout on the Rio Grande. The horse limped heavily, even without packing weight, favoring the left foreleg.

Slocum was afraid the horse might have cracked a pastern bone. If that were the case, the horse would have to be left behind somewhere along the trail. The brown was a game horse. Slocum hated to think of leaving the gelding alone, unable to run or defend itself from the packs of coyotes and wolves or the mountain cats that ranged in western New Mexico.

The animals now stood hipshot at the edge of the alkali-tainted stream, ears flopped in exhaustion. Dried sweat and lather on their necks and shoulders streaked white across their hides.

At least, Slocum thought, the flanks of the horses were no longer gaunt as a gutted possum from thirst. There was water. It wasn't fit for human consumption; the salts would give a man the green apple trots and belly cramps for days, but the animals could tolerate it well enough. Grazing was sparse here at best, but sufficient for a couple of days. They wouldn't be rolling fat, but they would have something in their bellies.

Even the badger-tough Kickapoo dun showed the strain of the miles. The dun and Jim Stonekiller's taller bay stood head-to-rump, tails occasionally flicking to brush the pesky flies away from each other's ears and eyes.

Slocum wondered if Stonekiller was human. He didn't seem the least bit tired.

The blocky half-breed stood beneath a wind-twisted cottonwood tree, slicing strips of meat from the hindquarter of the mule deer he had shot two hours ago. It looked to Slocum as if Stonekiller was going about the job a lot faster than was necessary, like a man trying to hack his way to inner peace through a hunk of meat hanging from a tree limb. The late afternoon sun that dappled through the cottonwood leaves winked points of light from Stonekiller's blade as his hands flicked over the hindquarter. He had already carved off more meat than they could use before it spoiled, and still he sliced away like a man possessed.

Slocum thought he understood. Stonekiller's inner demons were growing stronger as they made up ground on Bloody Hand's band. He was a man driven by hate, by hope, and by fear. Not fear for his own life, but for that of his woman. That they had not yet cut sign on Bloody Hand's bunch hadn't helped Stonekiller's disposition much.

Slocum's head snapped around at the click of a hoof against stone beyond the greasewood brush at a bend in the creek. He swept the new .44-40 Winchester he had bought in Santa Fe from the boot of the saddle at his side and racked a round into the chamber.

"Company coming, Jim," Slocum said softly. He knelt on one knee, shouldered the rifle, and swung the muzzle toward the edge of the thicket. His finger tightened on the trigger as the horse sounds neared the edge of the brush.

A rider came into view, a stooped old man on a ribby, shambling sorrel, leading a pack mule. Dragging the mule might have been a more accurate term. The long-eared animal sat back on the lead and looked to be about ten minutes from balking for good. Slocum heard the old man's steady mutter of curses as he yanked at the lead rope. The rider carried an ancient Colt Dragoon cap-and-ball revolver tucked into the waistband of soiled trousers. A Springfield single-shot rifle hung by a thong from his saddle horn.

"That's far enough!" Slocum called.

The old man's shoulders jerked at the unexpected yell. He yanked the sorrel to a stop and squinted at Slocum.

"Howdy," the old-timer said. He moved his hands well away from the grips of the handgun. "Didn't mean to ride up on you like that, friend."

"You alone?"

The old man nodded. "Sure didn't expect to see no white men around these parts. I don't mean nobody no harm, and I sure as hell ain't got nothin' worth stealin'. So I'd be much obliged if you was to point that there rifle somewheres else."

Slocum studied the man for a couple of heartbeats and decided the rider was harmless enough. He lowered the rifle but left the hammer at full cock, just in case. He chanced a quick glance toward the cottonwood. Stonekiller was nowhere to be seen. The half-butchered deer haunch twisted slowly at the end of the rope tied to the tree limb.

The old-timer nodded toward the fire. "Reckon you could spare some of that coffee, mister? Ain't had coffee in nigh onto two months now."

"Maybe," Slocum said, "if I decide not to shoot you after all. Mind my asking what you're doing out here?"

"Gettin' the hell out of them mountains back there, mostly." The old man turned his head and spat. "Up till a few days ago,

I was prospectin' over on the west slope of the Mangas range. Found me a silver vein, too. Just about the time I was lookin' to get rich, I got myself butt-deep in Injuns.''

Slocum lifted an eyebrow. ''Apaches?''

''Mostly. Some Comanch, a couple Kickapoos, a few Utes here and there. It don't figure, Utes and Kicks ridin' with 'Paches and Comanch. Never knowed them tribes to take much of a shine to each other.''

''How many altogether?''

''Didn't stop to count. They come moseyin' through in bunches. Anywheres from four at a time up to a dozen or more. Brung their women and kids along, too, and Injuns most time don't do that if they're just huntin' or even on a raidin' party. All I can tell you, mister, is I ain't seen so many redskins since I scouted for Gen'l Crook more'n a few years back.''

Slocum made up his mind. The stranger was no threat, and Slocum knew he was telling the truth. A man didn't ride away from a promising silver strike unless something had spooked him and spooked him bad. He lowered the hammer of the rifle and raised his voice. ''It's all right, Jim! Come on in!'' He sheathed the Winchester and nodded to the old man. ''Step down. Coffee's almost ready.''

Stonekiller suddenly appeared at the edge of the camp as if he'd materialized from the earth itself. That gave the old man another start. Stonekiller glanced at Slocum. ''He's telling the truth, Jim. He's alone.''

''Damn me for a short-tail possum,'' the old-timer said, glaring at Stonekiller, ''looks like there's Injuns everwhere these days.''

''This man,'' Slocum said pointedly, ''is my partner. I don't think it's a good idea to call him an Injun.''

''Nothin' bad meant. He's ridin' with a white man, I reckon he's okay.'' He held Stonekiller's cold gaze without blinking. ''You Comanch?''

Stonekiller's eyes were narrowed and cold. ''Half Kiowa. Other half's Irish.''

The prospector grunted. ''You won't have no trouble from me, then. Never cottoned to the idea of tanglin' with no Kioways. No offense, but the Kioways I've knowed's been meaner'n a long-tushed boar hog. Make the Sioux look plumb gentrified. Part Irish myself, grandma's side.''

"Then talk to my Irish half," Stonekiller said. "You going to sit that saddle all day, old-timer, or are you going to get down and tell us about these Indians of yours?"

The old man dismounted stiffly. Slocum thought he heard the creak and pop of joints as the prospector stepped down and dug a callused fist into the small of his back. "Coffee sure smells good," the old-timer said. "Name's Callishaw. Most folks call me Digger."

Slocum held out a hand. "I'm Slocum. My partner here is Jim Stonekiller."

Digger Callishaw took Slocum's hand. His grip was firm, the palms of his hands rough and callused from years of pick and shovel work. The handshake told Slocum that Callishaw was what he said he was. Only prospectors and hardscrabble dirt farmers had hands like that. Callishaw turned to the half-breed.

"Heard the name Stonekiller a couple times. Lawman up in Injun Territory. Treed the Lawton gang over in Arkansas. Even brought two of the six back alive for hangin'. You him?"

Stonekiller nodded silently.

Callishaw's weathered face cracked in a slight grin. "You'll do then. Anybody could handle that Lawton bunch is all right in my book." He shook Stonekiller's hand, then said, "You gents mind if I water this sorry bonebag of a sorrel and that cantankerous oversized jackass? Been a long dry since we left the mountains."

Slocum said, "Go ahead. Coffee'll be ready when you are."

Slocum added a dollop of water from his canteen to the coffeepot to settle the grounds and watched as Callishaw watered and hobbled the horse and mule and limped back to the fire, a blackened tin cup in hand. Slocum filled it. Callishaw took a hefty swallow of the strong, scalding brew and sighed.

"Damn good coffee, Slocum. I might near forgot what she tastes like. Much obliged."

Slocum sipped at his own cup and winced. Digger Callishaw's mouth must have been tough as an old boot. The coffee was past the scalding point. "About these Indians you've seen?"

Callishaw's leathery face darkened. "Somethin's up. I ain't sure what, but that many redskins headin' the same way spells trouble, sure as skunk shit stinks." He downed another swallow of coffee. "I was camped up in the high country overlookin' a little valley that's been a Injun trail since them Spaniards in tin suits brung horses to the redskins. First bunch come by six, eight days ago. Must of been fifty, sixty rode past that mountain 'fore I decided to light a shuck out of there less I got spotted and lost some hair.''

Stonekiller asked, "You say they were all headed the same way?"

"Straight toward Horse Springs. My guess is that part of the country's plumb covered up in feathers by now.''

A muscle in Stonekiller's jaw twitched as he glanced at Slocum. "Looks like we've found Bloody Hand's trail," he said. "You were right, Slocum. They must be using Horse Springs as a gathering point.''

Callishaw lifted wiry gray eyebrows. "You gents seem mighty interested in them Injuns.''

"We are," Slocum said casually. "They have some property of ours. We intend to get it back.''

Callishaw snorted in disbelief. "Just the two of you? Agin the biggest mess of Injuns since Adobe Walls?''

"Just the two of us," Slocum said, "unless you'd like to tag along.''

"No, sir! I ain't real anxious to get myself skinned alive and cooked over a slow fire.'' Callishaw drained his coffee and glanced at the lowering sun. "I reckon I'll mosey along. Like to get a couple more miles 'tween me and them Injuns afore dark. Much obliged for the coffee.''

Slocum watched as the old man creaked to his feet, mounted, and rode away, heading east. Callishaw's story bothered Slocum more than he let on outwardly. It was more than just the numbers, even if that meant Bloody Hand's band was growing stronger by the day. It was the mixture of tribes that was the most worrisome. If northern Apaches and Comanches were riding with Utes and Kickapoos, that could only mean an alliance that bucked centuries of tribal warfare. And it probably meant more warriors were on the way, coming from all directions. Which in turn meant bigger trouble than even the old prospector suspected.

Slocum pulled a skillet and bag of flour from a pack.

"Don't bother with grub, Slocum.'' Stonekiller's voice was hard and tight. "We're moving out.''

"I wouldn't recommend that, Jim—''

"Dammit, Slocum, Horse Springs isn't but sixty miles from here. We can be there in less than two days!"

Slocum held Stonekiller's glare. "You're not thinking straight—"

"The hell I'm not! Maria's out there! Damn you, Slocum, don't go getting weak in the knees on me now! We're riding, and we're riding now!"

Slocum stood. Stonekiller's eyes were narrowed and gleamed with the look of a wild man. His coppery face was almost black, lips twisted in rage.

"No," Slocum said softly.

"The hell you say! I'm going. With or without you."

"Can't let you do that, Jim."

Stonekiller took a step forward, fists clenched at his sides, his weight on the balls of his feet. "Think you're man enough to stop me?"

"Don't bet against it."

Stonekiller swung a fist. Slocum flexed his knees and ducked, trying to slip the punch, but the half-breed was quick. Slocum felt the skin split as Stonekiller's knuckles caught his cheekbone a glancing blow. Slocum stepped forward and slammed a fist into Stonekiller's gut, twisting his shoulders and snapping his legs straight as the blow hammered home just above the belt buckle. Stonekiller grunted, staggered back a half step, and started to lift his fist. Slocum grabbed the half-breed's wrist in his left hand and rammed a solid right into Stonekiller's chest just above the heart. The air left Stonekiller's lungs with an audible whoosh.

"That's enough, dammit!" Slocum barked. He thrust his face within inches of Stonekiller's. "Get hold of yourself, man! Quit thinking like an Irishman and start thinking like a Kiowa! We don't need this pissing contest right now!"

Some of the rage faded from Stonekiller's face. His chest convulsed as he tried to gulp air back into his lungs.

"Jim," Slocum said, "you told me to keep you reined in if it was necessary. I'm pulling those reins now. Look around you. Then tell me if you want to charge into Bloody Hand's camp on half-dead horses. And if you do, tell me just how the hell you expect to get out alive."

For a moment, Stonekiller glared hard into Slocum's eyes. Then the fury slowly drained from his face and the tension from his muscles. Slocum released Stonekiller's hand and stepped back cautiously, still wary and alert, ready to counter if the half-breed attacked again.

The caution wasn't needed.

Stonekiller's face colored again, but this time Slocum suspected it was the flush of embarrassment.

"Sorry, Slocum," Stonekiller said. "I lost control. It won't happen again. It's just—just the idea of being so close to Maria and not being able to do anything about it. You don't know what I've been through."

Slocum said, "No, I don't. I've never been in your position. I can't crawl inside your skin and know what's going on in your heart and mind. But I do know that if we make any stupid moves now, it would just get Maria and both of us killed."

Stonekiller's shoulders slumped. "So what do we do?"

"We stay here a day, rest the horses, get a little sleep ourselves. Then we do some serious thinking and planning." Slocum wiped a hand across his cheek. It came away smeared with blood. "First, we eat. You hungry?"

"Not sure I can eat. I think you stomped my stomach flat. For a *pistolero,* you pack one hell of a punch. I've never been hit that hard in my life." Stonekiller sighed. "I deserved it, Slocum. I won't fly off the handle again."

Slocum flexed his right hand. He suspected he would have some bruised knuckles, but nothing was broken. "I'll take your word on it. Just start thinking more Kiowa and less Irish."

"I'll do that." Stonekiller shook his head in disgust. "I don't know what came over me. I've never gone loco before."

"Because you've never had as much at stake before, Jim," Slocum said softly. "Let's get the venison in the skillet."

The sun was dropping toward the western horizon, the pounding heat from the hard disk softening as the sky turned from the pale, washed-out hue of afternoon to the deeper blue of approaching sunset, when Slocum stowed the last of the utensils from the evening meal. He refreshed the coffeepot, leaned back against his saddle, and studied Stonekiller seated across the way.

The half-breed had said little since the blowup earlier in the day. He sat with legs crossed at the ankle, his forehead wrinkled in thought. Slocum couldn't help but worry about Stonekiller. If he blew up like a cheap shotgun again at the wrong time, they could both wind up as hair trophies on a lodgepole.

Stonekiller glanced up, caught Slocum's eye, and seemed to read his mind. "I'll be all right now, Slocum."

Slocum nodded. He had two choices: trust the man or ride out. He knew he couldn't turn away. He had given Stonekiller his word. That was something Slocum never rode away from. And he owed the blocky half-Kiowa. He would have been buzzard droppings by now if Stonekiller hadn't come along.

Stonekiller said, "I've been thinking on what that old prospector had to say. If he's right, the odds against us just got a lot longer."

"I'm betting Digger was laying it out straight," Slocum said. "If that many Indians were coming down from the north, God knows how many others will have joined up with the renegade by now."

"Any ideas?"

Slocum pulled a cigarillo from his pocket and lit it with a twig from the fire. "We can't call in the Army, even if we knew where the nearest troops are. Not if we expect to get Maria back alive. One bugle call and Bloody Hand would kill the captives for sure." He dragged in a lungful of smoke and let it trickle from his nostrils. "Two men against the biggest war party since Little Big Horn. If I were betting on it, I'd put my money on the renegades right now."

"That would be the smart bet," Stonekiller said. He fell silent for a moment, rolling a cigarette. "I've been trying to crawl into that damn Comanche's head. And I'm thinking we're not the only ones with problems. Bloody Hand's got his share."

"Such as?"

"Too many chiefs. Every buck who leads a war party to join Bloody Hand is going to want to be the big stud hoss of the remuda before it's over. Could be some serious squabbles in the ranks. And he's got warriors from tribes that have spent too many generations fighting each other. Us Injuns never could tolerate other Injuns all that well. That's the main reason we don't own the land now." He lit his smoke with a twig from the fire. "There's an edge in that somewhere for us. All we need to do is find it."

Slocum poured himself a final cup of coffee, leaned back, and stared at the darkening sky. The yip and wail of a coyote sounded faint in the distance. The fading breeze rustled the leaves of the cottonwoods nearby. The first star of evening appeared overhead. From the thicket at the bend of the creek, a blue quail sent out its call, summoning other birds to the roosting site. The quail's cry changed pitch as an owl early to the hunt cruised on silent wings over the cottonwoods. The soft ripping sounds and occasional snuffle of horses cropping grass at the stream's edge was soothing to the ears.

It should have been a peaceful, relaxing camp, Slocum thought idly. It had always struck him as curious how such little things gained so much importance when a man didn't know how many more days he had to enjoy them. Slocum didn't fear death. It could come at any time for almost any reason and to anybody: man, woman, or child. That didn't mean he was in any particular hurry to give up living.

He finished his coffee and smoke and spread his bedroll for the night. He lay for the better part of an hour, studying the stars, thinking.

An edge, Stonekiller had said.

The half-breed was right. There was always an edge somewhere. It was just a matter of finding it.

The Kiowa-Apache called Natchee reined his prize paint warhorse to a stop at the edge of the arroyo and grunted in satisfaction.

The sun's rays rippled and glittered in the water trapped in the stone basins at the bottom of the gash in the earth. Water trickled slowly but steadily into the series of basins from a spring halfway up the northwest bank of the arroyo. A strip of green spread south from the stone shelves, the grass nourished by runoff as the basins overflowed. Driftwood carried by flash floods lay jumbled in the narrows and curves of the shallow canyon.

The view from the tallest point along the cut in the earth was good. As far as the eye could see, anything that moved would stand out against the sun-baked land. Only occasional patches of dull gray green greasewood brush, sage, twisted clumps of cactus, or low junipers stood in the way of the eye. There was little cover large enough to conceal a lone man on horseback. More than one man would raise a dust cloud visible for miles.

The site had all that was needed for a scouting camp.

Natchee studied the expectant faces of the four men remaining in his group. Two others already had ridden ahead, scouting far afield. Natchee had chosen his men well. They were all proven warriors, fine horsemen, well mounted and heavily armed. Natchee was still a bit angry with Bloody Hand for sending him out as rear guard when he should have been in his rightful place at Bloody Hand's side as the Indian band grew at the Horse Springs camp. But he would do his job. No man would surprise Bloody Hand from the rear. Natchee glanced at the sun. It was almost overhead.

"We will camp here," he said. "In two more suns, perhaps three—when we are sure no one follows—we ride back to Horse Springs."

Natchee's gaze lingered for a moment on the young Shoshoni woman called Willow. She sat with head held high, back straight, riding bareback on an old, sorefooted gray mare. Willow's hands were bound at the wrist, her slender fingers gripping the single rein of the old mare's crude hackamore. If she tried to escape, the ancient mare could barely run faster than a man afoot, and would tire within a hundred strides.

The woman showed no sign of exhaustion, even though they had covered many miles since sunrise. Natchee's gaze drifted up the young woman's legs; her doeskin skirt had crept up high on long, firm thighs. Her skin seemed to glow in the bright sunlight. The light played along the smooth skin of her legs and sparked highlights in the black hair that fell free almost to her slender waist. The old hag Crow Woman had done well in the purification rite. The Shoshoni woman was well scrubbed, the doeskin dress clean and brushed. The soft leather clung to her body, molded itself to her high, full breasts. Natchee felt the tightening in his loins. Tonight there would be no blood moon. Tonight he would take her. And if she did not please him, when the sun came he would give her, or sell her, to the others. Natchee felt a quick surge of satisfaction when their gaze met briefly; he thought he had seen a glint of fear in her dark brown eyes, though she tried hard to hide her feelings. *It is good,* Natchee thought; *perhaps she will struggle. It is always best when they fight.*

Natchee kneed his horse down the sandy side of the arroyo and dismounted at the water's edge. The others did the same, the woman nimbly stepping down from the gray mare despite having her hands tied. Within minutes The Place of the Water Stones had been turned into a comfortable camp. The horses were watered and picketed, a patch of ground cleared away, and a circle of stones laid for a fire. Natchee untied the woman's hands so that she could more easily tend to her camp chores. Other men spread blankets on chosen spots, taking care to make sure their rifles and other weapons were in easy reach. There were no lodges to erect. The scouting party traveled light.

Natchee squatted nearby and watched as Willow laid the sticks and dry wood gathered by one of the men, struck sparks from flint and steel, and puffed the wisp of smoke into a blaze. Soon the fire would die back until only coals remained for the roasting of venison brought from Horse Springs. There was no regular mealtime; the men would eat when they wished and rest from the long ride. When the sun went to rest as well, Natchee would take the Shoshoni woman to his blankets. Natchee checked the urge to take her now. There would be time later, when her chores were done and night came. He dug a sack of tobacco from a deerskin pouch, rolled a cigarette, and nodded to himself in satisfaction as he inhaled the smoke. It would be a good camp.

The sun's disk was halfway down the western sky when Natchee heard the hail from the lip of the arroyo. One of the scouts was returning, moving at a fast lope.

The scout kneed his horse straight up the rimrock and reined in at Natchee's side.

"What is it, Bear Skin?"

The wiry Comanche jabbed a thumb over his shoulder. "Riders. Headed this way."

"How many?"

"Two white men. Six horses."

"Only two men, eh?" Natchee scrubbed a palm across his chin. "Army scouts?"

"I do not think so. I circled behind them to look. I saw no sign of a large column. No dust cloud, no wagons. They ride alone."

"How far?"

"We could be there before the moon rises." Bear Skin put his fingers alongside his nose, blew the dust from his nostrils, and wiped the discharge on his pants. "They have camped at the buffalo wallow where we killed the Mexicans two snows back. I saw the smoke from their fire."

Natchee frowned, torn between the prospect of easily taking two scalps and half a dozen horses and lifting the skirts of the Shoshoni woman. But scalps and horses meant wealth, good medicine, power. It would raise his status with Bloody Hand. And if they were Army scouts, they had to be stopped before they found Bloody Hand's main trail. It should be no problem, Natchee thought. If the white men were camped in the buffalo wallow, they would be easy prey, as the Mexican traders had been. He wondered for a moment why the white men had camped in the wallow instead of atop the small butte overlooking the low place. He dismissed the idea with a snort of disgust. The white man was stupid. That was reason enough.

Natchee glanced at the woman and made up his mind. He had waited this long for her. Another night and day would not matter. There were more important things at hand. He turned from the scout to the others who had gathered around.

"Catch up your best warhorses and see to your weapons," Natchee said. "We go to kill some white men. Take only what you need for a night and a day. We return here after we kill them."

"What of the woman?" Bear Skin asked.

Natchee inclined his head toward one young warrior. "Bind her hands. She comes with us."

"It is not good medicine to take a woman on a raid, Natchee. Better to kill her now."

"No." Natchee all but barked the word. His tone let Bear Skin know who was in charge, and that Natchee expected no argument.

"Then leave someone to guard her."

"She comes with us. No man who rides with Natchee will tend squaws when there are horses and scalps to be won."

Bear Skin's frown deepened, but he said nothing further on the subject.

"Where is Two Toes?"

Bear Skin shrugged. "He went north. I rode west."

"It is no matter," Natchee said. "He can catch up with us later." Moments later, Natchee was astride his warhorse, waiting impatiently as some of the younger men took time to braid scalps and bits of ribbons into the bridles, manes, and tails of their war ponies. The woman mounted the limping mare. She did not look at Natchee. The Shoshoni, Natchee thought, was a proud bitch.

That, too, would end with the next nightfall. He would enjoy her whimperings.

The last warrior swung aboard his horse.

"We ride into the night," Natchee said. "Then we wait. With the sun we will attack. The white men will be asleep, their bladders full. It will be as easy as plucking the fruit from the prickly pear." He kneed his paint toward the narrow trail leading up the far side of the arroyo.

7

Slocum stepped from the black shadow of a juniper and lowered his rifle as Jim Stonekiller rode back into camp under the pale light of the high moon.

"Did he take the bait?" Slocum asked.

Stonekiller nodded. "Hook and all." He stepped from the saddle and flexed his shoulders. "Followed him all the way back to camp and watched them form up. They're not that far behind me."

"So we had it figured right," Slocum said. "He was a scout. The question now is whether he's one of Bloody Hand's bunch."

"He is." Stonekiller stripped the saddle from the tired sorrel and started rubbing the animal down with a wad of burlap. "I recognized the boss dog of the bunch. Mean son of a bitch. Kiowa-Apache called Natchee."

"You know the man?"

"He was one of the bastards who hit my place."

"How can you be sure of that?"

"A tribal star-packer has his sources," Stonekiller said. "Any coffee left?"

Slocum nodded, strode to the fire in the center of the buffalo wallow, and poured Stonekiller a cup. The Kiowa sipped at the liquid and grimaced. "That stuff would float a horseshoe."

"It has been on the fire a spell," Slocum said. "How many men has this Natchee got with him?"

"Half a dozen that I saw. Cut sign on one more, up north a few miles, headed back toward the camp. Probably another scout." Stonekiller's gaze settled on Slocum. "They have a woman with them."

"Maria?"

"No. If it had been, I'd have killed the whole damn bunch on the spot. She looks to be Shoshoni. I didn't know her. The way she moved and rode, I figure her hands are tied. That would make her a captive. Might want to keep that in mind when the shooting starts. I've killed a woman before. Didn't much like the way it felt, even if she would have blown my head off and laughed about it." Stonekiller worked the coffee cup for a moment in silence, his gaze locked on the western edge of the shallow buffalo wallow. The half-breed sighed. "Slocum, we can't let a mother's son of that bunch get away. Bloody Hand won't worry about his rear guard until he doesn't hear from them for a couple of days. That's two more days in our favor."

Slocum didn't reply. There was no need. Stonekiller's logic was sound. It had been sound since sunrise, when they had first spotted the Indian. For three hours, Slocum and Stonekiller had watched the Indian watch them, trying to give no sign that they had seen the scout. Slocum felt exposed the whole time, acting like an unsuspecting greenhorn and not sure that half a hundred warriors might be waiting just beyond the next rise. It had been a twitchy half day, but by the time he and Stonekiller deliberately stopped for noon camp in this shallow buffalo wallow, which offered no protection or defense, they knew the Indian was alone.

And they had come up with a plan.

If Bloody Hand bothered setting a rear guard, he must be getting nervous about something. Comanches seldom kept close watch on their back trail unless they expected pursuit. They usually sent scouts out ahead, or on the flanks to check out the countryside. They didn't worry all that much about where they had been.

Slocum and Stonekiller had to get past the rear guard somehow, or Bloody Hand would soon know they were on his trail—and that there were only two of them. Riding around the rear guard wouldn't work. The Indian scouts would cut their sign, sooner or later. That left them only one option. They had to bushwhack the rear guard. Take them down to the last man.

Slocum lit a cigarillo and turned the plan over in his mind for the hundredth time. It wasn't foolproof—nothing was when you faced a superior force—but it was the best option they had. Each of them had considerable skill at setting an ambush, and they couldn't have asked for better terrain.

The buffalo wallow lay less than a hundred yards west of a low butte, the only high ground for a mile around. The hill barely qualified as high ground; the gentle slopes of the plateau were barely a dozen feet tall. But the rim of the butte facing the wallow was studded with scrub juniper, greasewood brush, and Spanish dagger clumps, with a few sandstone rocks scattered here and there. It provided enough cover to give them an advantage.

Stonekiller knew Southern Plains Indian tactics even better than Slocum did. When the attack came, it would be just after dawn. Comanches and Kiowas alike were hesitant to fight at night, believing that the soul of a man killed in the dark was condemned to walk in darkness forever. They would attack from the west, confident of catching their quarry by surprise. That would put the sun in their eyes when the counterattack came from atop the butte. Two expert riflemen in the rocks and brush on the rimrock would have an open field of fire and decent shooting light. They could cut the attacking force to pieces in a matter of moments.

At least that's the way it worked in theory. The catch was whether the Indians could be tricked into charging the buffalo wallow.

"Got the dummies ready?" Stonekiller seemed to be reading Slocum's mind again. It was getting to be a bit spooky how the half-breed knew what he was thinking, Slocum thought.

"They're ready." Slocum had put the decoys together while Stonekiller tracked the Indian scout. Two bundles of brush and dry grass lay near the fire. In the faint light of dawn the bundles, tied in the rough shape of sleeping men, might pass for the real thing. Slocum would saddle the crippled brown horse and stake it near one of the bundles. One of the less valuable mounts taken from the outlaws would be hobbled at the head of the second bundle. Other horses would be on a picket line a few yards away. That would add a more realistic touch. Men in camp were seldom more than a few feet away from a horse at all times.

The bushwhackers would each have his top mount tied just out of sight beyond the rim of the butte in case something went wrong and they had to make a run for it. Slocum couldn't think of any possibility they hadn't covered. The plan was good. But he had seen other good plans go into the latrine trenches during the war. If there was one thing consistent about battle plans, Slocum knew, it was that things never quite went according to those plans.

Stonekiller finished his coffee, chased the rank brew with a swig from a canteen, and glanced at the lowering moon. "Think I'll grab a little nap, if you don't mind standing watch for a couple more hours."

"Take all the sack time you need," Slocum said. "You've been doing all the work today, anyway. I'll keep an eye on things."

"No need to fret much for a spell, Slocum. Not likely anything will happen past moonset. Nudge me awake then. Natchee'll be close by then, but they'll stop to rest the horses when the moon goes down. Us Injuns don't travel much when it's pitch black. Bad spirits about, you know."

Stonekiller was asleep within seconds, his breathing deep and regular, but Slocum knew the slightest out-of-place sound would bring the blocky man wide awake. Slocum slept that way himself. It was something a man learned when he rode dangerous trails.

He picked up his rifle and walked up the slight slope to the crest of the butte. He squatted on his heels beside a juniper and studied the horizon to the west. Dry grass rustled as a small night animal prowled nearby. A coyote yelped in the distance. Slocum stared intently at a faint movement a few yards beyond the wallow, then relaxed as a gray fox minced across a patch of moonlight, hunting.

It was a peaceful night, Slocum thought.

Come morning, it wouldn't be nearly as tranquil.

"Here they come," Stonekiller said softly. The half-breed lay five yards to Slocum's right, bellied down behind a clump of rocks. He had the dead bandit's spyglass in hand. The Ballard lay by his left elbow, several of the big .45 cartridges beside the weapon. The Winchester lay within easy reach of Stonekiller's right hand.

Slocum cracked the action of his .44-40 Winchester, made sure a load was chambered, and squinted into the faint gray light of dawn.

Eight horsemen approached the buffalo wallow from the west. They were moving cautiously now, unable to see the fake camp in the lowest part of the buffalo wallow.

"The one in front—riding the paint—is Natchee," Stonekiller half whispered. "The man to his right is leading the girl's horse." He slipped the spyglass back into its case and picked up the Ballard. "Natchee'll lead the charge. The others will fan out. You take Natchee first, then the ones on his left. I'll handle the ones on the right. Go for the horses if you don't have a clear shot at the Indians."

Slocum peered down the barrel of his rifle. The front post sight of the .44-40 was clear enough, even in the dim light. He took a quick glance at Stonekiller. The blocky man carefully adjusted the sliding bar on the tang sight of the big rifle, then settled down to wait. Slocum turned his attention back to the war party. The man on the paint horse checked his mount short of the far edge of the buffalo wallow, stood in the stirrups, and peered over the low crest. Slocum could only hope the Indian took the bait. From here, the two bundles lying beside the fire looked real enough, like a couple of men bedded down and sleeping through the dawn. Slocum had slipped into the fake camp a couple of hours ago and stoked the fire. The blaze had died now, only the specks of red embers and a wisp of lazy smoke remaining.

Slocum picked up his range finder, a single Spanish dagger plant with double stalks halfway beyond the fire and the far rim of the wallow. The blooms on the twin stalks were a pale white in the growing light. Slocum had stepped off the distance at a hundred and ten yards, well within accurate range of his finely tuned .44-40.

Natchee studied the campsite for what seemed to be a long time, as if something had raised his suspicions. Slocum hoped the man on the paint didn't smell a trap. Setting an ambush was like grabbing a rattler. Miss the first grab and the rattler could swap ends and bite you.

Slocum mouthed a silent curse as Natchee turned and apparently said something to his warriors. One of the men dismounted and crept toward the edge of the wallow, rifle in hand. A second grabbed the lead rope of the swaybacked horse the girl rode and led the gray out of sight behind a bulge in the wallow rim. Moments later, light glinted from a rifle barrel atop the bulge. Slocum's frown deepened. Matters were getting complicated in a hurry.

The sun's rays touched the far ridge of the wallow, bathing the raiding party in soft, gold light. Natchee had a revolver in hand. One of the warriors carried a lance, scorning the rifle hanging by a thong from his saddle. The gentle breeze from the west ruffled the trophy scalps lashed to the warrior's lance. The other mounted men had drawn rifles or handguns. And still, Natchee waited.

Slocum's heart beat a steady thump against his rib cage. The detached calm that he felt before a battle settled softly over his shoulders. "Come on, damn your soul," Slocum whispered aloud to the man on the paint. "Let's get the dance started."

The crippled brown horse staked by one of the dummies broke the silence. The horse looked up, ears perked toward the rim of the wallow, and whinnied.

Natchee dug heels into his paint, the four other warriors half a heartbeat behind. Shrill, yipping war cries split the air as five Indians charged into the buffalo wallow.

Slocum took a deep breath and held it for a couple of seconds, the sights of his Winchester lined on Natchee's chest. The paint horse charged past the Spanish dagger range finder. Slocum squeezed the trigger.

Through the billow of powder smoke, Slocum saw the stocky Indian jerk in the saddle, but he didn't go down. Stonekiller's Ballard thundered. The heavy slug walloped into a warrior at Natchee's left, lifted the man from the saddle, and threw him backward, rifle spinning. An Indian at Slocum's left abruptly reined his horse aside, attempting to flank them. Slocum racked a fresh round into his Winchester, swung the muzzle into line, figured a two-foot lead, and squeezed. The Indian's horse went down as the rifle thumped against Slocum's shoulder. The warrior hit the ground hard, rolled free of the flailing hooves, and sprinted toward the nearest cover. Slocum shot him between the shoulder blades. Two down, one hit. Slocum winced as a rifle slug spanged from a rock an arm's length away. One of those bastards on the far rim was a passing fair shot, he thought.

Stonekiller was almost as quick reloading the single-shot Ballard as Slocum was with the Winchester; the big rifle boomed again. A dismounted Indian kneeling on the far slope tumbled backward. Slocum didn't have time to admire the shot. Natchee had regained his balance and now charged toward Stonekiller's outpost. Fire winked from the muzzle of Natchee's handgun. Slocum snapped a quick shot at the Indian leader. The paint horse stumbled and went down hard. Natchee rolled, came to his feet, and dove behind the dying paint.

The warrior who had carried only a lance into battle reined his horse toward the downed Natchee, leaning low over the animal's neck. The man had guts, Slocum thought as he worked the Winchester. His shot skimmed past the horse's extended neck and rammed into the base of the Indian's throat. The warrior stayed on his mount for two strides, then slid from the animal's back and tumbled into the dust. The lance fluttered down almost atop the dead horse where Natchee had taken cover.

Powder smoke belched from beyond the paint's body. The slug from Natchee's pistol thumped into the rim two feet beneath Slocum. A second round buzzed over Slocum's head. He snapped two quick shots toward Natchee, not expecting to hit anything but at least keeping the Indian's head down. A rifle slug slapped into a stone near Slocum's elbow and sent rock shards nipping at his cheek. Slocum hugged the ground, thumbed fresh loads into his Winchester, and glanced up as Stonekiller's Ballard blasted again. Dirt flew inches from the head of the remaining Indian rifleman on the distant ridge; the head disappeared as the warrior ducked beneath the bulge in the rim.

"Slocum!" Stonekiller's call came as the big-bore rifle blast still echoed. "That's all of 'em except the one on the ridge! Keep this one pinned down! I'm going after the last one!"

Slocum nodded grimly and sent a slug toward Natchee's hiding place. The lead thumped into the dead horse's body. Slocum glanced at Stonekiller. The half-breed scrambled back from the rimrock, the Ballard in one hand and the Winchester in the other, and sprinted toward his horse tied to a juniper a few yards back. He thrust the Ballard into the saddle sheath, mounted with the Winchester in hand, and spurred off on a circular course that would bring him up behind the remaining rifleman.

Natchee's handgun coughed again, the slug knocking twigs from the juniper near Slocum's shoulder. Slocum snapped an answering shot, not expecting to hit the Indian, but just to keep his head down. There would be time to finish him later.

Slocum's head snapped up as hoofbeats sounded from the far rim. His heart leapt into his throat. The girl had broken away; she pounded her heels into the gray, trying to urge more speed from the animal, and she was headed straight across the wallow, apparently unaware that Natchee lay still alive behind the dead paint. She would be within Natchee's pistol range in a few more yards. Slocum frantically levered shot after shot toward Natchee, making no effort to aim, trying to keep the Indian's attention away from the girl.

The Winchester's hammer dropped on a faulty cartridge. The dull click and Slocum's barked curse came at the same time of the whack of lead against flesh in the wallow below. The old horse staggered as the report of a distant rifle shot reached Slocum's ears. The gray made two more strides and started to go down. The girl jumped clear as the horse fell, landed on her feet, and kept running toward Slocum.

"Watch out!" Slocum yelled to the girl. He yanked the lever of the Winchester. Nothing happened. The weapon was jammed. And the girl was almost within Natchee's range.

Slocum reacted without conscious thought. He dropped the useless rifle, drew his Colt, and sprang to his feet, boots skidding as he ran down the shallow slope of the butte. He hit the bottom at a full run and thumbed the Colt to full cock, hoping for a desperation shot. The odds were against him. From here, he could see only the top of Natchee's head, a target less than three fingers tall and better than fifty yards away. Sunlight glinted on steel as the barrel of Natchee's revolver flashed above the horse's rump and dropped toward the girl. Slocum fired by instinct, off balance, unable to aim. The slug went high. The girl was doomed.

She fell as Natchee fired.

Cold, blind rage swept through Slocum. He sprinted toward the downed paint, his heart pounding against his ribs. He was within thirty yards now.

"Natchee!" Slocum yelled.

The Indian's head lifted above the horse's rump. Slocum skidded to a stop, thumbed the hammer to full cock, and willed himself to take the half second he needed for an aimed shot. It almost cost him his life. Fire bloomed at the muzzle of Natchee's handgun. The slug tugged at the cloth of Slocum's shirt and left an icy track across the muscle of his upper arm. He steadied the Colt and squeezed. Natchee's head snapped back. A filmy mist seemed to hang in the air for a split second, a halo around the Indian's head. The head disappeared.

Slocum spun at the sound of footsteps, thumbing back the hammer, then lowered the weapon. The girl was back on her feet, running toward Slocum. He didn't know if she had been hit or not. Sand spurted near the girl's feet; a second slug buzzed past Slocum's ear. A split second later the reports of the distant rifle reached the wallow.

Slocum sprinted to the girl's side, wrapped an arm around her waist, and all but dragged her to the only cover available—behind Natchee's dead horse. He shoved her down and quickly lowered himself onto her, shielding her body with his own. He cocked the Colt and chanced a quick glance over the dead paint's rump. Smoke belched from the crest of the wallow a good two hundred yards away, well out of pistol range. Slocum ducked. A heartbeat later a slug splatted into the sand near the paint's hindquarters. Slocum lowered his revolver. The short gun was useless at that distance.

He instinctively reloaded the Colt and looked around, evaluating their position. It wasn't good. If they made a run for the bluff, they would be exposed to rifle fire from the Indian on the ridge. It was more of a chance than they could afford to take. All they could do was wait. It was up to Stonekiller now.

The girl had fallen across Natchee's lower legs. The Kiowa-Apache sprawled on his back, arms outflung. His eyeballs almost touched in the middle of a caved-in face. Slocum's slug had taken the Indian at the bridge of the nose and shattered the frontal bones. Blood and brain matter spread in a half circle a dozen feet behind Natchee's body.

A rifle slug thumped into the dead horse. The paint's carcass wasn't the best cover, but it would do—unless the shooter on the rim changed positions before Stonekiller got to him. Another slug kicked dirt behind the horse's rump. The crack of the rifle had barely reached his ears before two more shots came, the reports sharper, different from the others. Slocum figured Stonekiller had gotten his man. He gasped air into his lungs and heaved himself up on his elbows to take his weight off the girl. Her eyes were dark brown, wide with fright, her light copper skin pale.

"Are you hit?" Slocum said.

The girl shook her head, uncomprehending. Slocum switched to Spanish and got the same blank look in return. He tried Cheyenne. This time she understood.

"I'm not—hurt—" she gasped. "I just—tripped. Fell down. It is hard—to run with—one's hands tied."

"Good thing you fell," Slocum said, his words broken as his chest heaved for air, "or you'd have caught a slug for sure." With both of them winded, Slocum thought, this was going to be a choppy conversation for a spell. "What's your name?"

"I am—called—Willow."

Slocum eased his head up for a cautious look around. His shoulders sagged in relief. Jim Stonekiller rode casually down the far side of the buffalo wallow, rifle resting in the crook of an elbow. Slocum took a closer look at the girl still lying beneath him. She was young, probably not much past her teens. Her face was more oval than that of most Indian women, with deep brown eyes that were surprisingly calm, considering what she had just gone through. Even in his frazzled state, Slocum could tell this one was all woman. Any other time, he thought, he would be enjoying this position. The thought embarrassed Slocum a bit. He lifted himself from the girl's body.

Her deerskin dress was decorated in a Shoshoni pattern. Slocum was glad she spoke Cheyenne. His Shoshoni wasn't that good. The languages were similar on the tongue, but he had never grasped the subtle shadings of Shoshoni dialect. He had almost gotten himself lanced in a Shoshoni camp once over a casual remark that he later learned was a serious insult. He holstered his Colt, pulled his knife, and sliced the bonds from Willow's wrists.

"Are you sure you're not hurt?" Slocum's speech was almost normal now. He was getting his wind back.

"I'm sure," she said. She massaged her chafed wrists for a moment, then sat up and straightened her dress. "You?"

Slocum glanced at the torn sleeve, peeled his shirt down, and checked the bullet burn. The skin was barely broken. He shrugged. "It's nothing. Not much more than a scratch."   .

"I will tend it for you. Have you a name?"

"Slocum. You had me a bit worried there, Willow."

"I did not see Natchee lying behind the horse. I almost got us both killed."

"But you didn't, so it's nothing to fret over." Slocum started at the sharp crack of a rifle shot nearby. His right hand instinctively dropped to the butt of the Colt before he relaxed.

Stonekiller lazily racked a fresh round into the chamber of his rifle. One of the Indians in the wallow had still been alive.

Stonekiller checked the others, shot one more who might have had a flicker of life left, then kneed his horse up to Slocum and the girl.

"I suppose you got the gunner on the ridge," Slocum said.

Stonekiller nodded. "He was so busy taking potshots at you and the girl he never even knew I was around. Glad to see you two made it through in one piece."

"Not as glad as we are," Slocum said laconically. "Willow, meet Jim Stonekiller."

Stonekiller inclined his head in greeting and promptly rattled off a string of Shoshoni. Willow jabbered back just as rapidly. Slocum waited out the lengthy conversation and noticed for the first time that his mouth was dry. That happened often after a battle. Shooting and getting shot at pulled the water from a man in a hurry. He helped himself to a swallow from Natchee's water skin.

Stonekiller's face seemed to brighten as the jabbering continued. Finally, he turned to Slocum. "Willow was a captive in Bloody Hand's camp with Maria. They became friends. Maria's all right, at least so far."

"That's good news," Slocum said, relieved.

Stonekiller's gaze drifted over the carnage in the buffalo wallow. "Willow says all the men in Natchee's rear guard are accounted for. We got our extra couple of days, Slocum. Bloody Hand was camped at Horse Springs, like we figured. Willow says they probably have moved on by now, but at least we've gained ground on them."

Slocum stood and brushed the dirt from his clothing.

Willow said something in Shoshoni. Her tone sounded urgent.

"Would you two mind talking Cheyenne?" Slocum said. "I'd sort of like to be able to understand what's going on."

"Oh," Willow said, "I speak English."

Slocum's eyebrows went up. "Why didn't you say so before?"

"Until I knew who you were, I thought it wise to pretend I didn't understand." Willow turned back to Stonekiller. "We must find the American soldiers. Maria said if I managed to escape I must get word to the Army so they can stop Bloody Hand."

Stonekiller shook his head grimly. "No soldiers. At least not until I have Maria back. Bloody Hand would kill her if the Army attacked."

"But what can you—we—what can three people do against so many?"

"We'll think of something," Stonekiller said, frowning. "Do you know where Bloody Hand is headed?"

"Somewhere called The Place of the Bones."

"Skeleton Canyon," Slocum said.

"You know it?"

"I've been there once." Slocum's tone was grim. "It's a damn fortress, Jim. One way in and one way out. Half a dozen good riflemen could hold off a hundred attackers there. Not even the Tenth Cavalry could whip Bloody Hand in that place."

"We'll see," Stonekiller said. "In the meantime, let's get Willow mounted on a good horse and move out. I'd like to camp tonight at the rock basins Willow told me about. There's water and grass there."

"Whatever you say." Slocum's brow furrowed as his gaze swept the bloody buffalo wallow. "But there's a dirty job or two to do first." He stared at the brown horse staked beside the dummy. The gelding's back was humped, its head held low. A dark wetness smeared the brown's hide behind and below its ribs. The horse had been gutshot, hit by a stray slug. Slocum drew his Colt, strode to the brown, and shot the horse between the eyes. Dropping the hammer on the horse left a hollow feeling in his gut, even if it had been an act of mercy. Shooting Natchee had been a hell of a lot more enjoyable. He checked on the old mare that Willow had ridden. The mare was dead. Slocum ejected the spent cartridge, reloaded the empty chamber, and walked back.

Willow stood alone.

"Jim went for the horses," she said as Slocum strode up. She placed a hand on his forearm. "Thank you. For saving my life. I am in your debt. You did not need to risk your own for an Indian. And a mere woman, at that."

A hint of a smile touched Slocum's lips. Now that the excitement had died down, he could see that this was no mere woman who stood before him. She was tall for a Shoshoni girl, perhaps five foot six. The freshening wind rippled her long, black hair and molded the soft doeskin dress to her body. The supple material clung to high, firm breasts above a rib cage that tapered to a narrow waist before flaring over surprisingly full hips and long, firm legs. Slocum tried not to stare.

"No thanks needed," he said. "You owe me nothing."

Slocum glanced skyward as a shadow drifted over the sandy wallow. The damn buzzards were always around. At least, he thought, the scavengers of the desert would have plenty of grub tonight.

"They serve a purpose," Willow said.

Slocum glanced at her in surprise.

"The buzzards. They clean the land."

Slocum nodded. He couldn't argue the point. The carrion eaters did perform a service. But he was beginning to wonder if every Indian in the Southwest could read his mind. First Stonekiller, now Willow. And Slocum had always made it a point to keep himself stoic and unreadable in the eyes of others. He hoped she couldn't read his thoughts right now. He didn't want her to know about the tickle in his gut and the quickening of his heartbeat.

Stonekiller's arrival with the horses broke the awkward silence. Willow stepped easily into the saddle of a leggy red roan taken from the Rio Grande outlaw string. Her skirt rode up, exposing a bit too much smooth thigh for Slocum's comfort. The roan snorted and stamped its front feet, but quickly settled down under her firm hand and soft voice.

Slocum swung aboard the Kickapoo dun and waited as Stonekiller made the rounds of the Indian bodies, lifting scalps. There wasn't much of Natchee's hair left. A .44 slug at close range tended to tear up a lot of scalp when it came out. Stonekiller had more than a scalp in mind. He casually pulled his knife, decapitated Natchee, and dumped the still-bleeding head into a burlap sack. There were two lumps showing through the cloth.

"Why the heads?" Slocum asked.

"Never know when they might come in handy," Stonekiller said. "Besides, us Injuns got a reputation to uphold. Can't have you white-eyes thinking of us as anything but savages. Let's ride."

8

Slocum shifted his weight in the smooth niche carved and polished into a natural chair by wind and weather in an outcrop above the stone water basins, tongued a cigarillo, and listened to the soothing evening sounds of the camp.

Jim Stonekiller and Willow sat by the fire a few feet away, talking in muted tones. An awakening owl hooted sleepily in the distance. The lowering sun winked on the green feathers of a Mexican jay making one final feeding run to its brood nesting in a juniper across the way.

The broiling heat of the afternoon had faded a bit, bringing the promise of a pleasantly cool night, even though the basin stones would retain warmth almost until dawn. A light breeze drifted through the arroyo, rippled the waters trapped in the natural troughs below, and blew cool across Slocum's bare head. His hair was still damp from a bath and shave in one of the lower pools. He felt clean for the first time in days. Slocum liked the feel of a fresh shave and clean clothes against scrubbed skin. It was a luxury few townsfolk could really appreciate. Only a man accustomed to long rides and scarce water holes could savor the sensation of feeling clean. His belly was full, the camp meal topped by a shot from Stonekiller's whiskey bottle. He shouldn't have had a care in the whole world.

Except that a band of renegade Indians was only a couple of days' ride away. And the band was growing by the day. Little details like facing a nest of the Plains' best light cavalry troops in a fight that had to come soon, Slocum thought, could spoil a man's peaceful disposition if he were the fretting kind.

At least now he and Stonekiller had that edge they needed. The edge was Willow. The girl hadn't had her head under her wing while she was in Bloody Hand's camp. By the time they had reached the stone basins, Willow had told them a great deal about Bloody Hand and his renegade gathering. She had, in fact, told them more than she realized.

The gossip network among captives was a close bond. Beyond that, the Shoshoni girl had exceptional hearing and eyesight, and a quick, analytical mind.

Bloody Hand's band was growing, Willow had said, but still numbered less than fifty warriors at the time the rear guard was dispatched. That news wasn't particularly reassuring to Slocum. Fifty warriors was about forty-nine more than he was comfortable with. But as Stonekiller had guessed, some of them might be more trouble than help for the Kwahadi who would be king of the Plains.

Almost a quarter of the renegade's recruits were mestizos from northern Mexico—half Indian, half Mexican, and all superstitious to the bone. The mestizos were good fighters, but only to a point; they would panic, cut and run, if faced by a force they didn't understand. Many of the Apaches that had come were as superstitious as the mestizos. More than a few of the Kwahadi's cohorts were jealous of Bloody Hand or suspicious of his motives. Many of the tribes represented had been mortal enemies since time began, scornful of each other as less than human. It was a common viewpoint among the Indians. Almost every tribe referred to itself as "The People," or a similar phrase implying that all other tribes were inferior. The alliance Bloody Hand had built was a fragile one. Slocum knew that a shaky allegiance was one easily shattered if a man knew where all the Achilles' heels lay. Confusion, fear, and hate were the biggest enemy of any army, white or red.

Thanks to Willow's observations, they also had a good idea of Bloody Hand's timetable. By now the band would be on the move again, headed for Skeleton Canyon. The place was a fortress. History had shown it could also be a trap. The canyon was filled with evil spirits and the ghosts of the dead to the more superstitious Indians. The fact that there was only one way in and one way out could be used against Bloody Hand.

The glimmer of a plan had formed in Slocum's mind by the time they had reached the stone tanks. For the past three hours he had sat silently, thinking. The plan had more flesh to it now. It still needed more muscle and bone. Slocum tried to force the whirling thoughts from his mind. Sometimes the answers came more easily when a man quit thinking on them.

His gaze drifted back to the Shoshoni girl. She wasn't the least bit hard to look at, even squatting on her heels beside the fire. Her back was to Slocum, her long, dark hair riffling in the breeze. Her skirt was tucked up behind her knees, the soft doeskin clinging to her full hips. Slocum tried to ignore the stirring in his Levi's. It had been a long time since he had had a woman.

Slocum had tried to disguise his interest out of respect to the girl—only she knew what she had been through as a captive—but he couldn't blink away the memory of the expression in her eyes when their glances had met several times during the long ride from the buffalo wallow. Slocum thought he had seen something besides gratitude there during those brief moments of contact. He didn't put much stock in his observation. It was probably just wishful thinking on his part, he figured.

Slocum finished his smoke, frayed the stub of tobacco into slivers, and brushed sand over the remnants. He knew he had been sitting too long when the itchy feeling started in his thighs. He needed to stretch his legs.

Stonekiller glanced at Slocum and waved a beckoning hand. Slocum stood, brushed the thin layer of rock dust from his rump, and strode to the campfire. He nodded his thanks as Stonekiller poured him a cup of coffee.

Stonekiller said, "We'd better keep a sharp eye out. I doubt Bloody Hand will send more scouts out for a couple of days, but we're too close to him now to take anything for granted. I'm going to saddle up and take a little scout around. I'll be back about midnight."

Slocum nodded in agreement. "I'll take over then." He sipped at his coffee and watched as Stonekiller saddled up, checked his weapons, and rode off. The sun had set; only a narrow swath of salmon-tinted clouds low on the horizon marked its passing. The first evening stars already stood as sharp pinpoints in the deepening sky. Within minutes, Slocum knew, darkness would cover the land. Stonekiller would have little more than starlight to ride by until moonrise in a couple of hours.

Willow interrupted his musings. "This place where Bloody Hand is bound. Why is it called The Place of the Bones?"

Slocum stared into the distance for a moment, pulling the memories of a long-ago trip from his mind.

"It is known as Skeleton Canyon to the white man," Slocum said. "It is a narrow pass, less than half a mile wide at its broadest point, between mountains. It is just over a mile long. For most of its length there are human and animal bones scattered along the way."

"How did they get there?"

Slocum drained the last of his coffee and tossed the dregs aside. "Many years ago," he said, "there was a big battle in the canyon between the Apaches and the white man's Army. The Indians had only bows, lances, and a few rifles. The Army had cannons set up on each end of the canyon. They hammered the Apaches with shot and shell for three days and nights. But by then, most of the Indians had been killed by rifle and cannon fire—men, women, children. All their horses were dead. A few escaped on foot through the mountains. The bones of the others lie there still."

Willow's brow wrinkled. "And the Apaches did not return to bury their dead?"

"No," Slocum said softly. "The soldiers kept their cannon trained on the pass for weeks. It would have been sure suicide for any Apache to try to recover the bodies. The soldiers made no effort to bury the Indians. By the time the Army pulled out, the bones had been picked clean and scattered by buzzards and wolves. The skeletons lie there to this day."

Willow shuddered. "It must be a frightening place."

"It is," Slocum said solemnly. "I thought I had seen everything there was to see in the Civil War, but I have to admit my skin crawled when I rode through Skeleton Canyon. I didn't stop to camp."

Willow sat silently for a moment, staring into the dying fire. The glowing embers reflected points of light in her brown eyes and painted a reddish gold wash over her high cheekbones. She looked young and vulnerable to Slocum. He became aware that he was staring at her and averted his gaze.

She finally said, "Do you believe in evil spirits? The ghosts of the dead?"

"I won't say I do. I won't say I don't. There are many things I don't know, things I have seen and felt that made me wonder."

"Like when your skin felt strange as you rode through this canyon? As though unseen eyes were watching?"

Slocum nodded solemnly.

"There are ghosts, Slocum. I think that in this canyon you were riding among spirits. The souls of the unburied. I am Cheyenne. I believe. Most all Plains Indians so believe."

"Perhaps the Indians are right. Only the souls of those who walk the night know for certain, and they can't tell their stories." Slocum cut a quick glance at the girl. Her brow was wrinkled in contemplation. "Are you leading up to something, Willow?"

"Only a thought. Perhaps we could find ways to invent some truly bad spirits for Bloody Hand's camp in the canyon. Such a thing would cause many problems for him."

Slocum's brows arched in surprise. It was the same idea he had been chewing on for several hours. The Shoshoni girl had a brain at work behind those big brown eyes. "Do you have some specific spirits in mind?"

"Perhaps. I *am* Indian, you know." Willow smiled. Her whole face seemed to brighten with the flash of white, even teeth. "My mother was a medicine woman, but more than just a healer. There were those outside the tribe who believed she was a—a conjurer, I believe is the white man's word. Some say such gifts flow in the blood. I shall think on this more."

"Willow," Slocum said cautiously, "we might have to go into the canyon itself. Will the spirit presence there disturb you?"

Her smile faded, to Slocum's disappointment. "I would not be speaking the truth to say no. But one must overcome one's own fears when the need of others is greater." She placed a hand on Slocum's forearm. "I will be frightened, but I will not flee when I am needed, Slocum. We must save Maria Stonekiller. I owe her more than my life."

Slocum checked his curiosity. Whatever Willow owed to Maria was none of his business. It was enough that the Shoshoni woman was now an ally. Normally, Slocum avoided riding into a fight with a woman alongside. A man dodging lead and lances had enough on his mind without worrying about a woman's safety. Yet Willow wasn't the average female. He had seen that she was an expert horsewoman. Her courage was beyond question. She had shown that at the buffalo wallow fight. He had no qualms about her intelligence, and he had the feeling she could use a weapon, if necessary. Still, he would have to keep a tight rein on his natural instincts to worry about a woman. Especially as much woman as this one.

Willow interrupted his musings.

"Jim tells me you have spent time among the Indians, that you understand our thoughts and traditions better than most white men."

"I'm not sure how much I really understand," Slocum said. "Our cultures are very different. But, yes, I have spent a few seasons among the Plains tribes."

"Then between the three of us," she said firmly, "we will find a way to loose some bad medicine on Bloody Hand." Willow stood and brushed the sand from the hem of her doeskin dress. "Night nears," she said. "I need a bath."

She strode away toward the lower pool where Slocum had bathed earlier, hips swaying, her strides long. She stopped at the edge of the pool and stripped the dress over her head. Slocum tried to tear his gaze away as she stepped into the water, her body little more than a silhouette in the growing darkness. The faint light of dusk outlined high, full breasts, the sharp taper of rib cage to waist, and firm buttocks that flowed seamlessly into long legs that were full in the thigh and calf but trim in the knees and ankles. He thought he caught a glimpse of a dark triangle of hair where her smooth belly met her thighs as she turned slightly before lowering herself into the deeper water a few feet from the edge of the pool.

Slocum had to turn away. A man could tolerate only so much. He had never taken a woman unless she wanted to be taken, or unless it was her business. The latter case was the simpler of the two; a man paid his money, got his relief, and went on his way. No strings, no lingering attachments, just a simple cash payment for services rendered. Bedding a woman who didn't depend on her crotch for her livelihood was more complicated.

He spread his bedroll, tried to ignore the gentle splashings from the nearby pool, and removed his boots and pistol belt. He stretched out atop the bedroll. The night would not be cool enough for blankets until near dawn. He concentrated on the brightening wash of stars in the clear sky overhead, trying not to think of Willow. He identified a handful of constellations to occupy his mind before he dozed off.

A light touch on his shoulder jarred Slocum awake. His right hand had closed around the grips of the holstered Colt before he recognized the figure standing over him in the faint light from a sliver of moon. He moved his hand from the revolver.

Willow did not speak. She was still for several heartbeats, looking down at him, moonlight teasing ripples across her dark hair. Then she reached down, gripped the hem of her dress, stripped it over her head, and stood naked over Slocum.

Slocum's breath caught in his throat. For a moment he wondered if it was a dream, if he would awaken to a growing ache in his crotch. If he were dreaming, he didn't want to wake up.

It wasn't a dream. Willow knelt beside Slocum, the clean scent of freshly scrubbed skin and a faint hint of musk drifting to his nostrils. She took his right hand and raised it to her breast. He heard her sharp intake of breath as his palm cupped her breast and his fingers played softly over the erect nipple. The slight woman-musk grew stronger. Slocum ran his free hand through her hair, still slightly damp from her bath. The palm of his hand stroked her shoulder, slid down her waist to her hip. Willow's breathing became heavier. She reached for the top button of his shirt, shifted her weight, and spread her legs slightly, opening her crotch to his reach. His fingers snaked slowly across the smooth skin of her flank into the dense mat of hair between her legs. Slocum's chest heaved as his fingers eased deeper into the dark triangle and stroked the slit beneath it. He found a dampness there that was not from her bath.

Willow's hips moved against his hand, a gentle, rocking motion, her breath coming faster. Her fingers dropped from his open shirt to his belt buckle. Slocum's swollen shaft strained painfully against the confining cloth of his Levi's. The discomfort stopped as she flipped open the final button; her fingers closed around his thickness, freed him from the final restraints of cloth. Her hand was hot against his shaft as she stroked him gently. Slocum's scrotum tightened at her touch. He softly parted the warm wetness of the lips of her slit and gently massaged the swollen nub of her clitoris. She shuddered, her shoulders back. Then she straddled him, her knees alongside his ribs, and stroked his tight testicles. She reached back, parted the damp hair, spread the lips of her vagina, and guided him into her. She slowly lowered her hips.

Slocum almost lost control as her snug, hot wetness slid slowly down his shaft until he was completely buried in her. He managed to hold back his ejaculation; the girl deserved more than just a quick, sticky mess. For a moment she straddled him, not moving. Her breath came almost in gasps now. He felt the muscles inside her contract, relax, contract again. He moved his fingertip gently back and forth across her clitoris. She lifted her hips then, raising herself almost to the end of his shaft, paused for a heartbeat, and then slowly lowered her body until he was buried deep inside. Her interior muscles again contracted, as if she were stroking him with an unseen hand. She moaned and arched her back. He leaned forward, ran his lips along the side of her right breast, then softly tongued the erect nipple. She whimpered; for a moment Slocum was afraid he had hurt her. Then her hips moved again, more urgently this time, as she pressed her breast against his face. Slocum flicked his tongue back and forth rapidly across her nipple and lifted his hips to meet hers.

The movement of their hips became faster, more urgent, their pelvises meeting with increasing force at each thrust. Slocum leaned back, unable to keep his mouth on her nipple as his breathing quickened. The tension in his testicles grew with each stroke. Willow whimpered again, deep in her throat. Her entire body stiffened, then convulsed. Her breath came in a series of sharp gasps, almost grunting sounds; he felt her deep, powerful contractions against his shaft, then his own swelling, and a heartbeat later, the powerful explosion of his own release. His breath caught in his throat. He emptied into her, each convulsion of his shaft pumping more fluid; she pushed herself more tightly against him, her convulsions milking his testicles.

After what seemed an eternity but could have been little more than a handful of seconds, their convulsions slowed. Slocum felt the hot stickiness of the overflow ooze into his crotch hair and trickle down onto his testicles. He lay spent, his quick gasps slowing to a more normal breathing pattern as he began to go limp inside her. A drop of moisture pecked onto his cheek. He opened his eyes and realized the drop had been a tear. Willow was crying silently. On impulse, he reached up, cupped a hand behind her head, drew her face to his, and kissed her softly and gently. Her lips were moist and pliant. She lowered her torso onto his chest and sighed in contentment.

They lay for several minutes chest-to-chest, their combined sweat slick against their skins. He contented himself with the warmth of her, the feel of her hair as he stroked his fingers through the thick, damp strands. Still, neither had spoken.

Finally, Willow lifted her face to his, kissed him, and lifted her body. He felt his wet limpness slide from her, releasing more of their fluid onto his belly. She rolled onto her side and stared up at the stars for a moment. Finally, she spoke.

"I'm sorry to wake you," she said apologetically. "I couldn't sleep—"

Slocum shushed her by placing a finger over her lips. "Don't apologize, Willow. That was something I've been wanting to do with you since I first saw you."

"And I," she said, lifting his finger from her lips and kissing the heel of his hand. "I feel much better now. Thank you."

"The pleasure," Slocum said with a wide grin, "was all mine."

Willow's answering grin had a deliciously wicked twist to it. "It was not. Somehow, when I first saw you, I sensed the pleasure you could bring. It has been many months since I have been with a man." She sighed, contented. Moonlight glistened on her sweat-slicked breasts. "I do not choose just any man, Slocum," she said.

"I know that. And it's my turn to thank you." He pulled her to him and kissed her again. After a moment, she giggled and pushed him away. "Don't get me started again, or neither of us will sleep tonight," she said.

Slocum reluctantly rolled away. He couldn't think of a better way to spend the night, but he didn't force the issue. Indian women had a much better attitude toward sex than white women. They were open about it, asked no favor in return, and it seemed to Slocum they enjoyed it more. To most Indian women, sex was fun. As it was meant to be. He allowed himself a wry grin. There were things white women could learn from Indian women.

Willow sat up and reached for her dress. "I will sleep well now, but I must go to my own blankets. I would not sleep at all if I stayed here. Too many distractions.''

Slocum watched her stride away, her movements languid and relaxed. He idly wondered how old the Shoshoni woman might be. She could be sixteen or twenty-six; it was impossible to tell from her face or figure. He decided it didn't make a damn bit of difference. He crossed his arms behind his head and gazed up at the sky. Tonight had changed things. He knew now that when they rode into the fight with Bloody Hand, he would have to watch himself. A man who kept one eye on the enemy and another on his woman might wind up getting them both killed.

Maria Stonekiller crouched beside her cooking fire and gazed around the sprawling Indian camp in the canyon called The Place of the Bones. It was well named, she thought; a few strides in any direction brought one across a skull, a long bone, or ribs half buried in the sandy soil. Each discovery chilled her blood.

She sensed the same unease across the entire camp. Lodges dotted the twisting canyon floor for more than a half mile. Smoke from cook fires hung low over the lodges, drifted slowly and silently on the faint breeze, and cast an eerie gray pall over the camp. It was as if the sun and wind had chosen to keep them in shadowy half light, even at midmorning.

Maria was not overly superstitious, but she could not overcome tribal instincts of generations past. She still shivered from time to time as her gaze drifted along the steep canyon walls. It seemed a shadow flitted beneath every cedar or stunted piñon pine or ducked from sight behind a boulder a split second before the eye actually saw it. There was an ominous feel in the almost still air, a sensation of unrest that could not be denied. There were spirits here, ghosts of the dead stranded between worlds.

She knew the edgy feeling was not hers alone. There had been no stick and bones games, no horse races or other gambling, since the band had come to this place. The few women in the camp stayed in their lodges except when it was absolutely necessary to go outside. The half dozen or so young children did not run and play; they stayed close to their mothers, often clinging to skirts, eyes wide and round. One or two seemed to cry for no reason at all.

Even the sentries stationed atop the canyon rims stood watch in pairs. Maria could imagine how their hearts would pound and palms turn clammy during the darkest time of watch.

The mestizos felt the unseen presence more.

The small band, no more than thirty warriors, huddled in their camp pitched in the middle of the widest part of the canyon as if they could ward off the spirits simply by staying as close as possible to each other. Not even their bony dogs barked. The mongrels slunk about with tails between their legs and cringed at the slightest strange sound or smell.

Maria had overheard the argument when the small band joined them a day's walk from Horse Springs. The mestizos wanted to camp outside the canyon, or at least in the rugged, broken mountains surrounding the place of the dead. Bloody Hand stood firm. If the mestizos were so afraid of evil spirits, they could return to their barren, dry mountains and eat worms and bugs as they had done for centuries. There would be no share of glory or loot for them. Eventually, their greed—and possibly hunger—had been greater than their dread of the place. The mestizos were an ignorant people, poor, dirty, and cowardly. They had no lodges. What few horses they did own were shambling, ugly creatures. The mestizos owned few weapons beyond throwing sticks and poorly shaped lances. They were thieves. They would steal corn and jerked meat rather than ask for it. Worse yet, they had no pride. They were beneath the scorn of any Plains tribe. Being around them made Maria's skin crawl.

Her gaze drifted along the strung-out camp. Each tribe seemed to keep to itself. Only the Comanches, Kiowas, and Kiowa-Apache allies mixed freely. The Utes, Kickapoos, occasional Washita, even the few renegade Cheyennes, kept their own company. The steadily growing number of Apaches, mostly from the White Mountain and Chiricahua bands, kept their own counsel as well. The Apaches were perhaps the most fearless and best warriors of the lot, but they looked down their haughty noses at any man or woman whose blood was not Apache. And the Apaches were as frightened of this place as were the mestizos.

Maria stirred the stew bubbling in her cooking pot and flexed her shoulders. Her skin was still raw from the chafe of the carry straps of the heavy pack, but at least one good thing had come at this camp. She was no longer necked by the rawhide rope to the wagon, and her hands and feet were not bound at night. There was no need. Escape was hopeless here. And for two nights now,

Bloody Hand had been too busy to bother her. That was a luxury she welcomed but had not expected. Now, if she could only get a bath, to wash the dirt of travel and the hands of the Comanche renegade from her body, she could almost be at peace.

Even then, she knew, heaviness and worry would burden her heart.

The young Arapaho girl who had been hamstrung was dead, lanced in the back less than a half mile from the Horse Springs camp when she had tried to escape. The man who owned her had come back from the chase, laughing and joking about the girl's attempt to flee and the way the useless foot flopped as she tried to run.

There had been no word of Willow's fate. She might also be dead. Maria knew she wasn't the only one worried about the rear guard. Bloody Hand tried not to show it, but he was growing nervous. It had been four days since the renegade had sent Natchee and his men to watch the back trail. Last night, Bloody Hand had paced beside the fire long after the rest of the camp had gone to sleep. He paused occasionally to look back toward where they had been. This morning he had sent five warriors to check on Natchee.

Bloody Hand faced other problems, also. The wagon load of tiswin, white man's whiskey, and additional guns was overdue. There had been no sign of the Comancheros who were to deliver the goods. Without the fuel of liquor to flame men's courage, Bloody Hand would have a difficult time convincing his followers to engage in war against the white man. The battle was to begin in a few days, with the next full moon.

Despite her discomfort at being in The Place of the Bones, her sorrow at the crippled girl's death, and the uncertainty of Willow's fate, Maria found hope. Her husband was out there, closer now; she could feel his presence as strongly as if his hand rested on her shoulder. The hope was tempered by concern. It would be next to impossible for even a man so expert on the stalk as Jim Stonekiller to slip into the canyon camp, find her, and escape alive. She knew she had to come up with some plan to make his task less dangerous.

Her gaze settled on the small lodge set well apart from the others, smoke rising from the flaps atop the buffalo hides. It was the lodge where women in their blood moon were banished until their time had passed. Two women were inside the lodge now. When occupied, it was watched over by the older women. If a captive were inside, guarding the lodge fell to the toothless hag Crow Woman and a few of her wrinkled old crones. No warrior would dare venture near the lodge. The taboo was too strong. Perhaps, Maria thought, there was a way that could be used—

She flinched and almost cried aloud at the sharp, stinging pain in the tender flesh of her upper left arm. She leapt to her feet and spun on a heel. Crow Woman's shrill cackle sounded. The old hag's bony fingers held the sharpened stick she had just jabbed into Maria.

The blood rushed to Maria's face as she struggled to control her rage. She had no weapon other than her bare hands. And to kill the old hag now could mean a slow and painful death at the hands of Crow Woman's companions.

Maria glared into the old woman's eyes, barely visible behind the wrinkles. Then, slowly, deliberately, Maria dipped a finger into the trickle of blood from the fresh wound in her arm. She thrust both hands skyward, chanting in Cheyenne. Crow Woman took a step backward. She was not cackling now. Maria reached out with the bloodied finger, drew a small crimson half circle on the rough boards of the wagon bed, and dabbed two small dots below the arc. She turned to glare at Crow Woman.

"When the magic circle is closed and two moons become four," Maria said, her words steady, "Crow Woman dies. She will walk in darkness forever. It is so spoken."

The old hag instinctively raised the pointed stick as if to ward off an attack. Her eyes widened, her gaze flicking in confusion from the bloody sign back to Maria. Confusion gave way to concern, then a touch of fright in the beady black eyes. Her leathery skin seemed to grow pale. Crow Woman backed away slowly with shuffling steps, finally turned, and waddled away as rapidly as her thick legs would allow.

Maria didn't know if the old woman believed the makeshift curse. Crow Woman might not know the Cheyenne tongue. She might not believe in curses. But in this setting, where the bones of the dead lay scattered among the weeds, perhaps she would. If nothing else, it would give her something to think about. At least for a time perhaps Maria would be spared the old woman's torment.

She dabbed at the blood still trickling from the fresh wound and ignored the pain. She stood and stared toward the northeast, past the broken badlands beyond the canyon walls, toward the rolling dry hills of Horse Springs, and was reassured. The feeling in her breast grew stronger.

Jim Stonekiller was out there.

9

Jim Stonekiller squatted beside the crushed grass and poked his knife point into a pile of horse droppings. He speared one of the manure balls, broke it open, and held it to his nose.

"How long, Jim?" Slocum asked.

Stonekiller tossed the horse apple aside and wiped his knife blade on his pants. "Two days. Maybe three."

Slocum muttered a curse. "We should have been closer than that by now. We've had a good, clear trail ever since Horse Springs."

"We should be," Stonekiller said as he toed the stirrup, "but we aren't. Bloody Hand's pushing hard. We haven't exactly been lazing along admiring our shadows, and we haven't gained more than a few hours." Saddle leather creaked as the half-breed swung aboard his muscled bay. "Can we catch up before they reach Skeleton Canyon?"

Slocum shook his head. "They're probably there now."

"You know some way where we can cut across, maybe gain some time on them?"

"No. The one time I went through the canyon, I rode in on the southern trail. I've never crossed the country between here and there." Slocum spat in disgust. "If I tried, I'd just be guessing. A wrong guess would kill us all. An old scout once told me

104

it was a mighty long ride between water holes in any direction off the established trails.''

"Then we'll just have to follow Bloody Hand and hope he hasn't thought to foul the water between here and there,'' Stone-killer said. "We can't travel faster without wearing out our horses.'' He sat the saddle for a moment, studying the tracks. "Looks like the damned renegade picked up some new soldiers along about here. You two rest here a few minutes. I'm going to take a quick look around.''

Slocum watched Stonekiller ride a wide circle, stopping his horse occasionally to peer at the ground. Slocum's gaze drifted back to the Shoshoni girl riding at his side. She sat at ease in the saddle, her hands crossed over the horn. A Kennedy lever action rifle taken from one of the dead Indians in the buffalo wallow skirmish was slung in a makeshift scabbard in front of her left knee. The weapon was reasonably new, the stock decorated with untarnished brass tacks. It was a .45-60, an unusual caliber for a reservation-jumping Indian to be carrying. Slocum knew the girl could use the long gun. He had coached her a bit. She wasn't a crack shot, but most of the time she hit where she aimed. How she would handle the rifle under pressure remained to be seen. She also carried Natchee's revolver and gun belt around her waist, along with a skinning knife in a beaded sheath. The knife had belonged to the Indian who carried the lance. The lance now was strapped to one of the pack animals, the scalp locks along the shaft fluttering in the light breeze.

Sitting there on a good horse and armed to the teeth, Slocum thought, she looked like a competent Plains warrior. The fact that she was a woman didn't particularly damage the picture. Slocum had known of a few women who were fierce warriors in their time, feared and respected by enemies of their tribe. He had heard legends of other women warriors and of their tenacity and courage in battle. The Sioux, Cheyenne, and Crow tribes still sang of the feats of such women. Slocum wondered if future generations would sing of Willow's prowess in battle. With any luck, maybe they wouldn't have to. Slocum couldn't see her as a warrior. His mind wouldn't let go of the image of her standing above him, naked. He shook himself back to the present. Sitting in the saddle staring at a pretty woman was an enjoyable way to pass the time, but there were other chores at hand: like staying alive.

Stonekiller finished his scout. "Bloody Hand picked up some help here, sure enough," he said as he reined in. "I make it twelve warriors. They stopped to parley for a while a ways off the trail. Moccasin tracks say they were White Mountain Apache."

Slocum frowned. "I'd just as soon you hadn't said that, Jim. Those White Mountain warriors are all fight, horseback or afoot, night or day. They're as tough as the Chiricahuas. Not as mean, but maybe smarter—" He paused in midsentence. "What is it, Willow?"

The Shoshoni girl stood in the stirrups, a hand held above her eyes to cut the glare of the sun, staring toward the southwest. "A dust cloud, there." She pointed toward a rugged butte that shimmered hazy and blue beyond the heat waves. "People on horses, I think."

Slocum squinted toward the butte but saw no sign of a dust cloud. And his eyesight was keen. Either the girl was wrong, or she had eyes like an eagle.

"Could be mustangs," Stonekiller said.

"The dust cloud is too small for a wild horse herd," Willow said. "Four, maybe five riders."

Slocum said, "Could be Bloody Hand's getting nervous about not hearing from his rear guard and sent out a few more troops."

Stonekiller swung a leg from the stirrup, hooked it casually around the saddle horn, and reached for the spyglass. He stared through the instrument for a moment, then nodded. "Small bunch. Like Willow said."

Slocum thought he saw a faint movement, little more than a dot against the distant skyline. Bloody Hand's new rear guard must be a cocky lot, he thought. No competent scout ever topped a ridge like that, letting himself be skylined.

Stonekiller sheathed the spyglass, reached for his tobacco sack, and glanced at Slocum. "What do you think?"

Slocum's brow furrowed. "We could move off a ways and let them ride on past. Leave them watching an empty back trail and hope they didn't cut our sign."

"Could," Stonekiller said, "but I never warmed up much to the idea of having Indians at my back when I was riding into a fight. Even a little bunch of Indians."

"Me, either. But it could be chancy taking them down. We're not all that far from Skeleton Canyon. There could be others on the way, and if one of us should get hit—" Slocum's voice trailed away.

"Damned if we don't and maybe damned if we try," Stonekiller said. "God, I hate command decisions. That's why I worked alone when I was packing a star."

"May I speak?" Willow's tone was soft, thoughtful.

"You have a tongue, woman, and you're one of us," Stonekiller said. He lit his cigarette.

"I think we should kill them and take the bodies with us."

Slocum glanced at her, startled. "Why take the bodies?"

"For making bad medicine, evil spirits." Willow's brow wrinkled, her eyes narrowed in thought. "I had a dream last night. In this dream I saw things, terrifying things. Things we could use against the superstitious ones in Bloody Hand's camp."

"You had a vision?"

"Perhaps it was a vision, Jim. Perhaps only a bad dream." Willow seemed to shudder at the memory. "Either way, we must kill these who approach. Like you, I do not wish to have enemies behind me. Only in front."

Stonekiller took a drag at his smoke. "Slocum?"

"Never turn your back on a Shoshoni vision. Whatever she has in mind is more of a plan than the two of us have at the moment, Jim." Slocum lifted the slack from the reins. "Let's go find a good spot for an ambush and kill some renegades."

The Army ought to sign Willow up as a scout, Slocum thought as he watched the mounted men approach. She had called the shot on this one.

There were five Indians in the group. Three were Comanche, judging from their bearing and clothing. The other two wore costumes and carried equipment Slocum couldn't immediately put a handle on.

Whatever the tribal mix, they weren't very good scouts. All five rode close together, bunched up, easy targets. They had sent no one out ahead. Slocum figured they were either inexperienced or simply too sure of themselves to figure they might be riding into danger.

Slocum shifted his gaze from the approaching group for one final check on the ambush site. They had been lucky. This was the perfect spot for a blindside attack. The trail the Indians followed passed through a ten-foot-deep dry wash that narrowed sharply as it made a quick bend here. The wash was flanked on two sides by thick greasewood and sage clumps, with an occasional juniper clinging to the soil atop the rim of the wash. At the center of the bend, jumble of weathered rocks provided good cover and a clean field of fire. Slocum studied the rocks for a moment. There was no sign of Jim Stonekiller; the half-breed could melt into the sparsest cover and disappear, it seemed. Slocum knew he was there, Winchester in hand and the big Ballard within easy reach. Across the way, Willow waited in the thickest greasewood clump. Slocum saw the faint movement of a thin tube as she eased the barrel of the Kennedy rifle into position. Their horses were staked a hundred yards away, out of sight and with a quartering wind so they would not nicker at the approaching horses and warn the riders.

It would be close-range rifle work. As the band neared the bend of the wash, they would ride within thirty yards of Slocum and Willow. The lead horseman would be less than eighty yards from Stonekiller. The ambushers had the higher ground. The Indians were riding casually into a deadly crossfire, their weapons still stowed. The three Comanches carried lever action rifles. The fourth rider had an old Springfield slung across his back. The last man, who looked to be the oldest of the group, carried only a short bow and a quiver of arrows. Apparently he preferred traditional Indian arms to white man's weapons. Slocum shook his head in silent disbelief at the stupidity of the scouting patrol. No man, red or white, should be so dense as to blunder into an obviously dangerous spot, even if they felt sure no one would be waiting there.

Slocum lay belly down beneath a low, spreading juniper. A drop of sweat trickled in front of Slocum's right ear. The receiver of his Winchester was hot to the touch, despite the shade cast by the juniper. He settled the rifle against his shoulder and watched over the sights as the first Indian rode past. It was Stonekiller's job to open this dance. He would take down the lead rider, then Slocum and Willow would open fire.

A young Indian, barely past his teens, threw back his head and laughed at a joke from the older man with the bow as the group moved past Slocum. The young warrior checked his horse and dropped back as the trail narrowed. That made him Slocum's first target, quartering slightly away. Slocum lined the sights between spine and shoulder blade. At this angle, even if the slug didn't blow the Indian's heart out, it would still shatter a lung. At the edge of his vision, Slocum saw that the Comanche in the lead was almost to the bend in the wash.

Slocum heard the meaty slap of lead against flesh and the almost simultaneous crack of Stonekiller's Winchester. He squeezed the trigger. The muzzle blast fell atop the report of Stonekiller's shot. The young Indian pitched from his horse. The animal whirled and bolted, wide-eyed, headed back the way they had come. Slocum quickly racked a fresh cartridge home and snapped off a shot. The horse went down in a heap, hooves thrashing, blocking the narrow trail.

The blast of Willow's Kennedy put down a third rider. Stonekiller's slug hummed wide as the fourth Indian fought to control his panicked mount. Slocum shot the man through the ribs, then turned his attention to the remaining Indian. It was the older warrior. He bailed from his horse's back, bow already in hand and an arrow nocked. Slocum's heart skipped a beat as the Indian loosed the shaft on the run; the arrow sailed into the greasewood where Willow lay. The Indian dodged and ducked as he scrambled up the slope. Stonekiller's rifle cracked. The Indian stumbled, regained his footing. Slocum hurried a shot and cursed as the slug kicked dirt near the Indian's shoulder.

The warrior was almost to Willow's hiding place, a new arrow strung. He drew the bow. Slocum frantically levered in a fresh round and whipped the sights into line—and the Indian's head snapped back as powder smoke boiled from the greasewood barely a yard from his face. The warrior hurtled backward as if hit by a heavy fist, the arrow wobbling weakly into the side of the wash.

The gunfire abruptly stopped, the silence loud in Slocum's ears. "Willow," he called, "are you all right?"

There was no reply. Slocum darted from his hiding place, ran across the wash, and scrambled up the slope. Willow still lay on her stomach, her face pale, eyes wide, as she stared at the body of the warrior a few feet below. Slocum dropped to a knee beside her.

"Are you hurt?"

Willow blinked a couple of times, then shook her head as if fighting her way back to reality. "I'm—all right," she said, her voice wavering. "It's just—I never—killed anyone before."

Slocum sighed in relief. "I know." He patted her on the shoulder. "Taking a life isn't an easy thing. But it was something you had to do. Wait here. I'll help Jim clean up the mess."

Cleaning up the mess took a hell of a lot longer than making it had taken. Almost an hour passed before Slocum and Stonekiller got control of the spooked Indian horses. It took another half hour to tie four of the bodies in place on the backs of horses that snorted, pawed, and danced at the smell of blood and death. They didn't keep the man Willow had shot. They were short a horse. And there wasn't much left of the Indian's head, anyway.

By then, Willow had regained her composure. She helped calm the boogery Indian horses as Slocum and Stonekiller wrestled the last body into place.

Slocum took a quick inventory of the weapons taken from the dead Indians. Most of the firearms were little more than junk, the barrels shot out, metal pitted with rust, stocks scarred and weathered. The front sight of the aging Springfield trapdoor model was missing.

Slocum's frown deepened as he examined one of the rifles. It was a brand-new Winchester, caliber .44-40. Traces of packing grease remained in the action. The Indians might know how to aim and fire the new rifles, but they didn't know much about cleaning and caring for them. The serial number told Slocum the new rifle was from the stolen shipment he had been guarding when ambushed. There had been little doubt in Slocum's mind that the five warriors were from Bloody Hand's band. The rifle he held in his hands confirmed it.

Slocum put the new Winchester aside. It would join their growing arsenal. They didn't need more firepower. They had enough guns now to load down a strong pack mule. But he couldn't bring himself to discard or wreck a perfectly good rifle, and he didn't want to risk the chance of it falling back into Indian hands. He picked up the short bow lying beside the older warrior and was about to break the weapon over his knee when a call from Stonekiller stopped him.

"We'll keep the bow and arrows," Stonekiller said as he stroked the neck of a nervous little grulla war pony.

Slocum scooped up the new Winchester and carried the bow and quiver to the waiting half-breed. Stonekiller tested the draw of the bow and fingered an arrow shaft.

"Good bow," Stonekiller said. "Strong, tough. Osage orange, the best of all bow woods. This Injun knew his arrows, too. Straight shafts, three feathers. Could be we can use them later. You never know when we'll need to kill somebody quietly when they're out of knife range."

"You can use a bow?"

"Haven't used one in years, but I still remember how the trigger works."

"I can use one, too," Willow said.

Slocum lifted an eyebrow.

"I may be a woman," she said in answer to his unspoken question, "but I didn't spend my whole life chewing buffalo hides and sewing and cooking. I can hold my own with most men when it comes to using a bow." She took the arrow from Stonekiller and studied it, turning the shaft carefully in her fingers. "Jicarillo Apache," she said. "The man's medicine spirit was *lagarto*—the lizard. Thirty-inch shaft, traditional flint war point with blood grooves, sinew bindings coated with animal glue, probably antelope. Accurate to nearly a hundred yards with a good bow. This man was a senior warrior, the leader of many war parties."

Slocum was mildly surprised. "That's a lot of information to read from just one arrow."

"I'm Injun too," Willow said. She started to hand the arrow back to Stonekiller. He waved it off.

"You keep them," Stonekiller said. "I think maybe you're a better Injun than I am when it comes to using a bow." He wiped the sweat from his face and neck with his kerchief. "You did well, Willow. You've earned your first scalp and eagle feather here today."

"No one told me it would be so difficult, looking into a man's eyes before killing him. Does it bother you?"

Stonekiller's expression went grim. "Only when they don't deserve it. Otherwise, it's the same as shooting a wolf at calving time." He gathered up the reins of his saddle horse and glanced at the sun.

"We'd better get a move on. By sundown tomorrow, I'd like to know the lay of the land in Skeleton Canyon."

Bloody Hand squatted beneath the scant shade of a gnarled, misshapen cottonwood tree that still bore the scars of cannon shot and glared into the eyes of the lean, dirty man standing before him.

"You have heard this in council before, Koshay," Bloody Hand said, his words a menacing rumble. "I have said many times that this is where we stay until it is time to move against the white man. That time is not yet here."

Koshay did not blink under the cold stare. Bloody Hand did not expect him to blink. The war chief of the Mescalero band feared no man. His courage was beyond question. It was painted in blood across the border lands of the United States and Mexico. Koshay did not look like a formidable foe with his short, bowed legs, narrow chest, and head that looked too large for the lean body. Bloody Hand knew otherwise.

"I did not come to argue with Bloody Hand," Koshay said calmly. "I came only to say again that this place is not good."

Bloody Hand snorted in contempt. "Koshay, I did not expect you, of all warriors, to believe this canyon to be filled with evil spirits."

Koshay said, "What worries me more than any spirits is that this canyon can be a trap as much as it can be a stronghold. If the soldiers come, there will be no way out. To die a warrior is one thing. To die as a rabbit in a snare is another."

"There will be no soldiers."

"How do you know this is so?"

"There were none in the medicine visions," Bloody Hand said. "And the only soldiers our scouts saw were those few who passed several suns ago."

Koshay was not convinced. "My own runners have been watching them. They are but three suns' ride west of here as we speak. Where there are a few, there are many not far away."

The Comanche flicked his fingers as if brushing away a fly. "A handful of soldiers. Even if they come, they will be the first to die in our war."

"It might not be so easy as Bloody Hand thinks."

A fresh surge of irritation flooded Bloody Hand's chest. "Do these soldiers Koshay fears have the big guns on wagons with them?"

Koshay's eyes narrowed. "It is not a question of fear, Bloody Hand." His tone was hard and cold, a warning that he would stand for no more remarks about his courage. "It is a question of tactics. The soldiers have no big guns with them. But these are not ordinary horse soldiers. These are the buffalo soldiers of Colonel Benjamin Grierson. The colonel is no fool. If he finds us, he will have many troopers here before five suns have set."

"How do you know this, Koshay?"

The Apache shrugged. "It is my country."

Bloody Hand's anger at the Mescalero warrior dimmed. The news was not good. Koshay was not a man to state something as fact unless he were absolutely sure of it; there was no doubting his information. As much as Bloody Hand hated to admit it, Koshay was right. The thought brought a new sense of urgency. He would have to move up his plans, leave this place as soon as possible, even before all the recruits arrived. He had more than two hundred warriors in camp now. He needed at least half that many more before starting his campaign.

"Koshay's council will be heeded," Bloody Hand said after a moment. "We will leave this place soon. Within three or four suns our army will be strong enough to begin the war to crush the white man."

Koshay nodded. "Bloody Hand would be wise to move now. There are many here who are near to panic. Even the Mescaleros hear the moans of the dead in each whisper of wind through the mountains. The mestizos continue to spread fear. I do not think Bloody Hand's alliance of many tribes will last much longer in this place."

Bloody Hand bit back a curse. The damn superstitious mestizos were getting to be more trouble by the day. He inclined his head to Koshay.

"Tell my friends the Mescalero that there will be a new rifle for each of their number. That soon the lands that once were theirs again will be in Mescalero hands. Tell them that Bloody Hand salutes them as great warriors and welcomes their courage and wisdom into his army. And that Koshay is to take command, should Bloody Hand's medicine fail. This I have spoken."

Koshay turned and strode away. Bloody Hand watched him go, the Mescalero's short, bowed legs covering a surprising amount of ground at each stride. Of all the chiefs of all the bands, Bloody Hand needed Koshay the most, even if his warriors were so few in number. Bloody Hand knew he had made a mistake. He should never have even hinted that Koshay was lacking in courage. The wiry little leader and his handful of warriors had never surrendered. Not to the American army. Not to the Mexican *federales*. For years, Koshay's small band, less than thirty strong, had terrorized the border lands of the United States and Mexico from their stronghold deep inside the Sonoran Desert. The Mescaleros were worth a hundred mestizos and half a hundred Utes in this game of war. Thus the lies had fallen easily once again from Bloody Hand's tongue.

Already he had promised the upstart young Comanche White Shield a place at his right hand and new rifles for all his warriors. He had made the same promises to the aged chief of the White Mountain Apaches and the leader of the small Ute band. And to others. There were not enough new rifles left in the wagon to go around.

Bloody Hand turned to stare upstream toward the west and muttered a curse. There was still no sign of the damned Comancheros. The feeling of unease grew in Bloody Hand's chest. The Comancheros were to bring tiswin and whiskey. With the liquor, Bloody Hand could manipulate the various bands and factions. Keep them drunk enough that they cared not about evil spirits and ghosts. Whip them into a fighting rage and turn them loose on the white man. The Comancheros were also to bring repeating rifles—old rifles, but enough to arm another forty or fifty warriors. The rest would have to make do. By then Bloody Hand would have them so full of whiskey and promises they would charge the white man with a stone if necessary. But the Comancheros were late. They had to show soon.

Bloody Hand tried to push his worry aside. There were other problems to be solved. He considered banishing the mestizos, with their wide-eyed superstitions and ghost stories. He abandoned the thought almost as soon as it had formed. He needed the mestizos as he needed the Comanche, Apache, Cheyenne, and Kiowa. The mestizos were infantry, accustomed to fighting on foot. Best of all, they were expendable. Bloody Hand had plans for the mestizos. They would have the honor of leading the attack on the U.S. Army forts along the southern California trail. No one would miss the mestizos when they were killed in the attacks. And while they were occupying the soldiers, Bloody Hand's main army would bypass the forts and strike the settlers and supply lines from behind. Soon all the land that once was Indian would again belong to the red man. The buffalo would return. Life would again be as it had been in his father's father's time. One great victory over the whites and thousands of warriors would hurry to join Bloody Hand's army. They would pour in from every reservation and stronghold from California to the Mississippi River. Even the haughty Sioux Nation and the hated Crows would be forced to ally with Bloody Hand or be vanquished by his huge army. He and he alone would bring all the tribes together. And not even the white man's great father in Washington could defeat such an alliance. Bloody Hand would dictate the terms of peace.

It was a giddy thought: Great chief of all the tribes from Mexico to Canada. Wealth and power beyond belief. Songs would be sung of Bloody Hand, savior of the red race, for generations yet to be born. There were problems, yes. But it would be so. He had seen it in the medicine vision.

The idea brought a swelling to Bloody Hand's groin. He leaned back against the scarred trunk of the cottonwood tree and stared at the small figure squatting beside the fire near the wagon. The swelling grew.

Tonight he would take the Cheyenne woman.

10

The faint tick of hoof against stone brought Slocum to his feet in the deep blackness lit only by starlight.

He eased deeper into the inky shadows of the junipers, draped his left hand lightly over the backstrap of the Colt in his right to muffle the sound, and slowly drew the hammer back to full cock.

He mouthed a silent curse as the Kickapoo dun tied to a bush a few feet away snorted, the flutter of nostrils loud in the dead silence that blanketed the dry camp in the rugged breaks and badlands two miles from the north rim of Skeleton Canyon. Slocum wasn't the spooky type, but there were times when a little tingle of nerves meant the difference between staying alive or getting dead. This was one of them.

"Slocum."

The single word was little more than a whisper, but clearly audible. Sounds carried far on the cool, silky air. Slocum sighed in relief and lowered the handgun.

"Over here, Willow," he said softly.

A dark blob separated from the stand of piñon pines at the far side of the scouting camp and took shape. The nagging worry drained from his mind. He holstered the Colt. The Shoshoni girl, afoot and leading her horse, strode toward him. Her moccasined feet made no sound.

She did not speak again until she came into his arms. He held her for a long moment, soaking in the smell of her hair and the warmth of her, inwardly chiding himself for worrying so much about her. His brain told him Willow could take care of herself. His heart wasn't listening. Finally, she pulled back.

"Find anything?"

"It is as we thought," Willow said calmly. "There are pairs of lookouts posted at every high point along the southeast rim. Four sentinels guard the eastern pass, two on each side. There is one trail down into the canyon from the southeast rim. It is too steep and narrow for a horse, but a man on foot could make it. What did you find?"

Slocum thought back over his long night ride along the northwest rim. "About the same. The lookouts are in pairs there, too. The one trail into the canyon is treacherous. Loose shale, bad footing, and almost straight down, where the north rim makes a sharp turn to the southwest. It doesn't look too promising." He paused to scrub at the stubble on his chin. "I did find a passable camp a mile or so north of the rim. No human tracks around it. I doubt that anyone else knows about it. Unless Jim finds something better, it would do, at least for a short time."

Willow glanced at the stars. "He should be back soon. The sun will rise in a couple of hours."

Slocum knew how he wanted to spend those two hours. But that would have to wait. Willow was tired, and Slocum knew he wasn't fresh as a newborn colt himself. He twisted the cap from his canteen and handed it to the girl. She took a couple of sips and handed it back.

"This campsite you found," she said, "does it have water?"

"A small spring. Not much more than a seep, but the water is fresh, no alkali, and there's enough of it to keep us and our horses alive."

"Enough to bathe in?"

Slocum shook his head. "Barely enough for drinking and cooking—if we don't cook much."

Willow sighed in disappointment and ran a hand through her black hair. "I suppose I'll just have to stay dirty for a while, then. I must smell like a goat."

"No, you don't," Slocum said with a slight smile. "But when this is over, I'll scrub your back. Now, get some rest. I'll stand watch."

Willow put her hand on his forearm and squeezed. "I'll take you up on that offer, Slocum. The back scrub, I mean." She let her hand fall away, brushed twigs and rocks from the sandy soil, stretched out, and was asleep within moments. Slocum stared at her for a moment, then forced his attention back to standing guard. A man couldn't stay alert and think woman at the same time.

Stonekiller rode in as the first gray wash of dawn spread above the eastern horizon. The half-breed's face was drawn tight, his jaw set. A blood vessel pulsed in his temple. He dismounted and loosened the cinch of his lathered, winded horse. Slocum didn't have to ask how many miles Stonekiller had covered. The tired horse said it all.

Stonekiller squatted on his heels and rolled a smoke. He did not speak until the cigarette was gone. Then he looked up. In the faint but growing light, Slocum saw the glitter of hate and hurt in Stonekiller's dark eyes.

"I saw Maria, Slocum." Stonekiller's voice was as tight as his expression, the words low and cold. "I watched that red bastard Bloody Hand lead her into his lodge at sundown."

Slocum tried to think of something to say. There were no adequate words.

Stonekiller sat staring toward Skeleton Canyon for a long time, then sighed. "I'm going to gut that son of a bitch, Slocum," he finally said, his hand dropping to the haft of the big knife at his belt. "He's going to die hard. And slow." He abruptly stood. "Wake Willow. We'd best get back out of sight and compare tally books."

The sun had almost cleared the horizon when the three reined in at the shallow canyon where the spare horses were picketed two miles back. Slocum's nose twitched at the smell from the Indian bodies laid out on the arroyo bank. Even upwind of the slight breeze that now stirred, the corpses were getting mighty ripe under the hot sun over the last couple of days. Slocum and Stonekiller had had the devil's own time getting the stiff bodies laid out the way the half-breed wanted them and lashed to makeshift drags of poles and the dead men's own blankets. The corpses were beginning to bloat and blacken. Soon the stink would be enough to gag a stray dog off a gut pile. Willow winced at the odor, but Stonekiller didn't seem to notice the smell. Slocum figured the half-breed had other things on his mind.

"Might as well rest here for the day," Stonekiller said as he dismounted. "Odds against getting seen here are less than out in the open." He glanced at Slocum as he stripped the saddle. "You find a camp?"

Slocum nodded and told Stonekiller about the spring a mile from the canyon rim. "It's in a narrow box canyon tucked back in the badlands behind two fingers of mountain range," Slocum concluded. "Not much water, but enough if we're careful and don't overstay. Grass is scarce. There's a stand of piñons for cover. Only problem is that it would be impossible to defend. If Bloody Hand finds us there, we could hold them off for a while, but we'd never get out of that place alive."

Stonekiller grunted. "If they find us anywhere, we won't get out alive. The trick is not to let them find us." He propped the saddle on the ground, plucked a fistful of greasewood, and began rubbing the lather and sweat from his horse's back and shoulders. "It'll do. We'll headquarter there and make our raids at night. The next three or four nights will be mostly dark, with only a bit of moon, and that late." Stonekiller turned to Slocum. "Maria knows we're here."

"How does she know that?"

"I left her a message last night. A symbol she'll recognize, wedged under the rim of the wagon wheel by her cook fire."

"You went into the camp?"

Stonekiller shrugged. "I'm Injun. Us redskins are sneaky bastards."

"You were that close to Bloody Hand?"

"Within fifty feet. Could have shot the son of a bitch right there, but that would have got Maria and me both killed," Stonekiller said through gritted teeth. "Had to make myself think like a Kiowa instead of an Irishman."

"Jim," Willow said, "what was the symbol you left?"

"A small white feather from a dove's wing. I've been carrying it ever since I found the house burned and Maria gone. It's a private sign between us." Stonekiller's rigid expression seemed to soften a bit. "She'll know what it means."

Willow nodded knowingly, but said nothing.

Stonekiller pulled the coffeepot from a pack, then put it back. "Better not chance a fire. Bloody Hand could have scouts out. Finish up with the horses and we'll have us a war parley."

An hour later, Slocum leaned over to study the map Stonekiller had scratched into the sand with a twig. Slocum corrected the angle of a couple of bends, added the trail he had found, and traced a few rockfalls and tree stands from his memories of the trip through Skeleton Canyon years ago. He handed the twig to Willow. She scratched in a few of her own observations.

Between the three of them, the scout had been fruitful, Slocum thought. They probably knew as much, or, perhaps more, about the canyon layout than the Indians camped there knew. Willow noted something that had escaped Slocum. Even after sunset when the wind died in the mountains, a slight breeze blew from west to east down the canyon.

Stonekiller took the twig. "The Indians are scattered in camps all along the canyon, bunched up by tribe. Old habits die hard." He sketched a "B" near the center of the first bulge in the canyon floor. "Bloody Hand's camp is here. His Comanche and Kiowa buddies are with him." He quickly sketched other letters in the map of the canyon floor. "This M is the mestizos. They're camped at the widest part of the canyon, nearly a half mile across. They're spooked. One good 'boo' from somewhere, and they'll run like hell."

"How do you know that?" Willow asked.

"Walked up within ten yards of their camp."

"In broad daylight?"

"What better time for an Injun to sneak in to watch Injuns? Any sane redskin's got more sense than to do that." Stonekiller turned back to the map. "The U in the narrower canyon floor is the camp of the Utes, Kickapoos, Shoshonis, a sprinkling of other tribes. And here"—he indicated the letter A near the western end of the canyon—"is the most dangerous bunch of all. Apaches. Head man's a Mescalero named Koshay. Little bowlegged fellow with a big head." Stonekiller paused for a moment. "Koshay is bad medicine. One hell of a war chief. White Mountain and Chiricahua bands have joined up with him."

"That gives them a strong rear guard on the west," Slocum said, thinking aloud as much as anything else, "and Bloody Hand's Comanche and Kiowa troops hold the east pass."

Stonekiller nodded. "Not just for defense from attack, either, way I see it. I figure he set it up that way to keep the mestizos and other more superstitious tribes bottled up if they panic and try to run."

Slocum mouthed a quiet curse. "Our best chance is to get them scattered, confused. That camp layout could complicate things for us."

"Not necessarily." Willow's brow knit in thought. "Perhaps Bloody Hand has made a mistake. The Apaches have more reason to fear the canyon spirits than anyone else. It is their people who died there. Apaches are a brave people, but will they stand and fight against that which they do not understand or fear more than death itself? You can reason with an angry man. You can shame a timid man, bribe a greedy man. But the only way to stop a thoroughly terrified man is to kill him. Bloody Hand could wind up fighting on two fronts—east and west—just to keep his band together. And that," she concluded, "is no way to build loyalty among your followers."

A shadow flitted across the campsite. Slocum looked up and frowned. A buzzard sailed overhead, its battered wings missing a few feathers. Others soared on wind currents above the shallow canyon.

Stonekiller glanced up, then at Slocum.

"Something bothering you, partner?"

"Buzzards. They could lead Bloody Hand's scouts straight to us."

The half-breed shrugged. "Doubt it. Following buzzards is a white man's way of finding Comanches. They always hang around Indian camps. Indians don't give them a second thought, most times. There's a bunch of them hanging over Skeleton Canyon right now. Matter of fact, I think those birds can help us."

"What do you have in mind?"

Stonekiller rose. "Help me drag a couple of these dead Injuns out a hundred yards. We'll peel the blankets off their heads and let the birds at them. What's left of them after the buzzards get through will make an even bigger impression on our friends down in the canyon when the time comes to use them."

Slocum winced. He had walked over, around, and through bodies, some fresh, many bloated and swollen, numerous times on the bloody battlefields of the war. But he wasn't overly excited at the prospect of dragging dead men around. Killing them was one thing. Playing with corpses was another. He heaved himself to his feet.

The sun was directly overhead when the two men returned to the makeshift camp. Slocum wiped his hands on his pants again and tried to puff the smell from his nostrils. If they weren't short of water, he'd scrub his hands until they were raw.

Willow sat cross-legged in the scant shade of a stubby mesquite, the point of her knife teasing one of several round, green gourds that grew wild in the region. Slocum stopped beside her.

"Mind if I ask what you're doing?" he said.

Willow glanced up and half smiled. "Making a toy."

"Toy?"

"From my childhood days. We used to play with them all the time." She spooned out a knifeblade of pungent, reedy pulp from the gourd, carefully carved two small holes in the sphere, and threaded the split blade of a Spanish dagger plant through the center. "We used to call them buffalo roars," she said. "I'm making some changes. These will be called ghost roars." She cut two more holes and threaded a rawhide thong through the gourd. "It works better with wood carvings, but I think this will do."

"Do what?"

Willow winked slyly. "You will see. Or perhaps I should say you will hear."

Stonekiller strode up, shooed a lizard aside, and stretched out beneath the mesquite near Willow. "I'm going to catch a little nap, Slocum," he said. "Wake me in a couple of hours and I'll take the watch."

Willow said, "No need. I've had my nap, and you look tired, Slocum. I'll stand watch."

Slocum started to argue and decided against it. His eyelids felt like they were lined with gravel. He found a spot in the sparse shade of a low juniper and pulled his hat over his eyes.

"We'll move out just after sundown," Stonekiller said. "That'll put us in our new camp by midnight. We'll make our first move on Bloody Hand before dawn."

Maria Stonekiller stood beside the wagon wheel, her fingers stroking the smooth softness of the single white dove wing feather.

She no longer felt the aches and pains of exhausted muscles and stiffness in her hips and legs, or the crawling scratchiness of unwashed skin. Her heart soared. The touch of the white feather was like the touch of her husband's hand. He had been here. He had held the feather, their private symbol of devotion and love.

For an instant, sadness damped her singing spirit; she knew he would have to have placed the feather while she was in Bloody Hand's lodge. It must have cut him like a knife to have been so close, yet so helpless, knowing what was happening only a few yards away. She felt no shame, only disgust at the dirtiness of Bloody Hand's fluids that crusted her upper thighs. The uneasy feeling passed as quickly as it had formed. The rape of a captive was not the same as taking a willing woman to one's blankets. It was Comanche culture, not infidelity. Jim knew that. Maria knew that. She also knew they could both accept it, that it changed nothing. The feather told her so.

She lingeringly stroked the feather once more, then slipped it beneath the neck of her doeskin dress until it nestled against her breast, above her heart. Her gaze swept the rim of The Place of the Bones. She saw nothing. But Jim was there. She felt him as surely as she felt the caress of the feather.

Maria's thoughts sobered. It would be difficult, almost impossible, for Jim to take her from this place alone if she stayed in the open, in full view of the camp. She had to find a way to make it easier for him. First, she had to stay out of Bloody Hand's reach when the rescue attempt came, or the hated Kwahadi with the scarred brow would kill her. There was a way. There always was. She had only to find it.

She became aware of a crawling of her skin, as though a heavy bug scuttled about between her shoulder blades. It was the sensation of being watched.

Maria slowly turned. The toothless old hag Crow Woman stood a few yards away, the pointed torture stick gripped tight in a gnarled hand, hate glittering in black eyes bloodshot with age. Anger surged through Maria's breast. The old crone's torments would soon end. Maria's teeth closed on the inside of her lip until blood flowed. She touched a finger to the cut, turned, and added another inch of the blood mark to the nearly completed circle stained dark against the weathered wood of the wagon. She added another moon dot to the center of the circle and slowly turned to recapture the hag's stare.

Crow Woman's deeply wrinkled face paled. For a moment, fear and uncertainty flickered in her bloodshot eyes. Maria knew then that even though Crow Woman might not understand the Cheyenne words of the curse, she had grasped the intent. The hag stared past Maria at the closing circle and saw there her own approaching death.

Maria smiled at her.

Crow Woman abruptly turned. Her broad rear waddled almost comically as she scuttled toward the blood moon lodge. Maria laughed, a high-pitched cackle that she hoped sounded like the crowing of a madwoman. Apparently, it worked. The hag ducked from sight beyond the lodge. Maria glared toward the tepee for a long time as she renewed her solemn vow. If the opportunity came, Crow Woman would die beneath Maria's knife.

A sudden thought struck Maria. The blood moon lodge was more than a place that protected warriors from the bad medicine of menstruating women. It was a sanctuary, lightly guarded, and then only by women. No warrior would go near the place for fear of contamination. Maria's own blood moon had not yet come. She could not will it. She could not use the ploy that had worked for Willow. There was no bloody meat to smear over her crotch. Game was scarce in the canyon. There had been no fresh meat for two days. Yet, there was a way. It would come to her.

She stared again toward the high canyon rims with their jagged tops, deep notches, ridges studded with juniper, piñon pines, brush, and rockfalls. Her gaze settled on one particular deep cut in the north rim. It was a natural spot for watching the camp below. Jim knew where she was. Now she had to make sure he knew when she went into the blood moon lodge, to know where she was. Jim had always been a sundown stalker, a night fighter. He had told her more than once that was the best time to hunt dangerous game. It was a tactic that had kept him alive when others who wore the reservation badges died. Jim had no fear of death in the darkness, as did many men of red skin. It was, perhaps, the Irish blood in his veins, or his lack of belief in the traditions and taboos of his tribe. It mattered not to Maria—as long as it kept him alive.

She dropped her gaze from the notch in the rim. To show too much interest in it might draw attention. But she had committed the spot to memory. She need not look at it again. She knelt, fed small twigs and limbs into the embers of the fire in preparation for cooking the meal that would feed whoever wandered by for the remainder of the day. Bloody Hand would come for her again tonight, she knew. It was his pattern. Two nights in a row he took her to his lodge. The third night he left her alone. She knew she had to make her move before darkness fell today. Not just to avoid another time of humiliation and disgust on Bloody Hand's blankets, but to let Jim know where she was.

It would depend to a great extent on luck as far as timing was concerned, she knew. But she also sensed that the higher powers—the white man's one God or the deities of the Cheyenne—were with her, would guide her hand and watch over her. The feather resting against her breast told her that as well. She could feel the uplifting presence of the spirits as much as she could feel her husband's nearness.

All she needed was a tool, one with a sharp edge. She was allowed no knives except for skinning game, and those were immediately taken from her when the job was done. There were no sharp stones or edged flints within yards of the wagon. She had already searched, and found only a human thigh bone and lower jaw in the sage clump where she relieved herself a few yards from the wagon. She could not bring herself to shatter one of the bones. Her sense of respect—and, she had to admit, a lingering fear of the dead—would not permit it. The canyon floor was dotted with prickly pear and cactus, but the spines were not strong enough to leave more than a scratch.

She added larger sticks into the fire, feeding the ends in first instead of tossing the fuel haphazardly on the blaze. A fire laid Cheyenne style would burn steadily with less smoke, and needed less wood to maintain an adequate cooking blaze. She had learned the value of fuel at her mother's side at many Plains hunting camps.

Something that had escaped Maria before caught her attention. Somewhere during the long trip, an axle beam of the wagon had been damaged near the wheel hub. Cracks radiated from a gouge in the tough wood. Spikes of splinters angled outward from the oak beam. She glanced about. No one was watching. She reached behind the wheel. A splinter punctured a finger as she probed the

dent in the axle. She ignored the sting. Her fingers closed on a
wider slice of damaged wood and traced its pattern. She nodded
to herself; it would do. She wedged her fingers beneath the jagged
wood and pulled. The sliver parted with a barely audible crack.
The splinter was a foot long, thick at the base, and tapered to a
sharp point. It was more than a tool, she realized. It could be
made into a weapon.

She glanced about once more, determined that no one was paying attention to the woman hunched near the cooking fire, and
went to work on the splinter. She drew it across the iron tire rim
of the wagon wheel, each stroke smoothing and sharpening the
tough hardwood. Sweat beaded her forehead before the makeshift
wooden blade met her standards. It was ground and polished now
to a keen edge along one side, the tip sharp as any knife, the
thicker end smoothed enough to serve as a sturdy grip. She sighed
in satisfaction and tucked the wooden knife under her skirt until
it was held firmly at her waist by the rawhide tie of her dress.

Maria stood, massaged the muscles at the small of her back, her
gaze casually sweeping the camp. She was sure she had escaped
notice. No one paid much attention to a woman in a warrior camp
except for food or other pleasures. She stared for a moment toward
the council fire, which at the moment was little more than a wispy
smoke trail above a pile of ashes and embers. A wry smile touched
her lips. She wouldn't have to worry about Bloody Hand for a time;
the renegade Kwahadi had his hands full at the moment.

Bloody Hand glared into the shifty, deep-set eyes of the wiry man
seated across from him, trying to control the impulse to pull his
knife and gut the mestizo on the spot.

The man called José was nervous. He tugged constantly at the
sparse goatee on his receding chin and startled at the slightest
movement or sound in the canyon. The self-styled chief of the
mestizos looked more Mexican than Indian. Bloody Hand hated
Mexicans worse than he hated Americans. José was more peasant
than warrior. It showed in the rags he wore, in the ancient smoothbore Mexican musket he carried, in the dull and rusted butcher
knife thrust into the rope waistband of tattered and filthy trousers,
and in the hunched shoulders and shuffling gait when he walked.
His feet were bare, misshapen, callused, and white with dust up
to knobby ankles.

"Speak what is on your mind, José," Bloody Hand said, making no attempt to hide the disdain in his tone. "Do the mestizos see ghosts again?"

José's prominent Adam's apple bobbed. "Bloody Hand should not speak lightly of the spirits." The mestizo's thin voice quavered slightly. "We must leave this place—"

"We have spoken of this before," Bloody Hand interrupted. "We move only when the time is right. We will speak of it no more."

José lifted a hand. "It is not why I have come to Bloody Hand this day. I came to ask what the Comanche chief intends to do about the Kickapoos."

"What of the Kickapoos?"

"Last night they raided our camp again. They stole two bags of beans and a sack of corn as my people slept. Is it not enough that we must hear the spirits of the dead walk in the night? Must we starve as well at the hands of thieves?"

Bloody Hand sighed. Keeping the peace in this camp, he grumbled inwardly, was like trying to maintain order among squabbling children. "If the Kickapoos stole from you as you say, go get your goods back from them. There are more mestizos than Kickapoos here."

José swallowed again, his gaze darting about. "It is not so easy as that. The Kickapoos have much hate in their hearts for the mestizos. They have tormented my people since we first came to this place. If we go to them, there would be a fight."

"Do the mestizos fear the Kickapoos?"

"They have better weapons." José tugged at his scraggly chin whiskers again. "If there is a fight, men on both sides would be lost. Bloody Hand's army is not yet strong enough that he can afford to have warriors killed or injured fighting among themselves."

Bloody Hand's brow furrowed. The damned mestizo was a coward, afraid to face his own enemies. The mestizos were always afraid. But like it or not, José was right in bringing this problem to him. He needed every man who could handle a rifle, lance, or club—especially the mestizos. They were his cannon fodder against the soldiers. It did not matter to Bloody Hand whether the cowardly mixed breeds died hungry or with full bellies. It did matter that he kept them in the ranks until it was time for them to die in the proper manner.

"I shall speak to the Kickapoos. The mestizos will not go hungry. On this, you have Bloody Hand's word."

José nodded. Relief seemed to flicker in his eyes. "It is good." He stood, but made no attempt to leave. He shuffled his bare feet and swallowed.

"Does something else trouble you, José?" Bloody Hand said.

"Last night there was a bad sign."

Bloody Hand gritted his teeth to suppress a surge of anger. With the mestizos, there was always a bad sign. The superstitious fools saw bad signs in the lie of twigs in a path, in the rising of the sun, in a pile of animal droppings.

"What was this sign?"

A visible shudder twitched José's shoulders. His eyes went wide. "Evil spirits walked the night. My people heard their moans, the rattle of their bones. Our women are frightened, our children cry—"

"We were to speak no more of ghosts," Bloody Hand snapped.

"Hear me out, Bloody Hand." The corner of José's mouth twitched. "This you must know. Last night Medicine Woman saw a vision. It was a man who glowed like the sun, riding a pale horse—"

"An old woman's bad dream."

"Medicine Woman sees the future," José said. "She saw something else. Many dead mestizos lying before a thick forest of trees with no leaves, standing so close that the trunks of the trees touched."

Bloody Hand winced inwardly. He knew certain men or women within each tribe had medicine visions. Had the old woman seen his plan for the mestizos? That they were to be sent to certain death in a futile attack against the soldier forts? He tried to shrug away the thought, but something deep inside his brain turned cold.

"It is nothing," the Kwahadi said. "Bloody Hand's medicine is stronger than an old woman's bad dream. His vision is that once again the red man shall own the land of our fathers and their fathers before them, that the white man's face will not be seen west of the great river, that the buffalo will return. That the mestizos and all other tribes will have much wealth, many horses and slaves, and will forever live in peace. It is so spoken."

José didn't seem completely convinced. "The dark of the moon comes, the time when spirits walk. Bloody Hand must leave this place before then ."

"We leave when Bloody Hand says we leave," Bloody Hand snapped in irritation. "In the meantime, tell your people to have no fear."

José nodded and started to turn away, but paused. "There is one more thing. When do my warriors receive their gifts of new rifles and ammunition?"

Bloody Hand forced a reassuring smile. "When we are ready to begin our war against the whites. Each of your men will have a new repeating rifle and as much ammunition as he can carry. On this also you have Bloody Hand's word." The lie fell easily from the Kwahadi's tongue. He had no intention of wasting fine new weapons on mestizos, whose sole duty was to die.

José nodded. "My people will be ready."

Bloody Hand watched the mestizo leader walk toward his camp in that stoop-shouldered shuffle that reminded a real warrior of a peasant farmer who scratched in the dirt with a hoe like an old Caddo woman. Bloody Hand snorted in disgust. If he did not need them to keep the soldiers busy, he would tell the mestizos to go home and be content to breed more cowards.

He sighed and heaved himself to his feet, regretting his promise to José. He had to talk to the Kickapoos and tell them to stop their raids on the mestizo camp.

The knot in Bloody Hand's belly tightened as he strode along the shallow river. Commanding an army was becoming more of a task than he had bargained for. Getting the tribes together had been much simpler than keeping them from cutting each other's throats. And he had not heard from either the scouts watching the back trail or the Apaches tracking the horse soldiers. There was still no sign of the Comancheros and their wagons loaded with weapons and liquor. That was worrisome enough. And this constant yammering about ghosts and evil spirits and the dark of the moon and horsemen who glowed like the sun as they rode through the night—

Bloody Hand's heart skipped a beat as a low, wailing moan sounded along the canyon. He stopped in his tracks, stood motionless for a moment, then realized it was only the rising wind groaning through the rocks and trees along the canyon rim. He muttered a curse. Too much talk of evil spirits had started his own nerves to twanging like a bowstring.

His sense of urgency grew. He must leave The Place of the Bones soon, before his force scattered to the four winds or Grierson's soldiers discovered the stronghold.

Bloody Hand couldn't bring himself to admit that perhaps he, too, had begun to feel a presence in the canyon. He tried to push the sensation aside. It would not go.

11

Slocum came awake instantly, the hair tingling on his forearms, his right hand instinctively falling on the grips of the Colt at his hip.

A low, moaning hum droned against his ears, an eerie, tortured groan against the light breeze. The buzz grew louder, more intense, suddenly overlaid by a shrill, piercing screech like a woman being tortured. The scream died in a series of quick, gurgling cries, then abruptly rose again to an ear-splitting squeal.

Slocum whisked the Colt from its holster and sat upright. The unearthly cry faded, but not the goose bumps on his arms. He glanced around, located the source of the racket, and forced his jangled nerves to calm. His hand fell away from the revolver.

Willow stood fifty yards away, two round objects tethered together by a long rawhide thong slowly dropping from her upraised arm. She nimbly gathered in the thong as the gourds lost their momentum.

"Spooky little toy," Jim Stonekiller said from nearby.

"That's no lie. It sure as hell got my attention."

"It would grab you even tighter if you believed in spooks. Imagine what Willow's buffalo roar toy will sound like in the dead of night in a haunted canyon."

"Even if I didn't believe in ghosts, it would thin my blood in a hurry," Slocum said. "I've never heard anything like that in my life."

Stonekiller chuckled. "Just what we need. That girl's got some powerful medicine pumping in her blood."

Slocum stood and watched as Willow carefully coiled the thong, slung the loops over her shoulder, and strode toward them, the fist-sized gourds tapping against her ribs. She stopped before the two men and smiled.

"Well?" she said.

"Should make a lot of brave warriors piss in their breechclouts tonight," Stonekiller said.

"I never heard anything like that in my life, Willow," Slocum said. "How did you do it?"

The Shoshoni girl shrugged. "The low sounds come from the holes in the gourds. The high sounds are from the Spanish dagger leaves as the air blows through them."

"You learned that as a child?"

"Only part of it," she said with a smile at Slocum. "I worked out the dagger leaf sound while you two were asleep. Sorry if I disturbed your rest, but I wasn't sure it would work. I wanted to test it before we got too close to the canyon."

Slocum rubbed his forearms. "It works, Willow. Believe me."

Stonekiller glanced at the sun that had edged partway down the western sky. "We'd better get a move on, folks. I don't especially want to travel in daylight, but we need to get our base camp set up and have one last look around before dark. Willow, rig the drags back onto the horses. We've got some dead Injuns to move. Slocum, give me a hand with the buzzard bait."

Slocum followed as Stonekiller strode to the distant Indian bodies they had laid out for the scavengers. The birds hissed at them before lifting off on scraggly wings. Dust swirled in the buzzards' wake.

Slocum's gut churned at the sight. The birds had done their work. The exposed heads of the dead Indians were enough to give a strong man the wobblies. Where eyes had been, only raw sockets remained. The birds had torn the flesh from cheeks and ears until the bone beneath shone through. One corpse's nose and lips were gone, leaving behind only a hideously torn and twisted grin of bare, broken teeth. The stench was all but unbearable.

Stonekiller didn't seem affected in the least. He bent to stare into the mangled faces. "Buzzards did a good job. Let's wrap them back up and get them loaded. No need to waste any more time here."

Slocum gritted his teeth as he rebound the bloody, bird-soiled blanket around the ravaged face of one corpse. He was relieved to have the thing out of sight. The bitter taste of bile at the back of his throat slowly subsided. He wondered if he would ever get the stink off his skin and out of his clothes.

Slocum and Stonekiller heaved the bodies onto the makeshift drags behind the two still-skittish horses Willow led to them, then turned to the chore of wrestling the stiff remains of the other dead Indians onto similar rigs. Slocum was sweating profusely by the time they were finished.

"Slocum, you know the best and safest route to our base camp," Stonekiller said as he toed the stirrup and swung into the saddle. "Lead the way. And keep a sharp eye out. We're too close now to have our luck run out if that Kwahadi son of a bitch has patrols out."

Slocum mounted and kneed the Kickapoo dun into motion. He trotted out a hundred yards in front, then twisted in the saddle to check on his companions. Willow and Stonekiller had to fight the packhorses a minute or two before they got them lined out. Some attack force, Slocum thought; two men, one woman and a few decaying corpses to take on a canyon full of Indians. If he were a betting man, he'd lay odds against them. But he had faced long odds before. He reined the dun around an ocotillo, then gave the animal its head. At least he had the breeze in his face. He wouldn't have the gagging scent of death in his nostrils for a time.

Slocum tuned all his senses to the ride, his gaze constantly flitting across the rugged, broken badlands. He glanced at the lowering sun. Unless they were unlucky enough to run across one of Bloody Hand's patrols, they would be at the base camp below the north rim of Skeleton Canyon well before sundown.

Maria Stonekiller studied the shadows cast by the wagon wheel. The shadow of one spoke now covered the flat gray stone she used as a marker. When the stone was between the spoke shadows, Bloody Hand would come. He was predictable in his wants.

She rose and strode toward the low brush clump where she relieved her bladder. Inside the scant cover of the brush, she paused to look around. Assured that no one was paying any particular attention, she slid the makeshift knife from beneath the waist tie of her dress, hoisted her skirts above her hips, and squatted. She ran a thumb across the edge of the makeshift knife and nodded to herself. The wood was as keen as any metal blade. The oak would hold its edge.

She took a deep breath, spread her knees wide, and slipped the knife up her leg until the sharp tip dug into the tender fold where her upper thigh met crotch hair. She flicked her wrist and felt the sharp sting as the skin parted under the wooden knife. She ignored the pain and sliced again across the other thigh. Warm blood tricked over her skin. A thin but steady flow of crimson traced from the cuts. She had made her own blood moon.

Maria returned the wooden knife to its hiding place, waited a few moments longer, then rose and let her skirt fall. She ignored the sting of the cuts as she walked. The pain was nothing. Not if it kept Bloody Hand from her. Not if it gained her sanctuary in the blood moon lodge. Her spirits actually lifted as she strode back to her cooking fire beside the wagon. The discomfort faded beneath the gentle touch of the feather held against her breast by the caress of soft deerskin.

A few steps from the wagon, she cast a quick glance toward the notch in the canyon rim. And she knew he was there. Not at that particular spot, perhaps. Not watching yet, probably. But nearby. She could feel her husband's presence. She knew she was not out of danger yet; Bloody Hand might kill her when he learned of her blood moon time and decided he had no further use for her. Or he could sell or trade her to one of the other warriors. But she knew he would kill her for certain if he touched her before he knew of the blood moon. For a moment she was tempted to let him, for to touch such a woman would bring a lasting curse to a war chief. The impulse passed. The important thing now was to stay alive. If either she or Jim were to die, they would die together. She would not rob him, or herself, of that right.

On impulse, she dipped a fingertip into the blood on her thigh and closed the magic circle on the wagon bed. She thought for a moment about adding the final spot that would complete the curse, then decided against it. Let the old hag fret. If the opportunity rose and the time was right, she would place the final moon dot within the circle. It would be interesting to see Crow Woman's eyes when the death curse was complete.

Maria resisted the urge to look again toward the notch in the mountain and began preparing a meal. Food was growing increasingly scarce as the band of renegades grew in size. She had little to work with, but it was enough: a few strips of dried meat, wild onions, parched corn, edible tubers of various prairie plants, and a double handful of dried mesquite beans. It was more than she and Jim had in the beginning, when they fought to build a ranch. She sighed wistfully. They had been poor, but it had been a wonderful time of her life. They had each other. Young people starting a new life together, each so lost in exploring the other that the contents of the cook pot meant little. When Jim joined the reservation police to earn the cash money needed to expand the ranch, the cook pot was full more often. But her heart was empty more often. Her belly cramped each time he rode off into danger, on the trail of a violent and ruthless fugitive. She knew she might never see him again. Yet, it made the homecomings that much sweeter.

Maria glanced up from her work, surprised that so much time had passed. The sun had dropped lower in the west, almost touching the canyon rim. The white marker stone lay between the lengthening shadows of the wagon wheel spokes.

Bloody Hand would be coming for her soon.

The thought had hardly formed before she heard the whisper of moccasins on sand. She rose and slowly turned. The Kwahadi chief stood almost within arm's length.

"Come," Bloody Hand said. He reached out to grasp her.

"No." Maria stepped back.

Rage darkened the Comanche's face. He reached for the knife at his belt.

Maria hoisted her skirt.

Bloody Hand recoiled in revulsion, actually taking a backward step as he snatched away the hand that had reached for her. Maria knew then that if she had allowed him to touch her, she would be dead. Her heart pounded. She might still be slain, but not by the Kwahadi's hand. He would not risk the bad medicine that followed the breaking of such a strong taboo.

Bloody Hand turned away and barked a command in the Comanche tongue. Crow Woman waddled quickly to the Comanche's side, glanced at the blood on Maria's legs, and grunted. The renegade chief waved toward the blood moon lodge, turned, and strode rapidly away.

Crow Woman stared for a moment at Maria, a mix of hate and caution in the small, close-set eyes behind folds of fat and deep wrinkles. She raised the pointed stick clutched in her right hand as if to lift Maria's skirt for a closer examination. Maria tried to control the quickened pounding of her heart and maintain her calm expression. She had to keep the old hag from looking too closely and finding the cuts on her thighs. Deception by a captive meant immediate death.

Maria forced a twisted smile and pointed to the symbol etched in blood on the wagon bed. Crow Woman's leathery face blanched as she saw the completed circle with its three dots inside. A slight shudder sent the hanging folds of fat beneath her upper arms into a quiver. Relief surged through Maria's body. The toothless old hag was terrified. The ruse had worked; to die of a curse meant walking in darkness forever.

Crow Woman lowered the pointed stick and waved toward the blood moon lodge. Maria strode toward the isolated skin tepee, her back straight and head held high. As she neared the lodge, she glanced again toward the notch in the canyon rim above. A comforting warmth settled about her shoulders. She could not say how she knew, but she knew Jim was up there.

"That's her," Jim Stonekiller whispered, excitement and relief in his words. He lay on his belly at the bottom of the fissure in the rocks, Slocum at his side.

Slocum stared at the distant figure in the deepening blue haze in the camp below. He was too far away to tell what Maria Stonekiller looked like, but the easy, long strides of the woman heading for the isolated lodge left little doubt that there was a strength and confidence in the slight form. The woman ducked through the lodge flap and disappeared from view. The big woman who had been waddling along behind her stopped outside the lodge. Another woman stood at one side of the tepee. Apparently a guard, Slocum thought.

"That's the quarantine lodge for women in their blood moon time," Stonekiller said. "Now that we know where she is, it'll be a hell of a lot easier to get her out."

Slocum nodded. He knew the taboos as well as any Plains warrior. On the surface, it seemed a simple matter to steal into the camp, overpower the female guard, and get Stonekiller's wife out. The only problem was a couple of hundred or so Indians who would skin them alive and roast them over a fire if they were spotted. He studied Stonekiller's face for a moment in the fading light of dusk, trying to read what was going on behind the twitch in the half-breed's jaw muscle. Slocum knew that if it was his woman in that lodge, he would be champing at the bit to rescue her.

"So," Slocum said softly, "what's your pleasure, Jim? You've slipped into that camp before. You could do it again. We could grab Maria and get the hell out of here."

Stonekiller did not reply for a long time. Slocum sensed the ache in the Kiowa's gut. Finally, Stonekiller shook his head.

"The Irish in me says go now," Stonekiller said, his tone tight, "but the Kiowa in me says not yet. It's too chancy. Could get us all killed. And I've got to admit there's more at stake here than Maria. We've got to cut the *cojones* off these redskins first, or we'll have the blood of every innocent settler and tame Indian in the country on our hands. We have to stop Bloody Hand. But no matter what happens, that Kwahadi son of a bitch is going to pay for what he did to Maria unless he kills me first. When I rip out that bastard's liver, I'll be a happy man."

Slocum nodded. There wasn't anything to add. The former reservation policeman had said it all.

"There's one more thing," Stonekiller added. "We're partners. I made a promise to you, and I'll keep it. The price on Bloody Hand's head is yours."

"There are easier ways to make money."

"Nothing in life is easy, Slocum. If it's easy, it's not worth having." Stonekiller fell silent for moment, studying the canyon floor. "I figure we have two nights, three tops, to wreck Bloody Hand's medicine and get Maria back. We might as well get to work."

Slocum followed as Stonekiller squirmed back from the notch, then stood and strode to the horses tethered below the rim. Neither spoke as they reined toward the base camp to the north.

Slocum turned the plan over in his mind as he rode. He could see no flaws except the distinct possibility that all three of them could get seriously dead if anything went wrong.

Full darkness had fallen when Slocum reined in and glanced about the camp. Willow had already left on her mission. It was a long, circuitous ride to the east end of Skeleton Canyon.

"Worried about her, Slocum?"

"Yes."

"Don't. That Shoshoni girl is one hell of a warrior. She'll be all right. Besides, I need your complete attention on what we've got to do. We're looking at a tricky night's work."

Slocum crouched beneath a clump of Spanish dagger and peered into the faint starlight. The two Indian sentries posted on the rim above the mestizo encampment were dim black shapes against the inky sky.

The sentinels were less than thirty feet away. And they were jumpy. They stood hip to hip against the trunk of a piñon. Their voices were muted, but the few words they nervously muttered from time to time carried well in the clear night air. Slocum didn't understand the language. Stonekiller had said the lookouts were Apache. He had watched the changing of the guard before the thin sliver of moon slipped from the sky. Slocum glanced at the stars. They told him it was three in the morning. In a few minutes, Willow would open tonight's spirit dance.

Slocum's brow wrinkled in worry. Stonekiller should have been back from the western trail into the canyon by now. If he didn't make it back in time, Slocum had to go up against two men alone. He could think of a lot better ways to pass the late-night hours. He wiped a palm against his trousers and slipped the heavy bladed knife from the sheath at his belt. He preferred gun work, but guns made noise, and noise was their enemy. He had changed from his riding boots to a pair of Comanche-style moccasins with soles tough enough to turn the sharpest thorn but flexible enough to sense a small twig or loose pebble.

A flicker at the corner of his vision yanked Slocum's gaze from the two sentries and tightened his grip on the knife. Just as abruptly, he relaxed. Stonekiller was back. The half-breed lay motionless, barely visible beside a greasewood clump little more than arm's length away. Slocum hadn't heard or sensed his approach. The man was damn good in the dark. And, Slocum admitted, it was a relief to have him there. All was ready now. They were in position as planned. The horses waited almost a quarter of a mile back, out of sight from the canyon rim. The blanket-wrapped bodies of the two dead Indians savaged by vultures were with the horses.

Slocum waited patiently, senses tuned to each sound, thankful he had been blessed with good night vision and keen hearing, at least better than most white men's. Willow and Stonekiller seemed to be able to see through the darkness as though the sun was shining. At least Slocum's senses were acute enough that he and Stonekiller could communicate with hand signals. Slocum's heart thumped a steady, rhythmic beating against his ribs. The familiar, relaxed calm that came to him before a fight draped comfortably over his shoulders. He had slept less than four hours over the last day and night, but now he felt as alert and fresh as if he had come straight from a comfortable bed. It was the sensation of being alive. Slocum hoped he felt the same by sunrise. The thought ended abruptly as the hairs on his forearms prickled.

The sound was even more eerie than it had been in daylight. The low moan built into a deep, throaty roar overlaid by the high-pitched screech.

The two sentries stiffened, bolt upright, staring east, up the canyon. Neither moved or spoke. Slocum could almost smell the terror the two lookouts must feel. And he knew the ghostly cry would be even more unworldly on the canyon floor, carried to the Indian camps on the light breeze and intensified by the heavier air between the steep walls. If Willow's buffalo roar device was enough to give a man the creeping crawlies up here, he could imagine its effect on those in the canyon.

The screeching roar peaked, faded for an instant, then picked up again. Slocum glanced at Stonekiller and nodded silently. The half-breed motioned with a hand. Slocum would take the sentry on the right, nearest the canyon wall, while Stonekiller eliminated the second man.

Slocum turned his attention back to the sentries. Both still stood as if rooted to the spot, neither reaching for a weapon. Slocum thought he saw a faint shudder ripple one buck's shoulders. He eased his way from behind the Spanish dagger spines and crept forward, placing each moccasined foot with care so as not to snap a twig or loose a pebble. Moving without sound was second nature to Slocum. He had spent hours, days, even months silently stalking the woods and Union camps in search of targets for his sniper's rifle. But Yankees were not Indians, not attuned to the forest and plains. This was a different test of his skills. Fail now and the war was lost before it started.

He mouthed a silent curse. He was almost within arm's length of his target now, but the two men were pressed tightly together, their backs thrust against the trunk of the piñon. There wasn't much room to work. Slocum cut a quick glance at Stonekiller. The half-breed was already in position; he could almost reach out and touch the shoulder of the man on the left. And he had no better a target for a knife thrust than did Slocum. A quick slash from ambush was one thing. Battling a strong opponent on uneven ground was another. Slocum hesitated, unwilling to risk a scuffle, but knowing that time was running out. One of the sentries muttered something, a frightened stammer more than anything else, and reached for his rifle. Slocum drew in a slow, deep breath. He had to chance it, to make a move now. If the Indian managed to get off a shot, the whole plan went into the outhouse.

Stonekiller spoke. Slocum could barely make out the sound of the coarse whisper, little more than a grunt. But the man nearest Stonekiller turned toward the sound; his companion stepped away from the tree and started to lift his rifle. Slocum switched the knife to his left hand, took one final step, and clamped his right palm over the sentry's mouth. His blade slammed upward, glanced off a rib, and buried itself at an angle deep into the Indian's back. Slocum knew the knife point had hit the heart. He heard the low, gagging sound from the buck's throat as he twisted the knife, levered it back and forth, shredding the man's heart and lungs. The Indian tried to struggle free. Slocum tightened his grip over the man's mouth, put his knee in the small of the Indian's back, and arched his shoulders backward. The Apache's struggles grew weaker. Still, Slocum kept his grip firm. He knew it took more than a few seconds for a man to die, even with his heart and lungs torn apart. The sentry's body convulsed, quivered, and went limp. Slocum heard a faint gurgle to his left and let the dead man fall, ready to help Stonekiller.

Help wasn't needed. Stonekiller had the second lookout's hair firmly in hand, the buck's head tilted back at a strange angle, black liquid spurting. Slocum realized the sentry's neck had been all but severed by a swipe of Stonekiller's heavy blade. For a few heartbeats the two stood locked. Then Stonekiller stepped back. The Indian's body crumpled at Stonekiller's feet.

Slocum knelt to make sure no life remained in the man he had knifed, then looked up. Stonekiller casually wiped his hands and knife blade on the dead man's leather leggings and grinned at Slocum, his teeth showing a startling white in the faint starlight.

"You handle a knife pretty good for a white man, Slocum," Stonekiller said.

Slocum realized he was gasping for air. He had been holding his breath throughout the brief but intense struggle on the canyon rim. "Not my favorite way to fight, Jim," he said. "Give me a big-bore rifle and a long-range shot anytime. Using a blade gets mighty messy."

"Tell me about it. This son of a bitch bled all over me." Stonekiller sheathed the knife. "So far, so good." He cocked his head, listening. The screeching moans from the distance died away. A deathly silence held over the Indian camp below for a few heartbeats; then a child's keening wail sounded. "Let's finish up while those poor bastards down there are still too scared to do anything but slide around in that shit they just dumped in their blankets." Stonekiller shook his head. "That damn buffalo roar toy of Willow's made my skin crawl. Injun part of me showing, I reckon."

"You don't have to be Injun," Slocum said. He knelt and hoisted the body of the lookout he'd killed. The man wasn't overly big, but as dead weight he was heavy enough to bring a grunt of effort.

Stonekiller picked up the man he had knifed and tossed the body over a shoulder. The dead man would have weighed close to two hundred pounds, Slocum figured, but Stonekiller handled the load with no visible effort.

Slocum was breathing hard from exertion and soaked with blood and sweat by the time they reached the deep, narrow crevice and tossed the bodies inside. Slocum didn't think they would be found, but after another night or two it wouldn't matter. He scrubbed as much blood from his hands as he could on a clump of parched grass, straightened, and massaged the small of his back.

"We're halfway home," Stonekiller said. "Let's go finish up."

Slocum winced. Lugging a freshly dead body a couple of hundred yards was bad enough. Wrestling a maggoty, half decayed corpse with no face left wasn't high on his list of preferred amusements.

The stars stood at almost four o'clock before the job was done. Stonekiller stepped back and studied the stiff bodies that now leaned against the piñon tree where the sentries had stood. Starlight glinted from exposed bone where the birds had stripped away the flesh.

"That'll do," Stonekiller said. The man wasn't even breathing hard. "The next lookouts to come up here are in for one helluva shock. They probably won't stop running until they top the Mogollon Rim."

"Speaking of which," Slocum said, "let's get out of here before I start believing in ghosts and evil spirits myself. Everything go all right on the west trail?"

Stonekiller chuckled. "Couldn't have been better. Slipped past the lookouts and left a couple of souvenirs on the rocks down at the bottom of the trail. Nothing like walking up on a decomposed head with no body under it to get a spooked man's attention."

Slocum stood for a moment, listening. The babble of voices from the canyon floor carried clearly on the night air. Startled cries and shouts from the men mingled with the wails of frightened women and children. The Plains Indian tribes had been somewhat overrated in terms of being fearless and stoic in the face of danger and the unknown, he thought. Bloody Hand was going to have his hands full keeping that bunch in line come daylight.

"We'd best get on back to camp," Stonekiller said. "Wouldn't want Willow to get worried about us if we're not there when she rides back in." He broke a limb from a nearby juniper. "I'll brush out our tracks. Ghosts don't leave footprints."

The two men had been in camp more than an hour before Willow rode in, the short bow slung across her back and the quiver dangling at a hip, as the eastern sky began to pale. Slocum tried to look casual and unconcerned as he strode out to meet her.

"Any problems, Willow?"

"All went well. One of the sentries panicked and ran when the buffalo roar started."

"The other?"

"He didn't run. I put an arrow through his chest. This is a good bow. It drove the shaft all the way through him. I saved the arrow." She reached down and held a fresh scalp aloft, blood still oozing from the skin beneath the thick black hair. "My personal trophy. The man who wore this hair was in the group that captured me and killed my father and brother. He won't bother anyone else."

Slocum shook his head in silent wonder. He couldn't picture the gentle Shoshoni girl wielding a knife and popping the hair off a dead man's skull. Stonekiller had said she was a warrior. There was no doubt of it now. Slocum helped Willow unsaddle and tend to her tired sorrel and walked with her to where Stonekiller squatted, placing flat stones around a small pile of dry twigs.

"Soon as it's full daylight we'll have some coffee and breakfast," Stonekiller said. "Don't want to chance a fire until after sunup. You two hungry?"

Slocum's belly growled. He hadn't given much thought to food until now. Even though his hands and clothes still reeked of rotted flesh and fresh blood, he was famished. The belly didn't care much about the rest of the body or the state of a man's mind. When it had been empty for almost twenty hours, the belly got downright cranky.

Stonekiller listened silently to the Shoshoni woman's account of her night ride, then nodded his approval. "You did well, Willow," he said. He pulled the bottle of whiskey from a pack and popped the cork. "Might as well cut the dust some while we're waiting."

Slocum took the jug with a nod of thanks, downed a swallow, and offered the bottle to Willow. She shook her head. Stonekiller took two small sips, recorked the bottle, and reached for his tobacco. He glanced at the brightening sky. "Hurry up, sun," he said. "If I don't get some coffee soon, I'm going to turn downright grumpy. After breakfast I'll stand first watch. You two get some sleep." A wry grin touched his lips. "I doubt old Bloody Hand's going to get much rest for a spell. And come sundown, we'll deal him a real plate full of misery."

Slocum said, "Jim, we're going to have to get Maria out of there soon. Before Bloody Hand decides to kill the captives." He hesitated for a moment, then reluctantly added, "If he hasn't already."

Stonekiller shrugged. "He hasn't. I'd know it if he had. By sunup tomorrow, I'll have Maria out of there. Or we'll both be dead."

12

Maria Stonekiller crouched at the back of the blood moon lodge, her fingers trembling, the hairs on the nape of her neck tingling in the predawn blackness.

Even though she sensed the eerie noise was Jim's doing, it was still enough to chill her blood. It had hit others in the camp even harder. The deathly silence in the canyon camp had given way to a babble of noise as the roaring screech died. At first it was a subdued murmur, then a rising cacophony of shouts, whimpers, cries, and the nervous whinny of frightened horses stamping and lunging against their picket lines and hobbles. She heard the scurry of feet as men brave enough to venture outside their lodges or who slept in the open scrambled about in confusion and fear.

The two other women in the lodge, one Apache, the other Ute, huddled together at the center of the tepee. Maria couldn't see them in the pitch black interior of the lodge, but she heard their frightened whimpers. The scuffle of feet from outside told her the two women guards—the toothless old hag one of them—were scampering for the comfort of the ring of light cast by the council fire. This might be her best chance to add her evil spirits to The Place of the Bones. To be discovered outside the blood moon lodge would mean almost certain death. It was worth the risk.

Maria's fingers probed the rear skins of the lodge. They had not been staked down carefully. She could squirm beneath the hides. She slipped the wooden knife from beneath her skirt, placed it by one of the lodgepoles, lowered herself to her belly, and wriggled into the night. She crawled to the side of the lodge and glanced around. The camp was a whirl of bodies. Men, women, and children raced back and forth, most of them wide-eyed and obviously terrified. Odds were that one more woman dashing about would not be noticed.

She rose to her feet, took a deep breath, and scurried to the bushes she had used to relieve herself. She glanced about. Satisfied that no one had noticed her, she picked up the human leg and jawbone she had seen there earlier. She sprinted toward the milling bodies in the mestizo camp fifty yards away, praying there would be no challenge.

None came. The mestizos ran about, flailing their arms in the air, yammering their strange tongue, the whites of their eyes stark in the glow of starlight and campfires. She paused near the ashes of the head man's cooking fire, knelt, and placed the leg bone with care. She put the jawbone across the leg just below the ball at the upper end, the human bones in the sign of the cross. It would have special significance for the mestizos; they had been exposed to the teaching of the Catholic church since the days the first priests came to the hills of Mexico. It would be a double blow: the keening spirits of the dead and the sign of the cross combined would strike terror into any mind already confused and clouded by fear. She scrambled away, her heart pounding. Now she had to get back to the lodge unnoticed.

A sudden thought struck Maria. She scurried back to the wagon, paused long enough to squeeze a fresh drop of blood from the cuts on her thighs, and dabbed a fourth moon dot into the circle etched in dried blood on the side of the wagon. The curse on Crow Woman was now complete.

Maria tried to breathe normally as she made her way back to the lodge and wriggled beneath the skin as silently as she had stolen away. She found the wooden knife and slipped it back beneath her dress. She breathed more easily now. She didn't think the other two women had noticed her absence, gripped as they were by raw terror. She settled in to wait out the dawn. It was going to be an interesting morning in The Place of the Bones, she thought.

Bloody Hand glowered around the half circle of head men of different bands, all yammering at once, and tried to control the swirl of anger and fear that wracked his gut. He wouldn't admit that the sound last night had curdled his own blood. He did allow himself a silent vow that they would get out of this place as quickly as possible. He kept reminding himself he didn't believe in evil spirits. His gut wasn't listening. The echoes of that screech that was not of this world kept rattling through his brain.

The babble of voices as the head men shouted, muttered, argued, cursed, and gestured told the Kwahadi he was facing his biggest challenge yet in his attempts to hold his army together. The racket wasn't helping his splitting headache.

"Enough! Silence!" Bloody Hand roared.

The babble of voices slowly died away. Bloody Hand stared into each face in the half circle: White Shield, the surly young Comanche who was poised to challenge Bloody Hand's leadership; Koshay, the lean Mescalero with the big head; José, the spineless mestizo leader; the tall Ute with broad shoulders and powerful legs known as Wind Runner; and three other leaders of various loosely knit bands of Kickapoos, Wichitas, and lesser groups. Bloody Hand felt even the trust and confidence of his Kiowa and Kiowa-Apache allies slipping away. A wrong word now and the cause was lost.

"Are you women, who cringe in the dark, or are you warriors?" Bloody Hand's tone was heavy with sarcasm. "The sound you heard was nothing but the wind. There were no evil spirits." His gaze bored into White Shield's solemn face. "You, White Shield. Are you also a man-child who cowers at sounds in the night?"

Anger flashed in White Shield's eyes. "White Shield fears no spirit talk. And no man. Bloody Hand would be wise to remember the latter."

The Kwahadi let the challenge slide. Bloody Hand's turn would come. For now, he needed the insolent young Comanche and the men he led.

"And you, Koshay?"

The Mescalero's eyes narrowed. "These are not Comanche spirits who stalk this place. They are my people: Apache. Their souls have tired of waiting to be put to peaceful rest. Already they have spoken." Koshay gestured to two men who waited on horseback, blanket-wrapped bundles tied to their saddles.

The men rode forward, stopped at the edge of the semicircle, and untied thongs from the bundles. Bloody Hand recoiled in instinct as two rotted heads tumbled into the sand. A stunned silence fell over the gathering.

"My sentinels found these at the change of watch, at the base of the trail leading up the mountain," Koshay said. "Only the heads. Does Bloody Hand have an explanation for this?"

The Kwahadi stared at the deteriorating flesh for a moment, his blood cold. His mind stumbled upon itself. After a moment, Bloody Hand forced himself to approach the severed heads. He knelt and stared first at one, then the other, and finally grunted. At least he knew now what had happened to two of the scouts he had dispatched as a rear guard. He stood and scowled at the wide-eyed faces before him.

"This was not the work of demons or spirits." Bloody Hand hoped his words were stronger than the emptiness in his gut. "Those who walk in darkness carry no weapons. I know these two. I have ridden with them. What was done to them was the work of men."

"What men?" White Shield's tone held a challenge. "Our sentries and scouts report no sign of men. No tracks, no smoke from fires."

"Soldiers," José cried in alarm. "Grierson's buffalo soldiers." The mestizo glanced about nervously. "They are nearby."

"It cannot be," Koshay snapped. "This is not the way of the black soldiers with wooly heads. What of the bodies found with no faces atop the rim?"

Bloody Hand winced. He glanced inadvertently at the blanket-wrapped bundles beneath the cottonwood tree nearby. The sight of white bone shining where flesh should have been and dried eye sockets sent a chill finger along his spine.

"Killed by men," he said. "Men of flesh and blood."

"Koshay thinks it is not so," the Apache said, his tone firm. "This is the way of something, some being not of this earth. A thing that we cannot see or fight."

"Koshay speaks true," José said, his voice breaking. "The cross of bones before my fire," the mestizo chief José stammered, "and the dead man at the pass nearest the sun, scalped. Are these, too, the work of men like us?"

Bloody Hand leveled a hard glare into José's wide eyes. The man was about to soil himself, he thought in disgust. "What else could it be?"

"Something my people will not face," José said. "We cannot fight evil spirits. Already, half my people have left this place, Bloody Hand. The rest of us leave before the sun is overhead. Your medicine is not strong."

Bloody Hand's gaze never wavered from José's face. He whipped the knife from his belt sheath and flipped it underhand. The knife made a half turn and buried itself into José's chest. The mestizo staggered, took a half step backward, and sank to his knees. He stared in disbelief at the knife handle protruding from his chest. A gurgle sounded in his throat. He toppled onto his side.

"There is no place in this warrior alliance for cowards," Bloody Hand said. He strode to the body, yanked his blade free, and wiped the steel on the dead man's shirt. He stared into each face left in the semicircle. "Is there another old woman among you?"

The glares that came back unnerved Bloody Hand. White Shield and the Ute looked like they might accept the challenge. Bloody Hand sensed he had made a mistake in killing José. He could read it in the eyes of the others. He had lost face because of his quick temper. He kept his expression stern. "Is there no one else to question Bloody Hand's medicine?" After a moment's silence, Bloody Hand said, "It is good. Had José held his tongue, he would have known what I tell you now. Before the sun sets tomorrow night, we move from The Place of the Bones."

A couple of the men nodded in obvious relief. The Kickapoo leader shifted his weight. "Why do we wait another night? My warriors fear not, but the women and children now dread the sundown."

Contempt surged in Bloody Hand's chest. The Kickapoo lied; it was not just the women and children who were without courage. But he had to play the game. "The wagons of the traders come tonight," he said. The lie came easily. Bloody Hand had no faith that the Comancheros and their wagons would show up, or they would have been here by now. "Then each warrior will have a fine new repeating rifle and enough ammunition to kill many whites. We will begin our war. Go now. Tell your people Bloody Hand has spoken."

The gathering gradually dispersed until only Koshay remained behind. "My scouts have seen no wagons, Bloody Hand," the Mescalero said.

"They will be here. They come from the north."

Koshay's brows furrowed. The Apache knew full well there was no wagon trail from the north; it showed in the glitter of his narrowed eyes. He did not speak again. He started to turn away.

"Koshay, watch the mestizos. And the Kickapoos and the Utes. Do not let them run away. We will need them, you and I, when we begin our war. Koshay shall ride at my right hand when we leave here. He will have many guns, many horses, much wealth. Of this also I have spoken."

Koshay's face darkened at the request, but he nodded. Bloody Hand knew it was belittling to ask a war chief of Koshay's stature to herd mixed breeds and tribes of lesser courage than the Mescaleros. He also knew Koshay would not refuse the promise of a larger than average share of the loot and glory. Greed could be a weapon in the hands of a great leader like himself, Bloody Hand thought. He knew as well that the mestizos were afraid of the Apaches. They would stay until they fell before the guns of the soldier forts. When Koshay was no longer needed, it would be a simple matter to dispose of him. For now, it was more important that he keep his army together.

Bloody Hand had survived the strongest challenge yet to his leadership. He wondered why he did not feel a sense of victory. The unearthly wailing roar from the darkness still screeched in his mind. He tried to tell himself he was above superstition, that there were no ghosts. He considered breaking camp now. But he must wait at least one more day, until the arrival of the Jicarilla Apache and the Navajo warriors his runners had recruited.

Today he would make a show of placing his war medicine, the red hand, on the shoulder of his horse, to let everyone know that the great war was to begin. It would be enough. By nightfall, the timid ones among them would be too frightened to venture far from the strength of an armed camp.

Bloody Hand paused, his gaze sweeping the canyon rims around The Place of the Bones. He saw nothing. *Who—or what— is out there?* he wondered. *Who had killed the sentries, placed the rotting heads on the trail? It could not be ghosts or spirits. They did not exist except in the minds of ignorant savages.* He was not comforted. Bloody Hand had to admit he was as anxious as anyone to leave this canyon. Only one more night. That was all he needed.

A distant speck caught his eye, an eagle soaring in lazy circles on the hunt above the north rim, and he grunted in satisfaction. The eagle was his medicine animal. It was a good sign.

Slocum lay at the crest of the rocky butte, squinted through the midday heat waves, and muttered a bitter curse.

He was looking at trouble.

More trouble than the half a hundred or so Indians who had passed this way less than three hours ago.

This trouble rode two abreast, dark dots beneath the dust cloud stirred by the freshening south wind. Indians didn't ride in formation. Slocum had seen enough cavalry patrols in his life to know one at a glance. This was no mere patrol. It was at least company force, more than a hundred men.

Slocum had spotted the two separate dust clouds during a cautious early morning scout and ridden far afield to check them out. The risk of being spotted was outweighed by the need to know, so he had taken the chance.

The Indians, obviously bound for Skeleton Canyon, had made no effort to hide their trail. Now, wide-ranging scouts of the distant cavalry column were within a half mile of cutting the Indian band's sign. There was no doubt in Slocum's mind that they would. Grierson's buffalo soldiers, one of the toughest outfits on the southwest frontier, were on the prowl. Their Indian scouts were the best that could be had. They would find the trail, and the soldiers would follow the trail into the canyon stronghold. That would mean sure death for the captives in Bloody Hand's camp.

Slocum ignored the trickle of sweat on his forehead and the red ant crawling across the back of his hand. His gut iced despite the heavy heat as one of the cavalry scouts dismounted and knelt amid the tracks left by the passing Indian party. The scout followed the trail for a hundred yards on foot, leading his horse, then stopped and stared toward the canyon ten miles away. The scout mounted, reined his horse back toward the head of the cavalry column, and urged the animal into a swift trot.

Slocum's jaw muscles ached from the constant pressure of clenched teeth as he pondered his next move. He wasted no time fretting over the Indian band that had passed earlier. They weren't important. The cavalry company was the problem. And there wasn't a damn thing he could do about the soldiers. It was too late to stop them, and there was no way to delay them. He knew cavalry tactics. Before dawn they would be in position at the west end of the canyon. At first light they would charge into Bloody Hand's camp. That meant Slocum, Stonekiller, and Willow would have to move up their own timetable. That, in turn, meant making their move before moonset. It would be chancy. And they would be cutting it close. More than the lives of the captives was at stake, too. If the soldiers were unaware of the new rifles in the Indian camp, they would be outgunned as well as outnumbered. Grierson's black troopers would put up a hell of a fight, but it might not be enough.

Slocum winced as the red ant bit into the back of his hand. He squashed the ill-tempered insect with a thumb, then crabbed back from the rim of the butte and replaced his hat as he slipped and skidded his way down the steep slope to the Kickapoo dun tied at the base of the hill. There was no time to waste. He mounted and urged the horse into a fast trot back toward camp.

Jim Stonekiller's frown deepened as Slocum finished his report. Willow stood facing Slocum, concern plowing small vertical lines between her dark eyebrows.

"Damn it to hell," Stonekiller muttered. "Of all the times for the Army to show up, they had to pick now."

Slocum sipped at his coffee, knowing it would be his last cup for several hours. Maybe forever. "You know we have to get Maria out of there before the troopers attack, Jim," he said.

The half-breed didn't reply. Slocum didn't push. He left the man to his thoughts. Stonekiller had a hell of a lot more at stake here than Slocum did: his wife. All Slocum could lose was money. And maybe his life. He had lost money before. He had long ago come to terms with the idea that every man dies sooner or later.

It was Willow who broke the silence. "Perhaps we can use the soldiers—and help them at the same time," she said.

Stonekiller looked up. "How so?"

"A demoralized enemy is a beaten enemy. I have heard this spoken many times by my elders. A frightened army cannot fight. Bloody Hand's band already is afraid. If we strike at the proper time, many of his men will flee—into the guns of the soldiers. There will be fewer to chase us."

Slocum raised an eyebrow. "Do you have something specific in mind, Willow?"

The Shoshoni girl nodded. "A slight change in tactics. Last night, I overheard the sentries talking before I loosed the buffalo roar. They spoke of one called Medicine Woman, whose visions are strong and whose reputation as a seer spreads beyond her own camp. They spoke of Medicine Woman's vision: a glowing horseman who rode at night, the herald of many deaths. It is the talk of the entire camp, the sentries said. We have two bodies left. Perhaps if we gave them Medicine Woman's vision?"

Stonekiller glanced at Slocum. "Willow's on to something here. If that wouldn't booger a bunch of Indians, nothing would." A fresh gleam of hope sparked in Stonekiller's eyes. "In the confusion, I could slip into camp and get Maria out."

"And if we play the cards right," Slocum added, "the Indians who panic will run straight into the buffalo soldiers." Slocum stroked his chin, the scratch of dense stubble loud in his ears. "Timing is the key. And making sure we have a way out if Bloody Hand comes after us."

"I pray to the Christian God and all known Indian spirits that the son of a bitch does come after us if I don't get a crack at him in camp," Stonekiller said, his words tight and cold. "He owes me a liver." The half-breed walked off a few paces and stood staring into the distance.

"What do you think, Slocum?" Willow's words were so soft as to barely be audible. "Do you believe it would work?"

Slocum nodded solemnly. "It could. It has to, Willow. We're only going to get one chance."

After a quarter hour, Stonekiller returned, his strides long and confident, shoulders squared. "All right, here's what we're going to do . . ."

Bloody Hand stepped from beneath the cannon-scarred cottonwood tree and lifted an arm in greeting.

"Welcome, Wah-to-ke," he said to the powerfully built man on the spotted war pony. "I saw an eagle this morning. The spirit bird said my brother, the great war chief of the Jicarilla, would arrive today."

Wah-to-ke returned the greeting and dismounted, his movements fluid and smooth for a man so thick of chest and heavy of leg. The Jicarilla was a head shorter than Bloody Hand, but almost as heavy, most of his bulk in solid muscle.

"Greetings, Bloody Hand. It is good to see my old friend again." Wah-to-ke's voice was as deep as his chest. The Apache gestured to the men gathered around, a mix of Jicarilla and Navajo warriors, as he made the introductions. Bloody Hand made no effort to remember the names, but nodded a greeting to each man in turn. He struggled to keep the contempt from his eyes as the Navajos were introduced. He felt nothing but scorn for the blanket makers; as warriors, they were little better than the mestizos. A generation ago they were a proud people, before Canyon de Chelly fell to Army General Charlton and the small scout called Kit Carson. Then, as now, they were diggers in the dirt. Bloody Hand had little use for farmers.

The Jicarilla men were a different breed: warriors to the deepest bone. It showed in their eyes, in the set of their jaws. With Wah-to-ke's Jicarillas and Koshay's Mescalero band, Bloody Hand had his elite corps of desert fighters. The Apaches could use the land like a hunting wolf, unseen and unheard until they pounced, as much at home on foot as on horseback. They were a welcome addition to his own Comanche and Kiowa warriors, the finest and most fearless horsemen of the Plains.

"Come," Bloody Hand said. "We shall smoke and speak of our war against the white man. We shall speak of the sharing of great riches and the return of the buffalo. We shall speak of reclaiming the lands taken from us. Set your camp wherever you wish. My lodge is yours. Tonight there will be a great feast in honor of my brothers, the Jicarillas and the Navajos."

"Before we smoke, Bloody Hand," one of the Navajos said, "we were promised guns. New repeating rifles."

Bloody Hand fought back a surge of aggravation. The dirt-digger's tone held a hint of challenge. He nodded. "You shall have them, a fine new Winchester and ammunition for each warrior among you, when the sun rises tomorrow."

The Navajo wasn't satisfied. Suspicion flickered in the man's deep brown eyes. "Why not distribute them now? Does Bloody Hand not trust those who have ridden so far to join him?"

Bloody Hand's pulse quickened. The insolent Navajo was getting on his nerves. And the man had spoken the truth. Bloody Hand did not trust the diggers. The Navajos just might take the new weapons and disappear into the night. He forced a reassuring grin.

"My brothers, the Navajos, I trust with my own life," Bloody Hand said, "but the rifles remain under guard until it is time. There are mestizos in our camp."

The Navajo's humped nose wrinkled in disgust. The diggers hated the mixed bloods as much as every other tribe hated them. "Why mestizos? Your messengers said you had many fine warriors. He spoke not of mestizos."

"They have a place in our plans," Bloody Hand said. "You will see. Come. I will show you the rifles. Then we shall smoke to this great alliance of warriors."

The Navajo nodded grudgingly. Bloody Hand marked the man with the hooked nose in his mind. A bullet between the shoulder blades during the first fight would teach him some respect. Bloody Hand smiled inwardly. By the time he had eliminated all the troublemakers he had so marked, his rifle barrel would be hot. But by then his army would have tasted victory. It would not matter then that a few had died, as there would be no question as to who was the greatest of all war chiefs.

He led the way to the wagon and flipped up a corner of the canvas covering. Sunlight glinted on gun metal in an open crate. He reached into the crate, lifted out a new Winchester, which had an eagle feather tied to the front barrel band, and handed it to Wah-to-ke. The Jicarilla ran his fingers over the stock, stroked the metal of the receiver, shouldered the weapon, worked the action, and grunted in satisfaction. "It is a good rifle. Are the others the same?"

"The same type, my brother," Bloody Hand said warmly, "but this one is a special rifle, one whose bullets never miss the target. It has been purified at the hands of our eldest maker of medicine. It will be yours with the dawn. With this rifle in Wah-to-ke's hands, the white man shall flee in terror before a shot is fired."

The Jicarilla handed the weapon back reluctantly, his fingers lingering for an instant on the trigger guard. Bloody Hand idly wondered how many chiefs and senior warriors he had promised that particular weapon to. He had lost count. But it did not matter; one rifle was the same as another. He turned to the other men clustered about.

"Each of you will have such a fine weapon, and many bullets. Now come. We smoke."

Bloody Hand had grown tired of the Navajos, and even a few of the Jicarillas, before the elaborate smoking ceremony and extended council, followed by small talk, ended. He had forced himself to be the cordial host throughout, but was relieved that it was over. He had much work to do.

Bloody Hand found Koshay watching over the pony herd as it grazed in the west end of the canyon.

"Any word from your scouts?" Bloody Hand said by way of greeting.

"None." Concern wrinkled the Apache's brow. "They should have sent a runner back by now."

Bloody Hand shrugged, trying to conceal his own worry. One of the latest arrivals had mentioned hearing distant gunshots two days ago. Bloody Hand had replied it was nothing to be concerned with, probably shots fired by one of his hunting parties. But the nagging suspicion that something had happened to the scouts wouldn't go away.

"I will send more scouts," Koshay said.

Bloody Hand shrugged. "No need. They can catch up with us. We move out in the morning."

"I will not be sad to leave this place." Koshay glanced around. "The air here is bad. A worm crawls in Koshay's belly. Half a dozen of the mestizos and two Utes slipped away this morning, leaving their blankets behind. Others huddle together like children afraid of the dark, even when the sun is high overhead. All may bolt before dawn."

Bloody Hand snorted in disgust. "Cowards. They run before an old woman's dreams and the moan of the wind."

Koshay cut a quick, sharp glance at Bloody Hand. "Do not underestimate Medicine Woman's visions. Her mindsight is strong. The whole camp speaks softly and dreads the night."

Bloody Hand shrugged. "Nothing will happen tonight. I saw an eagle." He left the Mescalero and went to find Crow Woman.

She squatted beside the blood moon lodge, tracing a pattern in the dirt with her sharpened stick. Bloody Hand caught her eye and motioned her to him a safe distance from the forbidden lodge. He slipped a sheathed knife from beneath his belt and handed it to the toothless old hag.

"If anything out of the ordinary happens tonight," he said, "anything at all—kill the Cheyenne woman."

Crow Woman's eyes went wide; Bloody Hand thought he saw a flicker of terror within them. That was unlike Crow Woman. He wondered if the whole damn camp had gone crazy. Crow Woman opened her mouth as if to object. Bloody Hand cut her off with an abrupt wave.

"The Cheyenne woman has brought bad medicine among us." Bloody Hand's tone was cold and deadly. "I have spoken. If you do not wish to spend your last hours roasting over a slow fire, kill her."

13

Slocum made a final swipe with the cleaning rag over the receiver of the Winchester, thumbed cartridges into the loading port, levered a round into the chamber, lowered the hammer, and slipped the rifle into the saddle boot. A man who didn't care for his weapons didn't last long on the frontier. A bit of grit or grease in the wrong place could cost the shot that saved his life.

He glanced up at the sound of a soft footfall and shook his head in silent wonder. Jim Stonekiller was painted for war. Stripes of alternating vermillion and yellow angled from his breastbone down to the lower ribs of his muscled torso. An amulet of cougar claws and obsidian beads was strung on rawhide hung around his neck. The left half of his face was painted jet black, the other half stark white. Twin streaks of yellow paint ran from beneath each eye to his jawline, and a vermillion slash went straight across the center of his forehead. He wore only a breechclout and high-topped moccasins that reached almost to his knees. A yellow headband took the place of his hat. A beaded sheath held an oversized, wicked looking knife at his left hip. He carried the lance taken from the Indian at the buffalo wallow fight. He carried no rifle. The only thing that wasn't pure, traditional Plains warrior about him was the revolver that rode in the holster of the cartridge belt around his waist.

"No Irish in me tonight," Stonekiller said in reply to Slocum's raised eyebrow. "Gone Kiowa."

Slocum nodded. "Impressive."

"Might want to dab on a few smears of war paint yourself, Slocum. Don't know if Injun medicine works on you white-eyes, but it wouldn't hurt to ask for a little spirit help. Going to be a chancy night."

Slocum shook his head. "Thanks for the thought, but I'll pass on this hand. Paint might run. I tend to sweat when I'm spooked."

Stonekiller half smiled. "Any time you're spooked, Slocum, I'm going to get mighty worried. You all set?"

"A couple more minutes and I'll be as ready as I'll ever get."

"Me, too," a quiet voice said from behind Slocum.

Slocum turned. He hadn't heard the Shoshoni girl walk up behind him. He wondered if he was losing his touch, or if the woman was really that good on the stalk. He decided it must be the latter.

Willow also wore war paint, vermillion stripes over both cheekbones and two small black streaks across her chin. A thin line of yellow paint ran around her hair at the scalp line. Her hair was plaited into braids that fell over each shoulder, the tight weaves secured at the end by red cloth ties. Tiny green feathers from a Mexican jay dangled from beneath the end ties. She also wore a medicine amulet, a hammered copper bracelet around her upper arm. A strand of alternating wolf claws and seashells hung around her neck. She had changed from the familiar doeskin dress into a dark indigo cotton shirt and men's corduroy trousers, the legs tucked into beaded, high-topped moccasins. Leather straps crossed her chest, one holding the quiver within easy reach behind her right shoulder, the other containing cartridges for the Kennedy rifle. A revolver was tucked beneath her waistband. She still didn't look like a dangerous savage, Slocum thought. She looked like a pretty Shoshoni girl in costume.

Slocum shook his head in wonder. "I'm surrounded by Injuns already, and we're not even in the canyon yet." He softened the remark with a wink at Willow.

"Just remember, white man," Willow teased back, "they might not be as friendly down there as they are up here."

"I'll keep that in mind." Slocum made a quick final check of his weapons. He carried two revolvers, one holstered and one in his waistband; a knife in its sheath beneath his right elbow; his Winchester rifle; a bandolier of .44-40 ammunition draped over his chest; Stonekiller's Ballard rifle; and a pouch of cartridges for the big gun. He shucked his boots and pulled on a pair of moccasins.

"We've got a couple more guns in the packs if you need them," Stonekiller jibed.

"If I had a place to put them, I'd carry them," Slocum said. "But I suppose I'll have to make do with these."

"Man's entitled to his own idea of what makes war medicine." Stonekiller glanced at the sun. The joshing tone faded. "We'd better get moving if we're going to be in place by sundown. Bloody Hand wants a war, by God, we'll give him one." The half-breed reached for Slocum's hand. "Good hunting, friend."

"And to you." Slocum peered deep into Stonekiller's eyes. "Get Maria out, Jim. That's the number-one objective of this operation. Nothing else matters much."

"I'll get her." Stonekiller released Slocum's hand, gave Willow a quick hug, and strode toward the canyon. He would have to go in on foot. There was no trail down wide enough or safe enough for a horse.

"Let's go fetch our evil spirit and be on our way, Slocum," Willow said.

Slocum's nostrils pinched as they neared the pony staked apart from the other horses. The stench hadn't completely left him since they had spent better than an hour getting the body rigged. Even in broad daylight, the sight was enough to make a man's skin crawl, Slocum thought. The rotting body was wrapped in greasewood bundles and dry grass, held erect in the saddle by crossed cottonwood limbs lashed to rings of the rigging.

"Damn, I sure hate to do this to a horse. Even a sorry one," Slocum said.

"The pony won't suffer," Willow said confidently. "The lashes will part before the fire burns the horse."

The long-legged, boogery sorrel Slocum rode wanted nothing to do with the strange figure on the grulla pony. It took Slocum several minutes to calm the sorrel and coax the gelding close enough that he could take the lead rope of the pony carrying the grim load. At least, Slocum thought gratefully, the wind would be in their faces for most of the long ride to the eastern pass into

Skeleton Canyon. He checked the saddle scabbards to make sure the Winchester and Ballard hadn't been loosened during the fuss with the sorrel as Willow swung effortlessly aboard her chosen warhorse, a deep-chested roan that looked to have a lot of stamina and speed. She gathered in the lead ropes of Stonekiller's horse and a spare, saddled mount for Maria.

"All set?"

Willow nodded, her expression grim beneath the war paint. "Let's go."

They rode in silence for the first couple of miles, keeping to the draws and arroyos of the badlands for the roundabout ride. The sorrel had settled down some, but still wasn't exactly happy when the pony carrying the body edged up too close behind them. It could have been worse for the horse, Slocum thought. They had left one Indian corpse behind. One apparition should be enough. He studied the lengthening shadows and was reassured. They would be in position before the thin sliver of moon appeared.

"Slocum," Willow said softly, "when this is over, will you ride with me? Take me back to the reservation and my people?"

"Nothing would please me more, Willow," Slocum said.

The quarter-crescent moon cast a pale light over the steep south wall of the canyon rim pass as Slocum crept through the black shadows of a juniper stand. The low voices of the sentries were distinct now. Another few steps and he would be within arm's length of the two Indians.

Slocum paused at the edge of the junipers and muttered a mental curse. Taking these two out was going to be a lot harder than eliminating the pair standing watch on the other side of the rim had been. Willow had downed one with a single arrow. The blood of the second man was still sticky on the hand guard of Slocum's knife. The first two had been easy. Almost too easy.

These sentries hadn't made the same mistakes. Instead of huddling together and making easy targets of themselves, the two stood a good ten feet apart, in the open, away from any cover he could use in his final stalk. And they were nervous. Nervous men were more alert. That made them a hell of a lot harder to kill without using a gun. Firearms were out of the question. Gunshots would wreck the whole plan and probably get them all killed in the process.

Slocum hesitated, trying to work out a route of attack. The man nearest him had his back turned to Slocum. That sentry wasn't the problem. The other one was. He held a rifle, his thumb on the hammer. It would take him only a second to fire a shot. Slocum's mind raced, rejecting plan after plan. He was running out of time. Stonekiller would be in position at the base of the north trail now, waiting. Whatever Slocum did, he had to do it soon. The man with his thumb on the hammer muttered something to his companion. Slocum couldn't make out the words. They were in a tongue he did not speak.

Slocum's heartbeat picked up as the second man strode a few feet to the edge of a rockfall, propped his rifle against a boulder, and began fiddling with the buttons on his pants. Praise the saints for yelping bladders, Slocum thought. The odds still weren't good, but he figured he would never get a better chance. He waited a few seconds until he heard the first splash of urine against stone. He drew in a deep breath, told himself it was now or never, and tightened his grip on the knife.

He stepped from the shadows of the junipers, feeling the ground through his moccasin soles for the first, cautious step. He sprang the last three feet. His left hand clamped in the sentry's hair and yanked the head back. A quick flick of the right wrist sliced open the Indian's throat deep enough that Slocum felt the grate of blade edge against backbone. The Indian's body convulsed. A gurgling rasp sounded. Slocum dropped the man and spun—and knew he was going to be too late. The second sentry whirled, scooped up his rifle, his thumb groping for the hammer. Slocum's heart skidded. He could never reach the man in time. He had failed. The rifle muzzle lifted. Slocum braced himself for the shock of lead.

Something whirred past his ear. He heard a solid thump. The rifleman staggered back a half step as the feathered shaft drove deep into his left chest. Slocum was on him in two quick strides. He swept the knife up from waist level. The blade slit open the sentry's gut and buried itself deep under the rib cage, point driving upward. The Indian's scream came out as a strangled grunt. Slocum kept his body close to the dying man, shoving and twisting with the knife, oblivious to the blood and slippery guts around his hand and wrist. The man's eyes rolled back in his head. He went limp.

Slocum yanked his blade free, stepped back, and let the body fall. The arrow had driven almost through the Indian's chest. Slocum heard the slight crack as the wooden shaft broke under the man's weight.

He gasped in a lungful of air and turned at the rasp of leather on sand. Willow stood at the edge of the juniper clump, another arrow already nocked and the heavy bow drawn. Slocum stooped to wipe the gore from his knife hand on the dead man's shirt, then looked up as she stepped alongside.

"Girl," Slocum said, "I'm sure as hell glad you don't follow orders too well. If you had stayed where I told you, the whole stew pot would have got kicked over here."

The Shoshoni woman eased the draw of the bow and slipped the arrow over her shoulder into the quiver. "I saw the problem and thought you might need some help." She peered at the dead men, her face without expression beneath the war paint.

"You thought right, Willow. That's another one I owe you. I'll thank you properly later." He sheathed the knife as he rose. "Let's go. We've got work to do, and damn little time to do it in."

Slocum was winded by the time they had sprinted the hundred or so yards to where the spirit horse was tethered to a juniper stub at the base of the far canyon wall, out of sight from the rim. Willow, Slocum noticed, was barely breathing hard as she untied the buffalo roar from the saddle. She stepped clear and whirled the rig overhead. The low hum grew into the eerie wail, so loud at this range that it hurt Slocum's ears.

Willow worked the buffalo roar for what seemed an eternity, yet could have been little more than a minute, before the humming screech died away. She stepped to the far side of the skittish grulla pony. Slocum untied the single hackamore lead rein, wasted a second stroking the horse's neck as if to apologize, then dug in his pocket for matches. He handed one to Willow and struck the second on his belt buckle. He touched the match to the grease-wood and dry grass wrapped around the corpse. The flame wavered, then caught and quickly raced upward, fed by the tinder-dry grass and natural oil of the greasewood brush. He heard the crackle of flames from Willow's side as the first surge of true panic hit the horse. The terrified animal squealed and lunged against the lead rope. The skin of Slocum's palm burned against the sudden jerk. He held tight for another second until the corpse was engulfed in flames and the heat seared his cheek. He dodged a front foot, heaved the horse's head toward camp, and let go of the lead. He swept his hat from his head and slapped it against the horse's rump.

The horse was in a dead run within two wild lunges, headed toward the heart of the Indian camp below. Slocum stood for a moment, stunned at the sight he and Willow had turned loose. Flames flowed back from the corpse as the horse gathered speed. Cinders and sparks burst from the bundle; the flaming body swayed and lurched, but stayed in the saddle, held firm by the thick ropes.

"Good God," Slocum whispered in awe, "I know what it is and it still spooks the hell out of me." He tore his gaze from the fiery spectacle and glanced over his shoulder toward the east. A faint smudge of pale gray lay on the horizon. He grabbed Willow's arm. "Come on, girl. All hell's about to break loose down there. We've got only a few minutes to fetch the other horses and get into position."

Slocum chanced a glance toward the camp as he and Willow sprinted toward the horses across the open ground of the narrow pass. Stonekiller would be making his move any moment now.

Jim Stonekiller crouched close to the ground beneath the stubby piñon at the base of the narrow trail down from the canyon rim and stared in astonishment as the apparition charged toward the camp. His skin crawled at the sight of the flaming rider on the charging horse.

The first startled cries from the Indian camp jarred him back to his senses. He tore his gaze away from the ball of flame. The lone guard at the bottom of the trail stood ramrod stiff, his head turned toward the approaching ball of fire. Stonekiller stepped from beneath the piñon and slammed the lance tip between the man's shoulder blades. The guard's back arched in shock; he stood on tiptoe for a moment, one hand reaching for the spear point protruding from his chest. His knees buckled. He went down.

Stonekiller made no attempt to retrieve the lance. There was no time. He darted from one spot of cover to another, working his way toward the blood moon lodge a few yards away. Bedlam erupted as the terrified horse carried the blazing corpse into the center of the camp. Cries, shouts, and screams sounded over the occasional wild gunshot. Men scrambled from their blankets, dropped their weapons, and scattered in terror. The confusion grew as the fiery spirit horse charged through the middle of camp into the Indian remuda grazing to the west. The Indian ponies whirled with squeals of terror and bolted up the canyon toward the trail, hooves pounding. The fireball dropped from the horse's back, sparks flying as it struck the ground and rolled. The stampeding remuda swept over two mounted Indians. The horsemen disappeared under a growing cloud of dust thrown up by the horses' hooves.

Stonekiller was within thirty feet of the lodge now, crouched low, legs pumping and heart pounding, fighting his own fear. He knew it was all for nothing if Maria wasn't inside the lodge.

Maria Stonekiller scrambled to her feet, jarred from her light doze by the screeches and yells outside. She darted to the lodge flap and yanked it aside. Men, women, and children scurried about, dark shapes flitting through the weak light.

Crow Woman stood before the tent, rooted in terror. Maria did not know what the commotion was, but at the moment she had only one thing in mind. She slipped the homemade wooden dagger from beneath her dress, gripped it tightly in her right hand, and stepped from the lodge. Crow Woman turned as if suddenly aware of danger; firelight glinted from steel in her hand. The old hag swept the knife upward. Maria blocked the thrust with her forearm and lunged into Crow Woman, all her weight behind the upward thrust of the wooden knife. Crow Woman grunted as the makeshift blade slammed home. Her eyes went wide and her jaw dropped in shock and disbelief. The knife dropped from her fingers.

"The circle has closed, old hag," Maria said. She heaved again at the wooden knife handle. Her knuckles sank deep into the rolls of fat on Crow Woman's belly. Maria stepped back, a cold smile on her face. Crow Woman's gaze dropped to her stomach. She staggered and fell to her knees.

Maria spun away, leaving the toothless old hag to die. She stood for a moment, undecided which direction to flee in the uproar of the camp. She darted around the side of the lodge— and gasped aloud as a powerful fist closed on her upper arm. She tried to break free, flailing with her free hand at the dark shape that held her.

"Maria! It's me! It's Jim!"

Maria's knees buckled. She flung herself into her husband's arms. For an instant they clung to each other.

"I knew you were there, Jim," Maria finally said. "I found the feather—"

"We must hurry," Stonekiller interrupted. "There are horses waiting at the pass—" He stopped in midsentence as a voice sounded above the yells and screams, a bull-like bellow. The Kwahadi Bloody Hand stood less than a hundred feet away, trying to rally his people. Blood lust flared in Stonekiller's gut. He yanked the spare revolver from beneath his belt and thrust it into Maria's hand. "At the base of the canyon wall is a saddle-shaped boulder beside a piñon tree. You know it?"

Maria nodded.

"Wait for me there."

Maria grabbed his forearm. "What are you going to do?"

Stonekiller's heart pounded against his chest. "Kill that son of a bitch Bloody Hand, if I can. If I don't come for you in a few minutes, run. Work your way along the canyon to the east pass. Willow and a friend have horses there. Get out of this place as fast as you can ride. Be careful, and stay close to cover. There will be a lot of shooting soon."

"What of you?"

A muscle twitched in Stonekiller's jaw. "I'll catch up with you. First, I'll settle a blood feud." He turned away and sprinted toward the swirling mass of confusion in the middle of the camp. He had made only a few strides before the dust kicked up by hundreds of feet and the stampeded remuda thickened to a fog. He could see only a few yards through the dust and predawn gloom.

A hand grabbed at his arm. He jerked away from the terrified woman and plunged deeper into the growing dust and near darkness. He drew his revolver. A hazy figure loomed in his path, rifle raised. Stonekiller ducked without breaking stride as the slug buzzed overhead. He slammed the Colt against the rifleman's temple as he sprinted past. The man went down.

Stonekiller had covered only a few more feet before he was deep into the panicked mass of humanity. He didn't worry about being spotted. One more running Indian was just another Indian in this whirlwind of bodies. His breathing became labored as the dust grew thicker, and heavy with powder smoke from wild, unaimed gunshots. He skidded to a halt beside the lodge he knew was Bloody Hand's and squinted through the haze.

The renegade Comanche stood a dozen yards away, screaming orders at the handful of Indian men who stayed with him despite the panic along the canyon floor. Stonekiller cocked the Colt and drew a bead on Bloody Hand's chest. He squeezed the trigger. At the same instant a big man stepped in front of the Kwahadi. Stonekiller's slug hammered into the big man's back and knocked him down. Stonekiller barked a curse and thumbed the weapon to full cock, half blinded by the muzzle flash.

Bloody Hand disappeared in the second it took Stonekiller's vision to return. A half dozen armed men ran toward him. Stonekiller dropped one man with his second shot. He rushed his third shot and missed. The warriors were almost upon him. He wheeled and sprinted toward the canyon wall. A slug sizzled past his ear. He felt a blow against his upper left arm and the icy-hot sting of lead. He ignored the wound. He ran past the blood moon lodge and abruptly changed course, darting to his left. If he were run down, at least he could lead them away from Maria.

He was almost at the canyon wall now. Lead kicked at his heels, spanged from rocks, and thumped into the side of the sheer cliff. He heard approaching hoofbeats and cast a quick glance over his shoulder. Two men had managed to mount up. They were closing fast. He wasn't going to make it.

Fire blossomed from the rocks off to his right. He heard the whap of lead against flesh atop the flat bark of a handgun, a quick grunt of pain and the thud of a body hitting the ground. Stonekiller flung himself to the earth as hoofbeats closed on him, rolled onto his belly, and lifted the Colt. A mounted warrior was close enough that Stonekiller could identify the markings on his horse. He snapped a quick shot at the Apache. The slug went wide. Stonekiller braced himself for the impact of a bullet as the Apache raised his handgun. The warrior's pistol flashed, but the shot went wide as the Apache suddenly stiffened in the saddle. A second handgun report sounded atop the shot fired by the mounted man. The Apache's horse instinctively ducked aside, a rear hoof narrowly missing Stonekiller's head. Stonekiller steadied his revolver and drove a slug into the Apache's back. He bounced to his feet, aware of the shouts of the men on foot, closing in. He threw himself behind a small juniper and turned to face his attackers. He had one cartridge left in the handgun and no time to reload.

Stonekiller braced himself for death, a strange calmness settling about his shoulders. He aimed with care and squeezed the trigger. The man in his sights threw his hands high and went down. The warrior alongside stumbled and fell at the same instant. Stonekiller watched, confused; no single bullet could have taken down two men that far apart.

The attack suddenly broke. The remaining two warriors spun and ran back toward the camp. Stonekiller ejected the spent cartridges and reloaded the Colt, then came to his feet and sprinted toward the rocks and piñon at the trail.

He almost ran over Maria before he saw her. She crouched beside a low boulder, the spare revolver in her hand, a good forty yards from where she was supposed to be waiting. Stonekiller knew now where the shots that had saved his hide had come from. He skidded to a stop and knelt by her side, gasping air into winded lungs.

"I saw you were in trouble," Maria said calmly. "I wasn't going to give you up that easily, Jim Stonekiller. I'm not through with you yet." He reached for her hand. She ignored it. "We'll court later," Maria said. "For now, hand me some more shells."

Stonekiller had to grin through the ache in his chest. He dropped cartridges in her palm. "You're a hell of a woman, Maria," he said. In the few seconds it took her to reload, Stonekiller had caught his breath.

"We've got to get out of here," he said. "In a few minutes, there's going to be one hell of a gunfight going on. Ready?"

"Ready."

Stonekiller glanced toward the camp, disgust and relief mingling in his heart. *If there's a white man's God or a decent Indian spirit*, he thought, *I'll get another chance at Bloody Hand*. He dismissed the Kwahadi from his mind and stared at the east pass, starkly outlined in the first gray light of dawn. It seemed a hell of a long way off.

"Let's go," he said.

Slocum dug his elbows into the sand atop the south rim of the canyon pass, his breathing finally returning to normal. It had been close, but they had pulled it off. They were ready.

His sorrel was tied twenty yards down slope, out of the line of any stray slugs. Willow waited on the far rim, her own horse and the two intended for the Stonekillers near at hand. The sky was brightening fast. In five minutes or so, the light would be good enough for accurate shooting.

The barrel of Stonekiller's Ballard rested across a pad of juniper branches, a crude but effective shooting rest. Slocum racked the tang sight up to the five hundred yard notch. That, he figured, would give him several chances with the single-shot before he had to reach for the Winchester at his side. A half dozen of the big Ballard cartridges waited near his right hand.

Slocum glanced toward the far rim, but caught no sight of Willow. He had no doubt that she was ready. Or that she could handle the rifle. Still, he couldn't fight off his nagging concern for her safety. A lucky shot or a ricochet when the dance started— He forced the thought from his mind. Other things needed his undivided attention.

He stared into Skeleton Canyon. The pall of dust and weak light on the canyon floor concealed most of the activity in Bloody Hand's camp, but Slocum's ears told him what his eyes could not yet see.

Distant cries of confusion and terror still filled the canyon air. Frequent gunshots penetrated the din. Slocum wondered how many of Bloody Hand's people had killed each other with their wild, panicked firing. He could only hope Stonekiller and Maria hadn't been among those to go down. There had been no sign of them yet. There was nothing Slocum could do about that. Either they would make it or they wouldn't.

The dust from the stampeded pony herd had settled a bit in the west end of the canyon. Slocum could see the bodies swarming like ants, Indians trying to flee the evil spirits and death that had come in the night. A hundred Indians, perhaps more, crowded into the narrow pass.

The fleeing Indians suddenly scattered, a number of them lying motionless, specks in the distance. A second or so later, Slocum heard the rattle of a volley of rifle shots. A slight smile touched his lips. The Indians had ridden straight into the waiting cavalry troops. The reports of .45-70 government-issue carbines were impossible to mistake. Echoes of the first volley blended into an almost constant crackle at the far end of the canyon. Slocum knew some of the Indians would escape. Many of them would not. Soon the ambush would sprout into a cavalry charge whipping through the camp. It was going to be a hell of a long morning for Bloody Hand. It was only a matter of minutes until it got a tad busy here, too. The Indians had no place to go except straight up the canyon, into the guns of Slocum and Willow. Two good shots could hold out for a long time from their vantage points. Bloody Hand was really going to piss in his pants when he found himself caught between the U.S. Army at his back and sharpshooters at his front.

A flicker of movement at the base of the canyon wall, away from the dust and smoke haze, caught Slocum's eye. Two figures worked their way along the scrub brush and fallen rocks. They were almost two-thirds of the way to the pass. There was no sign of pursuit. Slocum sighed in relief. Stonekiller and Maria had made it at least this far.

"Come on, you two," Slocum whispered, "just a little farther—" The soft words died in his throat as the first wave of mounted horsemen broke from the thin cover of the dust cloud below, racing toward the pass. He drew the heavy hammer of the Ballard to full cock and lined the sights on the Indian leading the retreat. "All right, you bastards," he muttered aloud, "come to some more bad medicine."

14

The Ballard slammed against Slocum's shoulder. Fire lanced from the muzzle at the thunderous muzzle blast. Boiling powder smoke obscured his vision for an instant, then wisped away on the breeze.

Slocum saw the body of the Indian who had been in his sights flopping in the dust. He took his time, ejected the spent brass, slid a fresh cartridge into the chamber, closed the rolling block action, and picked another target.

The charging Indians had covered another sixty yards before the heavy Ballard slug hammered into a war pony. The rider flipped over the horse's ears as the animal went down, crushing the Indian as it rolled head over tail. Slocum reached for another cartridge. The crack of Willow's .45-60 sounded. A split second later, a warrior jerked in the saddle and slumped over his pony's neck. Slocum took the time to slip the rear tang sight down to the three hundred yard notch and drew a bead on a warrior at the left end of the line. He squeezed the trigger and muttered a curse as the shot sailed high.

The Indians' flight wavered as riders checked mounts or reined aside in confusion at the unexpected attack. One rider made the mistake of pulling his horse to a stop. A slug from Willow's rifle put him down. Slocum's fourth shot walloped through the thigh of one rider, ripped into the ribs of the Indian's horse, and staggered the pony. Slocum squinted through the pall of powder smoke and dust as he chambered the fifth round in the Ballard. His heart sank as an Indian yelped and gestured toward the canyon wall. The buck had spotted Stonekiller and Maria clambering through the rocks and brush. The remaining warriors yanked their horses toward the two figures on the canyon wall, still a hundred yards away from the safety of the rockfall at the base of the pass.

Slocum drew a deep breath and swung the Ballard muzzle toward the lead rider. It was a quartering shot at a fast moving rider—not the easiest target a man could have. He instinctively calculated the lead and stroked the trigger. The slug took the rider in the ribs and slammed him from his horse. Slocum put the Ballard down and grabbed his Winchester. The Indians were almost upon the Stonekillers now. Slocum's jaw clenched; they weren't going to make it.

Smoke belched from the side of the canyon wall and one of the Indians twisted in the saddle. An instant later Slocum heard the flat bark of two quick handgun shots. Willow's rifle cracked and an Indian pony went down. The rider rolled to his feet, tried to run, and went sprawling as a pistol slug whacked into his back. The remaining Indians scattered, riding hard for the canyon wall.

Slocum slapped a quick shot at one of the warriors, missed, and worked the action as the Indians dismounted and scrambled for cover. They had the Stonekillers bracketed. Slocum instinctively ducked as a slug splatted against the soil two feet below him. The Indians were about to make a fight of it now. A brave poked his head above a boulder only a few yards from the rocks where the Stonekillers had taken cover. Slocum levered two quick shots. Both missed, but the Indian ducked from sight.

The firing became almost a constant crackle. Dust and gunsmoke blended into a haze at the base of the canyon wall. Slocum swore bitterly. The Stonekillers were going to be overrun, and there wasn't a damn thing he could do about it. They had been so close.

Slocum's gut went cold as he glimpsed a flash of cloth darting down the steep side of the pass. Willow was sprinting toward the Stonekillers. "Dammit, girl, you're just going to get yourself killed, too," Slocum barked aloud. A rifle slug hummed past his ear. Slocum ignored the buzz of lead, concentrating on the Indians on the canyon wall. One of the braves stood as Willow darted into view. Slocum spent half a heartbeat to draw a fine bead and squeezed the trigger. The Indian's rifle whipped skyward and blasted harmlessly as Slocum's slug took him. Slocum got a better look at Willow as she crossed ten yards of open space, a brace of rifles under her arm.

Slocum emptied the Winchester as fast as he could work the action, wild, unaimed shots intended only to keep the Indians' heads down. His heart skipped a beat as he saw Willow stagger, then regain her footing. Two strides later, she was behind the boulders. She tossed a rifle to Stonekiller, threw herself prone, and fired. Her shot slapped into a bush and brought a squawk of pain. Slocum hurriedly crammed cartridges into the Winchester, his fingers moving by instinct, afraid to take his eyes from the battle below.

Two Indians went down as Stonekiller and Willow cut loose with the rifles. The flat blast of a handgun sounded between cracks of the long guns. A slug spanged from the canyon rim, kicking dust and gravel into Slocum's cheek. He ignored the sting. An Indian had worked his way up the canyon side. He had a clear shot down toward the three people below. Slocum forced himself to take his time and aim with care. His shot thumped into the warrior. The man's body slumped, rifle dropping away.

The attack on the hillside broke, the fight knocked from the Indians by unexpectedly heavy losses. The warriors scrambled away, remounted, and whipped their horses back toward the Indian camp. Slocum took advantage of the temporary lull in the firing to reload the Ballard. He became aware of the distant thump of handguns and crack of carbines, the thunder of horses' hooves beneath the blanket of dust in Bloody Hand's camp. Through a momentary break in the haze he saw horsemen tear into the west end of the camp, handguns barking, light flashing from sabers. Slocum didn't have to be there to know the cavalry troops were decimating Bloody Hand's band. He breathed a sigh of relief as three figures darted from the canyon wall and scrambled up the steep side of the pass. Willow, Stonekiller, and Maria were safe. It would all be over by full daylight.

Slocum almost didn't see the lone horseman.

The rider burst into view through the dust cloud that hugged the south canyon wall, leaning low over the withers of a gray horse, riding hard. Slocum recognized the horseman from the red handprint on the pony's shoulder. Bloody Hand had abandoned the fight and was fleeing for his life, trying to save his own hide.

Slocum whipped the Winchester to his shoulder and tried to line the sights. Bloody Hand might be a coward, Slocum thought, but the man was no fool. He reined the horse first one way and then the other, an erratic and unpredictable path. Slocum tried to guess Bloody Hand's next move. He squeezed the trigger. The shot went wide as the gray horse darted to one side. A second shot kicked dirt at the pony's front feet. Then Bloody Hand was riding against the base of the pass, hugging the canyon wall, out of Slocum's line of fire. A couple more minutes and the renegade would be racing through the pass and into the badlands beyond.

Slocum grabbed the Ballard, leapt to his feet, and sprinted a dozen yards to the canyon wall overlooking the center of the pass, hoping for a last crack at the fleeing Comanche. He dropped to one knee and shouldered the Ballard. He knew he would have only one shot. His finger tightened on the trigger as the sound of hooves drew closer. Bloody Hand whipped past an instant later, quirting the gray to still more speed. Slocum forced himself to wait for a clear shot.

Bloody Hand was better than three hundred yards away before he made his mistake. He kept the horse in a straight line for several strides. Slocum pulled the sights fine and squeezed the trigger. The Ballard's muzzle blast hammered Slocum's ears. A second later he heard the meaty slap of slug against flesh. Through the powder smoke, Slocum saw the gray stumble, then regain its footing.

Slocum knew the big slug had taken the horse hard. The gray wouldn't make half a mile before it went down to stay. Slocum saw a flicker of movement from the edge of his vision. Jim Stonekiller was in the saddle, his horse skidding and sliding down the steep trail into the pass. A Kiowa war whoop sounded as the horse reached the level ground at the bottom of the hill. Stonekiller leaned low over his mount's neck, urging the horse into an all-out run. Across the way, another rider headed down the trail. Maria Stonekiller was following her husband.

Slocum fought back the urge to swing aboard his own horse and join the pursuit. There was still a chore to do here. He scrambled back to his post and flopped down as the first wave of Indians fleeing the carnage in camp broke through the dust cloud. Only a few were mounted. The others ran, legs churning, as they sought refuge from the buffalo soldiers. The sound of pistol shots and screams was closer now. Slocum figured the troopers had swept over the last of the camp defenders and were closing in on the remaining Indians.

He nestled the Winchester against his shoulder and squeezed the trigger. A mounted warrior toppled from the back of his horse. A second man went down as Willow's Kennedy cracked. Slocum settled into a deadly routine, picking his targets. He put down three more men. Willow nailed at least that many more before the Indian flight broke, swirling back upon itself in confusion. Slocum swung his rifle to his left—and almost shot a U.S. Army trooper. The soldier was riding hard, leading at least twenty men into position to block the eastern pass. Slocum lowered his rifle as the troopers dismounted, knelt, and laid a blistering volley into the Indians. Slocum knew the rout was complete.

He sprinted to his horse, paused long enough to reload the Winchester and Ballard, sheathed the weapons, and spurred after Stonekiller and Bloody Hand. His horse skidded to the floor of the pass in a cloud of shale and stones. At the same time, Willow's mount plunged the last few strides down the far wall. Slocum checked his horse until Willow was alongside.

"Are you hurt, Willow? I saw you almost fall," Slocum said.

"I'm all right." The Shoshoni girl's face was dusty, sweat streaking the smudged war paint on her face. "We can't do any more good here. Jim could be in trouble. Let's ride." She kneed her horse into a run.

They had covered less than a mile before they sped past the body of the gray horse. Slocum saw at a glance that the rifle was still in its saddle boot, pinned beneath the dead gray. He heard the pistol shots—three quick, coughing explosions—just before they topped a low rise in the eastbound trail. He whipped his Colt from its holster and thumbed the hammer in one smooth motion as his horse reached the crest. He reined in abruptly. Willow, riding at his side, also brought her mount to a sliding stop.

Stonekiller stood in the middle of the wagon road, feet spread, knees flexed, his Colt cocked and ready in his right hand. Blood stained his left sleeve. Maria stood beside her horse ten feet away, a rifle shouldered.

Bloody Hand faced Stonekiller, a smear of crimson spreading across his ribs, a smoking revolver in his fist. The hammer of the Comanche's handgun clicked on an empty chamber. Maria sighted her rifle.

"No, Maria!" Stonekiller snapped. "Don't make it easy for him!" He never took his eyes from the renegade's face. "You're not much of a hand with a pistol, you son of a bitch." Stonekiller's voice was hard and cold. "You any better with a knife when you're facing somebody besides women and kids?"

For a tense moment, the two stood silent, glaring at each other. Stonekiller tossed his handgun aside and swept the heavy bladed knife from its sheath at his belt.

"Jim, no!" Maria's tone was near panic. "Don't—"

"Stay out of it, Maria! This is between me and him!"

A murderous confidence flared in Bloody Hand's eyes. He dropped his revolver and reached for his knife.

"Maria's right, Jim," Slocum said calmly. "Let's just shoot the bastard and be done with it."

"Not until I've cut his liver out," Stonekiller said.

"Whatever you say." Slocum lowered the hammer of the Colt, but didn't holster the weapon. If the Kwahadi got a blade into Jim, Slocum intended to put a slug between Bloody Hand's eyes. For the moment, he would stay out of it; this was a personal fight. One Jim had earned.

Stonekiller held his knife below waist level, the cutting edge up, as the two men cautiously stepped toward each other. Bloody Hand's blade was at shoulder height. They closed to within six feet, both men on the balls of their feet, shoulders hunched, knees flexed, as they jockeyed for an advantage. Slocum figured the contest was a toss-up. The Comanche had the height and reach advantage, but Stonekiller was quick as a scalded cat. Stonekiller might have an edge—if he hadn't lost too much blood from the wound in his shoulder.

Bloody Hand lunged, his blade flicking toward Stonekiller's gut. The Kiowa twisted, parried the blow with his left forearm, and swept his own knife upward. Bloody Hand jumped back, but not before Stonekiller's knife sliced across the Comanche's chest. The two circled again for a moment, staring into each other's eyes.

Stonekiller feinted an upward slash; Bloody Hand dropped his left arm to block the blow. The Kiowa abruptly whipped his blade back and overhand. The keen tip narrowly missed Bloody Hand's neck. The Kwahadi ducked low and thrust his knife toward Stonekiller's ribs. The blade struck a glancing blow. Slocum heard Stonekiller's quick intake of breath; when Stonekiller spun away, Slocum saw the thin line along a middle rib. Blood welled from the cut.

The two again circled warily in the grim dance, each now aware that one wrong move would end the battle. Both men were breathing hard.

Bloody Hand sprang to his right, spun a complete circle on his heel, and whipped his knife toward Stonekiller's throat. The Kiowa snapped his head back. The blade whistled close to his neck. Stonekiller's knife flicked out. Bloody Hand grunted as the blade sank into the skin above his hip. He abruptly lunged toward Stonekiller, his knife flashing toward the Kiowa's collarbone. Stonekiller grabbed the Comanche's knife wrist as the two men's chests met with an audible thud. Bloody Hand's fingers wrapped around Stonekiller's forearm in a desperate grab. For an instant they stood locked in a test of strength and will, muscle against muscle, neither able to power his knife point past the other's grip. Muscles knotted and tendons strained. Bloody Hand's knife began to inch toward Stonekiller's chest. The Kiowa abruptly took a half step back and yanked on the Kwahadi's knife wrist. Bloody Hand was off balance for an instant. Stonekiller slammed his chest against the Comanche's, hooked a foot behind Bloody Hand's heel, and shoved. The Comanche staggered, knife hand flailing, and almost went down. Stonekiller was on him in a split second, his blade slicing between Bloody Hand's ribs.

The Comanche's knees buckled. The knife dropped from his numbed fingers. Stonekiller held the taller man upright, his left forearm jammed beneath Bloody Hand's chin. The Kiowa's shoulders bunched in effort as he drove his knife deeper, then slashed from right to left. Blood spurted from the wide, deep gash across Bloody Hand's ribs. The Comanche's eyes went wide.

Stonekiller stepped back and let Bloody Hand fall to his knees. He put a foot against the renegade's shoulder and toppled him onto his back. The shrill victory cry of the Kiowa warrior burst from Stonekiller's lips. He shifted the knife to his left hand and rammed his right fist deep into the cut across Bloody Hand's ribs. The hand came out covered in blood that spurted from a fistful of liver. Stonekiller crouched over the Comanche and plopped the torn, gory organ onto Bloody Hand's chest.

The Comanche died with a silent scream on his lips.

Slocum breathed a sigh of relief and holstered his Colt. It was over.

Stonekiller stood for a moment, bloodied, chest heaving as he gasped for air. Maria dropped her rifle and ran to Jim's side. Slocum started to follow—and pulled up short at the barked order from behind.

''That's enough!''

Slocum spun, his hand darting toward his holster.

''Don't try it!'' The voice had the ring of authority. Slocum froze. Half a dozen black Army troopers stood beside a white lieutenant, .45-70 muzzles pointed at Stonekiller, Slocum, and the women. Slocum cursed himself silently. He had been so intent on the knife fight he hadn't heard the troopers approach. And it looked like that could cost them their lives.

The officer nodded toward the quartet. ''Shackle them, corporal,'' he said to the big buffalo soldier at his side. ''It looks like this is the last of the bunch.''

Slocum realized with a start that Stonekiller and Willow still wore war paint. He raised a hand.

''Hold up a minute, lieutenant,'' Slocum said. ''We're on the same side here.''

The officer's eyes narrowed in a lean face streaked by powder residue, sweat, and a heavy layer of dust. ''You've got about ten seconds to convince me of that, mister.''

Slocum glared back. ''I'll do exactly that, lieutenant. It's going to take more than ten seconds.'' He jabbed a thumb over his shoulder. ''The man in the Kiowa war paint's a reservation policeman, name of Jim Stonekiller. The woman beside him is his wife. We've tailed Bloody Hand all the way from Kansas after he kidnapped the woman and ambushed my freight wagon.''

The lieutenant's frown deepened. ''Were you the one up on the east rim?''

Slocum nodded. ''One of them. Stonekiller was in the camp when the fracas started. Willow—the Shoshoni girl—was with me on the rim.''

The officer paused for a moment, thinking, then shrugged. "All right. Lower the weapons, men. We'll hear them out."

The sun was halfway up the eastern sky when Lieutenant Jacob Dalton dismissed yet another courier bringing reports from the battlefield and turned back to Slocum.

"All right, Mr. Slocum, what you say jibes with everything I've seen and heard since we first got word that Bloody Hand had jumped the reservation." Dalton offered a hand. "Looks like the U.S. Army owes you a formal expression of thanks."

"Don't bother," Slocum said with a wry half grin. "We got what we came for. No need to go through any more paperwork."

"Nonetheless, you and your friends helped avert a bloodbath on the frontier and saved some troopers' lives to boot. The rumors that Bloody Hand was putting together an army of renegades were true. There isn't much left of his army now." He nodded toward the body lying in the trail. "Or Bloody Hand himself, for that matter. Or Koshay of the Mescaleros, White Shield of the Comanches, Wah-to-ke of the Jicarillos, and a half dozen lesser war chiefs of other bands. The power of the troublemaker tribes was gutted here today. It will be a cold day in hell before any other wild bucks try something like this. Much bad medicine handed out to the Indians this morning."

The officer mounted and started to rein away, then hesitated. "By the way, we recovered all but a few of the stolen rifles. We'll have to confiscate them, of course."

Slocum nodded.

"We also recovered quite a sum of money from the wagon. I'll see that the personal funds taken from you when you were ambushed are returned before we break camp. I'll wire ahead as soon as we reach a telegraph. The reward on Bloody Hand will be waiting when you reach Fort Concho on the way back to the Nations."

Slocum lifted his hat and wiped the sweat from his brow. "One thing still bothers me, lieutenant," he said. "How did Bloody Hand know which wagon the arms shipment was in? The decoy wagon wasn't touched."

Dalton's chapped lips turned down in a frown. "He had it from the horse's mouth, so to speak. My scouts worked over—perhaps I should say interrogated—a few of the less stoic prisoners. The man who tipped off Bloody Hand was none other than A. W. Smalley, owner of the freight line. He was in cahoots with Bloody Hand from the first day. A warrant will be wired for his arrest, and I will personally see to it that he spends many years in the federal pen—if he doesn't hang for inciting war against the government and accessory to murder.''

"If he doesn't hang," Slocum said coldly, "the son of a bitch will answer to me."

Dalton stared at Slocum for a moment. "Since you've made that threat in my presence, Slocum, I must advise you of this." The hard glare faded. "If it comes to that, I'll personally reimburse you the cost of ammunition it takes to kill the greedy bastard."

The officer reined his horse about, the patrol falling into step behind. All told, Slocum thought, it had been a reasonably good day. Jim Stonekiller had an impressive collection of fresh cuts and a shallow gunshot gouge across the meat of his upper left shoulder. Nothing serious. He would heal quickly. Most importantly, he had his wife back. The buffalo soldiers still hadn't finished counting bodies in Skeleton Canyon, but it appeared that more than 100 warriors were dead, caught in the crossfire and confusion. The rough estimate was that more than 150 Indian men and a sprinkling of women and children had been captured, along with 500 horses from the pony herd.

The Army's losses were light. The couriers had reported three troopers dead and seven wounded. The losses weren't light for the three dead soldiers, Slocum thought solemnly. He glanced at Bloody Hand's body. A swarm of blow flies buzzed around the blood-soaked corpse. The chunk of liver still lay on the Kwahadi's chest.

The lieutenant would order no burial details to dispose of the Indian dead. The man knew Indians, Slocum granted; the spirits that stalked Skeleton Canyon would have reinforcements now. No Plains Indian was likely to come within a hundred miles of The Place of the Bones for decades.

Slocum strode to where Maria Stonekiller was tending her husband's wounds with Willow's help. The Shoshoni girl still wore her war paint. It showed faint through the heavy coating of dust, powder residue, and sweat streaks on her face. She glanced up at

Slocum. The ferocious look of the war paint melted away beneath her smile.

"Jim all right?" Slocum said.

"Hell, yes, I'm all right," Stonekiller said. He cocked an eyebrow at Slocum. "You fight damn good for a white man."

"Hush up, Jim Stonekiller, or I'll never get this cut closed," Maria groused. "I swear, I've spent more time stitching your hide back together than I've spent sewing clothes."

Stonekiller winked over her shoulder at Slocum. "Maria's going to be fine, Slocum. She's grumbling again. So help me, the thought of living the rest of my life with such a cranky old squaw"—he yelped as Maria gave him an extra stab of the needle—"is enough to give me second thoughts about whether my own medicine's gone bad."

"You haven't seen trouble yet, you lazy half-breed. Just wait until I get you home. Now hold still, or I'm going to have to get rough with this needle."

"*Get* rough? Woman, you've got a streak of rattlesnake in you. I always heard Cheyenne women were good at torturing captives."

"And I've always heard that Kiowas whimper over the least little thing. Our kids are going to be raised Cheyenne, by God. Now, quit squirming."

Slocum grinned. To an outsider, the exchange might sound like the makings of a domestic fuss. But Indians had a sense of humor. Teasing was just one way they showed affection.

"If it gets to the point you can't stand her anymore, just boot her out of the lodge, Jim," Slocum said. "She can move into my blankets."

"The hell she will, Slocum," Willow snapped. "There won't be room enough in there for three of us. Besides, I'm not so sure you could handle two women."

"Maybe not. Might be fun to try, though." Slocum ducked the stone Willow threw at him and went to tend the horses.

Slocum lay on his bedroll and stared up at the stars winking on to stand watch over the coming night. He was a contented man, content for the first time in months. A full belly, a fresh bath and shave, and a good cigarillo, topped off by the last of Stonekiller's whiskey stash, had a mellowing effect on a man.

Their second camp out of Skeleton Canyon was the best yet, Slocum mused; nothing like almost getting dead to make a man appreciate the finer things in life. The rustle of the cool breeze through the cottonwood leaves overhead and the distant hoot of an owl blended with the soft ripping sounds as the horses grazed along the grassy, spring-fed creek that gurgled past, a few feet away. The gentle splashes from the deep pool where Willow bathed added to the peace and tranquillity of the meadow.

Stonekiller sat by the small fire a few feet away, his arm around Maria's waist. The soft murmur of their voices added a further soothing touch to the silky night air. Slocum figured they were talking about their future. He felt an additional sense of contentment that he had been able to help.

Last night in the dry camp twenty miles back, Slocum and Stonekiller had held a parley. Slocum did most of the talking.

"Jim," he had said, "nobody likes money more than I do. But that thousand dollar reward on Bloody Hand is more than I need. I'm splitting it with you—"

"The hell you are," Stonekiller interrupted. "That's your money. That was our deal. I got Maria back. That's all the reward I want."

"As Maria said back in the pass, hush up and quit arguing," Slocum said. "We went into this as partners. We came out of it the same way. I'm not going to insist you take the money as a gift. Wouldn't want you beholden to any white-eye. But it's going to take money to rebuild and restock your ranch, and I won't have Maria starving to death in the meantime. So I'm putting five hundred of *my* dollars in your hands. Call it a loan and pay it back when you get to be the richest Irish-Kiowa cattleman in the Indian Nations."

Stonekiller shook his head. "Can't do it. I don't accept charity."

"Damned if you're not as bullheaded, stiff-necked proud as you are ugly, Jim Stonekiller," Slocum said. "It isn't charity. It's a loan, for God's sake. I know I'll get the money back. Take the offer, or I'll just squander the money on slow horses, fast women, whiskey, and four-card straights."

Stonekiller was silent for a moment, then sighed. "Whiskey, women, and poker sounds like a good investment to me," he said. "I have to admit I've been worried about the expense of starting over from scratch. I guess the least I can do is save a friend from a life of wild debauchery. But before I say yes, we have to talk about this loan. I insist on paying interest.''

"What did you pay for Maria?"

"Ten ponies. Eight good ones and two worthless plugs."

"Then the interest on the loan will be five good horses. No plugs, cripples, windbroke nags, or outlaws.''

"Payable when?"

Slocum shrugged. "Whenever you're showing a profit.''

"And how do I get the money and horses to you?"

"I'm a drifter. I'll drift back through the Nations sometime."

Stonekiller rolled a cigarette, lit it, then nodded and held out a hand. "Agreed. A loan. And they'll be good horses. Thanks.''

"Don't thank me. Just build a good ranch, breed up a houseful of little Irish-Kiowa Cheyennes, and have a meal and a jug ready when a certain saddle bum drifts through.''

A movement at the campfire brought Slocum back to the present. Stonekiller tossed his bedroll over a shoulder, reached for his wife's hand, and led her toward the stand of cottonwoods. *Looks like Jim's healing faster than anybody expected,* Slocum thought. He took the final drag of his cigarillo, crushed the butt into the sand, and tugged his hat down over his eyes.

A soft footfall sounded near Slocum's head. He pushed his hat back and looked up. Willow stood over him, naked. Starlight glinted from water droplets on her full breasts, in the dark triangle at her lower belly, and danced across the hair that clung damp against her face and neck. The sight put a hitch in Slocum's breathing and a stir in his crotch.

"You're out of uniform, soldier," she said softly.

"Oh? How's that?"

"You still have clothes on." She knelt beside him and reached for the top button of his shirt. "I'll fix that for you. By the way, I have a question." Willow's voice was low and husky.

"Hmm?"

"You remember I asked you to take me back home? To my people on the reservation?"

"I remember."

"I just wondered something." Her fingers flipped open the last button and pushed the cloth of his shirt aside. She lowered her head and touched her lips to his chest. "We don't have to be in any real hurry to get back, do we?"